DEFENDING JUSTICE

JUSTICE TEAM SERIES

MISTY EVANS

ADRIENNE GIORDANO

ALG PUBLISHING

DEFENDING JUSTICE

Former prosecutor turned hotshot defense attorney, Jackie DelRay, is a star in the shark-infested judicial waters of Washington, DC. Behind her take-no-prisoners façade, she hides a painful secret, and a longing for FBI Special Agent Beckett Pearson—the man who captured her heart during a passion-filled weekend in college. The same man who still holds a grudge over a case Jackie refused to prosecute several years ago. When Beck is arrested for the shocking murder of the FBI director's estranged wife, Jackie breaks every rule about being emotionally involved with her client - knowing the risks to her heart and her career - and rushes to defend him.

Former model and football star, Beck has finally found his home with the Bureau. He wants nothing to do with the sexy lawyer who left him without a goodbye twelve years ago and then destroyed his first, and most important, missing persons investigation. Now, with his freedom on the line, Jackie's brilliant legal mind may be his one hope at staying out of prison.

When their investigation is mired by political alliances and reckless greed, Beck and Jackie battle corruption at the highest levels. That battle includes resisting the long-buried passion they shared twelve years ago, but will a killer bent on stopping their investigation give them a fight they are bound to lose?

To Frank Paine.
Thank you for your generosity and kindness toward a stranger.

1

$\mathscr{T}$he bass of *Hot Child in the City* pounded from giant speakers as Beckett Pearson walked onto the stage and straightened his tie. Bright lights, lots of screaming women —ah, yes, he'd missed the days of walking the runway.

Not.

Being a model in college had given him extra cash. A lot of headaches as well. Beautiful, sexy headaches, but damn, tonight's bachelor auction aside, those days were long over and he was glad.

As Nick Gilder sang about a runaway girl, the room of women watched Beck strut his stuff. The MC—Caroline Foster, a former FBI agent helping out tonight like he was—spoke over the noise, giving the potential donors his curriculum vitae.

Born and raised in Georgia, four brothers and four sisters, helped support himself in college by working as a Vogue model.

A fresh round of cheers erupted. A few catcalls echoed through the room over the heavy bass tempo.

Beck stopped and smiled, giving his fans a wave as he gritted his teeth. Yep, when Taylor got back from her vacation with Matt Stephens, Beck was going to kill her for setting him up like this.

"Hey, Beck," she'd said with that big ol' toothy grin of hers. *"Wanna help a good cause?"*

"Sign me up," he'd replied without asking for the deets, because Taylor, head of the FBI Missing Persons Unit, and his friend, always had his back.

Big mistake. Like Grammie always said, the devil was in those pesky details.

Which was why he was doing a pseudo-Magic Mike impression tonight to raise money for the St. Agnes Women's Shelter and Sydney Banfield. Minus removing his clothes.

Not that he didn't want to support the shelter—he did. One hundred percent. The place offered battered women and their kids sanctuary. Sydney made sure they were safe and helped find them the services they needed. She also lined up educational opportunities and job fairs for them.

Beck just wished Taylor hadn't volunteered him for this particular task. A bachelor auction? Really?

Suck it up. If he was going to strut his stuff and raise money for the shelter, than he was damn well going to give it everything he had.

As he hit the end of the runway and cocked a hip, Caroline mentioned the fact that along with being lead investigator of a missing persons team with the FBI, he had a genius IQ of 144.

And then the real clincher—his former defensive lineman status from his days with the University of Alabama. At her pause, Beck smiled for real at the women cheering for him. "Roll Tide!" he yelled.

His new fans went crazy.

"Bidding starts at three-hundred dollars," Caroline said.

Three hundred? That's it?

He couldn't help it. He gave her a look. Caroline, being

Caroline, was totally unfazed. "Did I mention that Agent Pearson is also a talented Reiki masseur?"

He nearly had to slap his hands over his ears as exuberant cheers nearly drowned out good ol' Nick. Technically, he didn't do massages, but whatever. This crowd couldn't have cared less, so he struck his favorite Vogue pose, crossing his arms and placing a finger to his jaw as he made eye contact with the blonde in the first row of tables.

"Three-fifty!" she shouted.

Yep, he was definitely going to get the highest bid and the biggest donation tonight.

And he was just getting started.

Dropping his hand, he rolled his broad shoulders and unbuttoned his suit jacket, using both hands to pull the sides away from his chest. Hands on hips, he gave them a little roll and shot the brunette next to the first bidder a sexy grin.

"Five hundred!" she shouted. The blonde gave her a look, not believing her friend would bid against her.

And so it went. By the time Caroline called *going once, going twice...sold!*, Beck had raised three thousand dollars. The only issue now was the fact that the woman who'd bought a date with him was the estranged wife of Byron Lockhart III.

He was about to escort the wife of the freakin' Director of the FBI to dinner. Oh joy.

Sure they were in the midst of a divorce, but still.

Not much made Beck nervous, but meeting up with Annabelle Lockhart backstage a few minutes later had him sweating like a whore in church.

"Special Agent Beckett Pearson." She extended a well-manicured hand. Thin and model-height in her stilettos, she could nearly look him in the eye. Impressive, since he was 6'4". "I believe you owe me dinner."

He guessed her age around forty, although she might have

had some work done. "Yes, ma'am. Thank you for your generous donation to the shelter."

Her red lips parted to show perfect white teeth. Either she had amazing genes or enough caps to cost as much as his townhouse. "I'm sure you're worth every penny," she purred. Slim fingers snaked out and raked across his chest as she leaned closer, putting her mouth close to his ear. "I can't wait to experience your magic hands."

Still smiling like the cat that ate the proverbial canary, she straightened, but left her hand on his shirt, dipping it down to his belt. The way she looked him over from head to toe made him feel like raw meat in front of a starving lion.

Cougar is more like it.

Even if he hadn't been an expert in nonverbal social cues, her bold, suggestive gaze told him everything he needed to know—she expected the night of her life with a side of hot, unabashed sex for dessert. The cherry on top for Annabelle was the fact Byron would find out one of his investigators had played slap and tickle with her. The fact she'd kept the Director's last name so far spoke volumes—she still had a thing for the man.

Can anyone say awkward?

Although Beck found her attractive, he wasn't into casual hookups. He was thirty-two and ready for a meaningful, long-lasting relationship. Marriage, kids. The whole shebang. He wanted magic and love and all that shit. He didn't mind being admired and lusted after—hell, he loved it—but he had no intention of being bought, and he'd hang up his cleats before he let anyone use him to get back at their almost-ex.

Make the best of it. Wining and dining Annabelle might be fun and he'd make it his mission to leave things on a good note. No sex, but she was still going to have the time of her life after shelling out three thousand dollars.

"Let me take care of everything," he said, offering his arm. He liked taking care of people, and outside of Taylor and the other team members, he rarely got to flex his instinct to do so. Now that Taylor had Matt, he had one less person to play big brother around.

At least there's Tink. His cat still needed him, at least as much as any feline ever needed an owner. He winked at Annabelle. "I have the perfect evening planned for us."

The cougar licked her lips. Her arm slid through his. "Let's stop at my place first, okay?"

It wasn't a question. She was going in for the kill, no holds barred.

Good thing he loved a challenge. This one was going to rate right up there with the game of '07 against LSU. Nasty one, that, but the Tide had prevailed, thanks to him.

But damn it, he was definitely going to ring Taylor's neck come Monday.

"It's your night, Annabelle," he said, already strategizing how he was going to get out of sleeping with her.

Under a pitch-black sky, Jackie stood on the steps of the U.S. District Court in DC waiting for the cameramen to assemble themselves for the defense's impromptu press conference. She didn't need a podium for this show, just the hungry batch of reporters awaiting her post-verdict statement. And they'd get it, despite the late hour and her thoroughly trashed mind and body.

Every inch of her ached, but the long days – and nights – had been worth it.

A spotlight flashed and she dropped her gaze from the harsh glare to her previously unwrinkled suit. Damnit. The navy Chanel number her mother bought her for her very first case looked like an army had marched over it. And not because it was nearly ten years old. Fifteen hours she'd been in this suit. Now, after six hours of deliberations in a case that had monopolized not only her time, but just about every emotion she possessed, she was...numb. Completely pulverized by waves of self-doubt regarding her performance.

"Ms. DelRay," the reporter from DC's ABC affiliate called. "What are your thoughts on the verdict?"

Her thoughts? Oh, she had plenty of those. The reporters closed in, shoving microphones at her, intensifying the already thick air of an unusually warm fall evening. She pushed her shoulders back, taking it all in. The five-deep crowd, the cameras, the reporters jockeying for the best vantage point.

Her moment. Right here. Right now. Her mother had better be watching.

"Obviously," she said, "we're pleased. We've said from the beginning the evidence in this case was suspect, at best. Clearly, the jury agreed."

Beside her, Josh, the young lawyer she'd snatched from the D.A.'s office six months earlier, stood a little taller. As hard as he'd worked, he deserved this moment as much as she did.

"What about the DNA evidence?" a blonde from CBS shouted. "How big of a factor do you think that was?"

Um, how about the biggest? "Critical. There was no smoking gun here, people. The entire case was strung together based on detectives' hypothesizing. Yes, they had my client's blood in the bathroom, but – hello – the man lived there. For God's sake, he shaved every morning in that bathroom. Of course his blood would be there. The question to ask is why the criminologist felt it wise to package together and ship multiple pieces of evidence to the lab. They obliterated the control sample. When you co-mingle evidence, it's contaminated. Useless."

If Josh wasn't her employee, she'd have kissed him right on

the mouth for discovering the shipping info. Hell, she'd have even slipped him the tongue.

From there, it hadn't taken her long to figure out the evidence could be tainted. In a case involving a United States senator and his murdered wife, the whole thing screamed reasonable doubt.

And they'd gotten a not-guilty verdict on the biggest case DC had seen since that four-star general got busted sharing top-secret intel with his mistress.

We did it.

"Ms. DelRay," a CNN reporter called, "what if the government appeals? Will you stay on?"

Bet your sweet ass.

"We'll decide that later. Right now, we're going to get Senator Watkins settled and give him time to grieve for his wife." Jackie held up her hand. "Thanks, all. That's it for now."

Josh stepped in front, making himself a human bulldozer, shredding the crowd as reporters screamed questions Jackie wouldn't answer.

Now she needed her bed and sleep. Peaceful sleep that wouldn't be interrupted by anxiety and the ever-present mind-racing that came with a case of this magnitude.

At thirty-four years old, she'd just defended a United States senator.

And won.

Go, Jackie.

A black stretch limo pulled to the curb, catching Jackie's attention. The rear window slid open and the glow of the streetlight illuminated a man's face. Familiar craggy lines registered and a burst of energy expanded Jackie's chest. *He came.* He waved her over and the window slid closed.

She clutched the sleeve of Josh's cheap suit, reminding herself to give the kid a raise. After this win, she could afford it.

Yep. DelRay and Associates just catapulted itself to the top of the hot-shot lawyers list.

Josh glanced at the limo, then to Jackie. She jerked her head. "Our ride is here."

The limo door flew open, revealing her father in dark dress pants and a gray blazer. He slid across the seat and Jackie piled in to find her mother and brother on the adjacent seat. Mom wore her usual pantsuit, blue this time, with a white shell under the jacket. Her ash blond hair fell to her chin, the ends curling up a bit from the humidity. Even with the stray curls, her mother pulled off 'poised and polished'. She'd built a career on that look.

And she'd come to celebrate with her daughter.

A huge win and now Jackie had her family. How good was life? She let out a squeal.

Before the mob of reporters could flash photos, Josh shoved her over and slammed the door behind him. Jackie launched herself at her father, squeezing him tight as the limo lurched from the curb leaving the shouting reporters behind.

"I can't believe you came."

Her mother held her arms out. "A little bird told me the verdict was in. We wanted to be here."

"How did you get here so fast?"

Her mother gave her a bored look. "Darling, I'm the Mayor of Philadelphia. I have a helicopter."

"Holy crap," Josh blurted. "That's cool!"

Calvin, her PITA of a brother, held up his hand. "Hey, sis. Don't mind me. I'm just along for the ride."

Always a smartass. That's what coming from a family with three lawyers got her. "Hey, Cal." She plopped on the seat between Cal and Mom, then gave him a squeeze and a smack on the cheek. "I can't believe you guys are here."

"What?" Cal asked, "You think we're gonna let you celebrate the biggest case of your career alone?"

"At ten at night? Yes, besides, if my estimate is right, when you left Philly, you didn't know I'd won."

"True," Mom said. "But I had no doubt. My girl destroyed the prosecution."

Being a career prosecutor, her mother would know. Her family. Unbelievable. A bunch of hard-noses, all of them, but this impromptu visit? Crazy devotion. Jackie tucked her hair behind her ears and let out a breath.

"Lord, I feel ninety years old."

Mom's gaze moved to Jackie's mangled suit. "Sorry, honey, but you look it, too."

Yep, same old Mom. "It's been a long day." She elbowed her brother. "And, silly me, I forgot to check my lipstick before I went into court."

Mom would have. Even as a lowly prosecutor on a tight budget, she'd amped up her beauty queen appearance. Now that she had money and the title of mayor, she didn't leave the house without designer duds and perfect makeup. Elegant and strong. That was her mother.

Jackie may have inherited Mom's legal prowess, but when it came to her appearance, she just hoped her blouse matched her suit. One of the main reasons she stuck to solid, easily matched colors. The family joke had long been Jackie's need for adult Garanimals.

"Jon and Will wanted to be here," Dad said. "They couldn't swing it. Will is on call and Jon has court in the morning."

Will, the next oldest from Jackie – yes, she'd dealt with three older brothers – was a heart surgeon. Mom liked to joke that with three out of her four children being lawyers, she'd somehow gone astray with Will.

"Where to?" Dad asked. "Have you two eaten?"

Jackie pondered the question, then looked at Josh. "Did we eat?"

"Yesterday, I think."

9

"We'll fix that." Mom hit the button to lower the glass screen separating them from the driver. "Take us to Charlie Palmer's. We have celebrating to do."

Jackie, still wedged between her brother and Mom, gripped both their hands and rested her head back. So much for sleep. Who cared? She had her family and the biggest win of her career. What more did she need?

2

*B*eck made it home before midnight, letting out a sigh of relief as he tossed his car keys into the dish next to the door and laid his jacket on the table to take to the cleaners the next day. It had been one long, crazy evening, and he was ready to shower off Annabelle's perfume, forget all the groping and fondling she'd done to him, and spend his weekend hoping Byron Lockhart III didn't show up on his doorstep to punch him out.

"Tink?" he called.

He wasn't surprised when there was no response. The cat could hold a grudge like nobody's business. The styrofoam carryout container in Beck's hands might be his savior.

The stop at Annabelle's had resulted in a drink and her trying to seduce him. He'd dodged that bullet as gracefully as he could and managed to get her out to dinner at Flat 1776. The place had opened only a few weeks ago and was booked months in advance, but Kershaw, one of his old college buddies and part owner, had done him a solid. Thank God he'd had the sense to set the whole thing up before the auction—the nine p.m. reservation had saved his bacon. They'd enjoyed a lovely four-course meal and Annabelle had nearly drunk herself under the table. She could now tell all her friends at the country club she'd eaten at the hot, new 5-star restaurant in town with her runway-model/former-football-star boy toy.

Begging off from returning to her place afterwards had been much easier than he'd anticipated, but she'd already texted him.

Sexted him was more like it. He hadn't even made it out of her long, winding driveway when she'd sent him a picture of herself in sexy lingerie and asked him to come back.

No way in hell.

As expected, Tink was on Beck's pillow, face buried in the covers. He no longer made up his bed because it did no good. The cat—a stray who had shown up on his doorstep just before Christmas—always undid his work.

He opened the container with the leftovers from his meal and waved it in front of her nose. "Look what I brought you."

She peeked one eye open and gave him a scornful look, then tucked her head back down.

Hello, cold shoulder.

"Your loss." He set the container on the floor near the bed, knowing she'd eventually come around. "I'll leave it here for you, and remember, tonight was for a good cause, not because of work."

She burrowed farther down.

After his shower, he found the container licked clean and Tink had moved over to her side of the bed. He got in and turned on ESPN. Once he was caught up on the various scores of his favorite teams, he picked up the book on criminal sociology from his nightstand. The shower had done some good to clear his head, but he still couldn't get the sight of Annabelle in her lingerie out of his mind. She might be divorcing Byron, but it still seemed wrong to know she liked pink satin...it was like seeing the Pope in his skivvies.

Sometime later, a loud noise woke him with a jerk.

ESPN hummed in the background and the book lay open in his lap. Tink was curled next to him, having forgiven him. But at the noise, she came to attention.

Bambambam. Tink hurled her chubby body off the bed and Beck sat up, rubbing his eyes. The bedside clock showed it was nearly one a.m. *Who the fuck was at his door at this time of the morning?*

God help him, it was probably Theresa, or one of his other siblings, needing a handout. He hadn't heard from any of them in over six months now, and then it had only been Corey texting him for bail money.

Or worse than his criminal family, it might be Byron Lockhart coming for his balls.

Bambambam. A man yelled his name.

He never slept in anything, so he threw on sport pants and headed for the door.

"Just a goddamn minute," he shouted back. "I'm coming."

His townhouse was in a decent neighborhood, but, as he hadn't recognized the voice, he still checked the peephole before opening the door.

What he saw made him pause before deactivating his security system. Two uniformed cops stood on his doorstep.

"Beckett Pearson," one called through the door. "This is DC Metro. Open the door."

What the hell?

Beckett flipped on the porchlight and unlocked the door. Cool night air met his bare chest. "What's going on, fellas?"

"Beckett Pearson?" the taller of the two asked. The guy behind him had his hand on his weapon.

Shit. Byron must be really *pissed...*

"Yeah, I'm Special Agent Pearson."

"Mr. Pearson, please turn around and put your hands on top of your head."

"What?"

In the next second, cop number two pulled his weapon. "On your knees!"

"Whoa." Beck raised both hands. "I think there's been some kind of mistake."

"No mistake." The bigger cop waved down his sidekick, taking out his handcuffs and motioning for Beck to turn around. "Mr. Pearson, you're under arrest for the murder of Annabelle Lockhart."

3

---

*H*alf comatose from the most amazing New York strip she'd ever tasted, Jackie pushed through her apartment door, double-checked the lock and hung her keys on the hook before heading to her bedroom.

The day had been long, the evening, despite the lovely surprise from her family, even more so. Now they were on their way back to Philly and every inch of her ached. It was a jazzed-up tired though. One that came with the knowledge her family loved her enough to fly down and celebrate her largest victory to date.

Had to love those DelRays.

Even if they drove her half-crazy sometimes.

Hell's bells, her body protested every tiny movement. She passed the small bedroom on the right that doubled as her home office and made her way into her room. Slivers of moonlight through the blinds gave her rumpled sheets an eerie glow. This morning, like every one for the last month, she'd left in a hurry. What did an unmade bed matter when she'd been the only person in it for over a year?

That's what happened with smart-mouthed career girls.

Throw in a hot temper and men tended to run screaming. She didn't have the time – or compulsion – to chase them. Not when her trusty vibrator got the job done.

Oh, Maurice, how I love you.

Distracting thoughts of Maurice caused her to trip on the small mountain of dirty laundry at the foot of her bed. Now that the case was over, she'd start doing it again rather than dumping it all at the cleaners.

Not bothering with the light, she tossed her briefcase on the chair by the bed and kicked her shoes into the open closet.

Bed. All she needed now was a solid ten hours of sleep. Something she hadn't had in...hell, she didn't know. Tonight she'd get it. Even if the building fell down around her. Even if the earth opened up and swallowed the entire block.

She'd declared tomorrow her own holiday and told Josh to take the day off. They both deserved it. Time to get their lives back in order. Pay bills, watch television, grocery shop, and *here's a novel idea*, call a friend. Assuming she still had any after the lack of contact.

This life. Who the hell lived like this?

Her mother, that's who. Did Jackie want that? Barely seeing her loved ones and then, when she did, battling to stay emotionally present. That's how it had been. Mom coming and going while Dad provided the steady guidance. Her father had been Mr. Mom when it wasn't exactly status quo. It had worked, but...

Sigh. In Jackie's Career vs. Family war, the battles raged on.

"I'm tired," she said to no one. "That's all."

Just as her fingers reached her skirt's zipper her cell phone rang. No way. Seriously?

She peered at her briefcase spewing the offending sound.

Ignore it.

Phone calls at one a.m. were never good. And with her

family on their way back to Philly? What if the chopper crashed?

An irrational panic rattled her. Damned helicopters. She hated those things. *Tired. That's all.* Holding her panic in check, she hustled to the chair, dug in the front pocket of the briefcase and checked the phone.

Chessie. Her investigator. She punched the screen before the call dropped. At least her family hadn't perished in a fireball dropping from the sky.

"Chesley Morton, this better be good."

"It is."

When Chessie said it was good, it usually was. At fifty-eight years old, he'd spent thirty years as a homicide detective with the PD. Now retired and working for her full-time, he had enough contacts to keep her well-informed.

Jackie's fatigue took a backseat to the burst of adrenaline plowing from her brain.

She closed her eyes and forced herself to focus. "What is it?"

"Just got off the phone with one of my guys. Annabelle Lockhart – estranged wife of the director of the FBI – was murdered."

Jackie drew a hard breath. "When?"

"Tonight. Her throat was slit. They arrested someone."

Already? Either they got seriously lucky or someone confessed. "Captured at the scene?"

"Nah. This thing sounds...eh."

In Chessie-speak, *eh* meant sketchy. "What's the problem?"

"They got the guy down at the PD in an interview room. No phone call yet."

Meaning the detectives were more than likely stalling in allowing this poor schmuck to call his lawyer. "Unbelievable," Jackie said. "I guess they haven't learned much from the beating I just gave them."

"It gets better. You're not gonna believe who they pinched."

"Who?"

"Your buddy, Beckett Pearson."

Beck.

For a few long seconds, it didn't sink in. She'd definitely heard the name. Had even, on some level, processed it. But...Beck?

She pictured him in his slick suits, his perfect cheekbones and immaculately groomed hair that never, ever, dipped below his ears. At least these days.

Then there were his eyes. Oh, my, that intense blue did her in every time. Made her think about Mr. GQ butt naked on a bed in a crappy motel room.

Ft. Lauderdale. Spring break. They'd met during her senior year and had a fling that included copious amounts of fantasy-worthy sex. She'd been sucked in by his muscles and easy swagger. She'd also been pleasantly surprised by his ambitions. He had a brain behind the brawn and a soft spot for the underprivileged, lost, and abandoned. Hell, she'd barely known him when she'd refused to give him her number, but gave him everything else.

Fast-forward five years and there she was, a prosecutor in DC, when glamour boy showed up in her courtroom. Not as a defendant, but as an FBI agent with a light in his eyes and a case to win.

Beck.

God. What could he have gotten into? And if he hadn't been given his phone call yet, it meant no attorney.

Huge problem. One she could avoid.

She moved to the closet and scooped up her shoes. She should change into a fresh suit but...no. Even a few minutes could cost him. On her way out of the bedroom, she grabbed her briefcase and then her car keys from the hook by the kitchen entry.

"Did I lose you?" Chessie asked.

"No, I'm here."

"I figured you'd want to know," Chessie said. "Given the high profile of it."

"You figured right. If it's Beck, he knows to keep his mouth shut. I can't believe the cops are screwing with an FBI agent. A damned good one too."

"Probably waiting on him to get good and tired, see if he'll slip."

"That's not gonna happen. Not if I can help it."

Twenty minutes later, Jackie stormed into the police station lobby where a desk sergeant tucked behind a glass enclosure glanced up from a computer. At this hour of a weeknight, the lobby was quiet with only one other person sitting on a bench against the wall.

Who knew what the man was here for. In DC it could be anything.

"I'm Jackleen DelRay," Jackie told the sergeant. "Attorney for Beckett Pearson. Where is he?"

Technically, Beck hadn't hired her yet, but they'd worry about that small detail later. The man needed an attorney. Even if he didn't want her for the long haul, for now, she'd keep him from doing any damage. An FBI agent accused of killing the estranged wife of the director of the FBI? Talk about tabloid fodder.

Beck better have kept his lovely mouth shut.

The desk sergeant took in her mess of a suit and more-of-a-mess hair and a smirk formed on his mouth. She resisted the urge to tell him she'd been at it for over eighteen hours and he could shove his opinions straight—and all the way—up his ass.

So tired.

She needed to stay cool here. She jerked her chin at the door leading behind the glass. "Buzz me in."

"Give me a sec."

He picked up his desk phone, speaking softly and well out of her earshot before hanging up.

"Davis," the sergeant said to another officer, "take her to interview two."

Interview room two. The big one. She'd been there plenty of times as a prosecutor, but never as the defense.

The inner lobby door buzzed and she whipped it open. Knowing the way, she charged forward, leaving the cop in her wake as her heels clickety-clacked against the linoleum.

"Guess you know the way," he cracked.

"You bet."

She took the first right, walked ten feet and halted. This was it. She breathed in, fighting the aftereffects of a blood rush that left her mind and body feeling like a hundred-and-twenty pounds of sludge.

Her vision blurred against the stark white of the wall and she blinked. Time to focus. She set her shoulders, and did that little chin lift her mom had taught her. That and the mental benefits had saved many a case.

The cop set one hand on the door, turned the knob and Jackie focused on her entrance. That moment when she'd march in and take over a room.

Shark Jackie.

He pushed the door open and – show time – she sailed through.

A shirtless Beck – Yoi, the man's chest was still a finely sculpted work of art – sat with his hands neatly folded on top of the metal table. He faced a two-way mirror where Jackie surmised a prosecutor watched the festivities. Beck's gaze snapped to her and his perfect eyebrows shot up. Two detectives. Muldoon and Brasich – she thought – sat across from him. Both angled back, spotted her and, if she wasn't mistaken, Brasich groaned.

Excellent.

"Gentlemen," Jackie said, "I'll forgive you for keeping me from my beauty sleep since I got lucky and found a spot in your back lot." She offered up a winning smile. "Now you won't have to validate my parking."

She tossed her briefcase on the table. The buckle thwacked against the metal surface and the reverberation sharpened her senses.

Full bore, baby.

"And," she said, "I sure as hell hope you're not violating my client's rights by questioning him without his attorney present."

Beck's gaze was hot on hers. "What the hell?"

She met his stare and pointed. "Have you said anything?"

"You're not my lawyer," he said. "I want Fleming."

Fleming? She should be insulted. She *was* insulted. That idiot was useless when it came to actually arguing a case. Before jumping the aisle, Jackie ate him for lunch on an eight-month trial that won the prosecution – eh-hem, *her* – a guilty verdict. And Beck was ready to toss her for that guy? Puh-lease.

Had to be because of their sordid history. In short, he despised her.

She liked to believe it was due to their spring break inter-lude. The glamour-boy jock from the University of Alabama was just coming off an ugly break-up and she couldn't risk the heartbreak. No flippin' way. Not after acing her LSATs with law school looming. Back then, like now, she'd been too focused on her work and had virtually ignored the male sex.

Of course, their history didn't end there. The Donlin case two years back didn't help. She'd refused to bring charges on a murder case they'd never win. Sure, he'd done the work – damned good work – and gathered as much evidence as he could, but it was scarce. No DNA, no fingerprints, no blood. A mountain of circumstantial evidence existed, but the case had been forensically bankrupt. What they'd had would never stick. Even if they'd made it to trial, a guilty verdict would have been impossible.

Beck hadn't liked hearing it and had gone over Jackie's head. Her boss agreed with her and somehow it all became Jackie's fault. But that's how it went when FBI agents and detectives were pissed at prosecutors.

All that ended when she jumped the aisle to the defense side.

Rolling right over Beck's objections, she waggled her finger at the detectives. "Give us a second. I need to confer with my client. And, we're going across the hall. To the room that doesn't have recording devices." She pointed at Beck. "Come with me."

"For the love of God," he said, "she is *not* my lawyer."

Beck shook his head vigorously as the two cops who'd been interrogating him stood to leave in the wake of the hurricane known as Jackie DelRay.

Chair legs scraped against the concrete floor, like fingernails on a chalkboard, setting his teeth on edge. The cocky, confident glint in DelRay's eyes did the same.

Muldoon unlocked him from the table, but left the cuffs on. "Do not leave me alone with her," Beck begged the detectives. He swiveled to follow the two men—*damn cowards*—with his gaze. "I want my phone call. *I want Fleming!*"

Muldoon held the door on the opposite side of the hallway open. "You've got two minutes."

The door banged shut behind Muldoon but not before the guy smirked a *good luck, buddy* at Beck.

When I get out of here, I'm gonna make your life hell, you coward.

"Stop being a baby," DelRay said, shoving one of the chairs

out of the way and squaring up the other across from him. Her gaze dropped to his chest and did a slow perusal. "Where's your shirt?"

The cops hadn't allowed him to grab one before they'd handcuffed him and read him his rights. He was lucky they even let him put on shoes.

Beck sighed heavily before dropping into a chair and trying not to like having Jackie's eyes on him. He wished he could pause and look at the stunning defense attorney for a moment like any red-blooded man in his right mind would do, or have a normal, civilized discussion with her about the mess he was in. Because, jeez, it would be nice to have someone in his corner right now. But Jackie did not do *normal*. For Jackie, everything was an engagement, a skirmish. A fight.

Beck had fought her once. And lost. The Donlin case still made acid rise in his throat.

Not to mention the way Jackie DelRay had run out on him in Ft. Lauderdale back in the day.

This room, like the previous, was a freezer, the good ol' detectives having turned down the heat since Beck was half naked, hoping, he guessed, that a little physical torture along with their endless, stupid questions would make him confess.

Fat chance.

"Why are you wearing two different colored shoes?" he fired back at the hotshot attorney.

Not much took Jackie aback, but she glanced down and seemed to notice for the first time they didn't match. Same conservative pump, but different colors. She blinked twice and went back into pit bull mode. "Maybe because it's the middle of the night, I'm half dead from exhaustion and didn't bother to peruse my closet before racing down here. To, I might add, help someone who clearly does not want my services. A simple thank you would be nice. Besides, my shoes are not the problem here."

"Your suit might be. Is that the same one you wore two years ago as a prosecutor?"

A brow cocked upward and at the same time, she ran a hand over the lapel of the jacket. "I love this suit. It's my lucky one. And in case you haven't noticed, you are handcuffed and sitting in an interrogation room on charges of murder. You have bigger things to worry about than my wardrobe."

No shit. Annabelle was dead and he was the easy suspect – the *only* suspect. Cops liked easy. He folded his fingers together and considered his options. He didn't have many. "What are you doing here, *Ms*. DelRay?"

"Defending you, what else?" The ass-kicker shifted facades. Her defenses lowered slightly, her face softening. "And stop with the Ms. DelRay stuff. I know we've had our issues, but we're on the same side. Even if you want that idiot Fleming, right now, I'm here and this case is going to explode. Let me help until you get an attorney."

"You don't even know what happened."

"I know enough and you're going to fill in the rest."

How much *did* she know? The cops didn't have a clue as to what had really happened. All they had was circumstantial bullshit and conjecture. Unfortunately, that might just be enough. An attack on the Director's wife was an attack on all of them and with Beck in custody, they wouldn't look anywhere else. "What did they tell you?"

"That you killed Annabelle Lockhart." She leaned closer, getting right in his face, those beautiful brown eyes searching his, as if he would melt and tell her his deepest, darkest secrets. "Did you?"

He caught a whiff of her perfume, something sexy and mysterious with a little tuberose, and was that vetiver? For a split second, his old fantasy of stripping her clothes off – those awful, out-of-date suits in drab colors – and seeing the real woman underneath flashed through his brain. "I thought defense attorneys never asked questions they didn't want to know the answer to."

She sat back, rolled her eyes. "Stop playing me, Beck. I know you didn't do it."

"Bullshit." This was no game to him – his life was on the line here. He wasn't going to be her next high-profile case. "Then why did you ask?"

She flipped open her battered briefcase, took out her phone and punched up a recording app. "Start from the beginning. What happened tonight? Were you with Annabelle?"

"Turn off the recorder. You're not my lawyer. You of all people should recognize conflict of interest."

Her slender fingers traced the outline of her phone, and she paused before hitting the button, a tiny smile quirking the corner of her lips at his concession. "It's not a conflict of interest if I'm not your permanent counsel. Although why you don't want me to record this is beyond me, since currently I *am* your attorney. Go ahead." She motioned with her hand and hit record. "Start at the beginning."

Damn hard-headed woman. "I attended a bachelor auction at the Hay-Adams."

"Fancy place."

"It was a charity event for the St. Agnes Women's Shelter."

"And you were on the auction block?"

He nodded. The light came on in her eyes as she pieced together a part of the puzzle. "Annabelle bought you?"

"Considering who my boss is, it was an uncomfortable situation to find myself in."

The smile that had threatened earlier broke free. "Big, bad Beckett Pearson unraveled by Annabelle Lockhart? I met her once. She didn't seem too scary to me."

Was Jackie afraid of anyone? He gave a derisive grunt. "She made it very clear she bought me for a reason."

The smile fell off her face. "You slept with her?"

"What? No." God. He sat back, totally pissed and completely on edge. How had this happened? It was like living a bad dream. Kicking his feet out, they bumped into Jackie's and he had to shift sideways in order to extend his legs all the way. His ass hurt from sitting on the cheap plastic chair and he was beyond exhausted, his temper a short fuse. "I danced around her blatant advances all night. We stopped at her place for a drink before dinner, we ate at Flat 1776, and I dropped her off afterwards. That's it. That's all that happened."

"So why do the cops think you killed her? What's your motive?"

"Everything they have is circumstantial and I don't have motive." He'd heard their spiel, the list of 'evidence', over and over. "I was the last one to see her. To be in her house. After I left, she sent me a text. A suggestive one with a picture of her in lingerie. She paid three grand for this date and the cops think I slept with her. They believe the autopsy will reveal my...*trace evidence*, but they won't find any, I assure you."

"Meaning, no semen? No condom in a garbage can? Nothing?"

Jeez. Of course, she would spell it all out in black and white. "None."

"Good. Then let's get you out of here and work on carving these charges up."

If only. "What they will find – on my suit jacket – is her blood."

Jackie's calculating mind went berserk behind her eyes. This time both brows climbed skyward. "Well, *that's* a problem. Explain."

Beck wished someone could explain this whole goddamn situation to him. *Deep breath. Focus.* "When we were at her place before dinner, she dropped a wine bottle and cut herself. Her blood is on my jacket because she grabbed my arm with her bleeding hand when I tried to help her clean up the mess. I'm guessing the jacket is at the lab. Crime techs were already searching my place by the time I had cuffs on."

"Her throat was slit."

"Yep, and they're saying it was done by a piece of glass from the broken wine bottle. She left it in a grocery bag on the counter when we went to dinner."

"Did you touch the bottle at all?"

"What do you think?"

Shit was written all over Jackie's face. "Was there anyone else at the house when you were there? Did you see any cars in the driveway when you dropped her off? Did she mention anyone living with her? Any hired help? Any enemies who might want her dead?"

"We didn't discuss her domestic help, and silly me, I didn't think to ask about her enemies. Great dinner conversation, thanks for the tip. I bet that's why you're so popular, isn't it? All the guys love you grilling them about their enemies and who might want them dead."

She flinched slightly, but didn't acknowledge the dig. "Was there anyone else in her house?"

"As far as I know, she lives alone. Byron moved out four months ago according to gossip around the office."

"Okay," Jackie said, blowing out a breath. "You were the last one to see her, your fingerprints are on the weapon, and her blood is on your jacket."

His fingers impatiently drummed on the table. It was a slam-dunk case. *Fuck.* "I wasn't the last person to see her. The killer was."

"I'm looking at it from the prosecution's point of view."

And now he was the one who knew better than to ask a question he didn't want an answer to. He asked anyway. "And?"

Jackie punched the recording off, tossed her phone in her briefcase and stood, smoothing down her jacket and glancing at her mismatched shoes again. "I'd say it's a good thing I came down to help you because you're in a world of hurt. Fleming would screw this up so many ways you couldn't see straight from your prison cell."

Before he could respond, the door to the room flew open, bouncing off the wall.

"Time's up," Muldoon said. "Back across the hall."

"Fine," Jackie said. "We're through anyway, and my client won't be answering any more questions tonight. It's late and he's tired. Get him processed."

She waited for Muldoon to escort Beck back to the interview room they'd started in, where he stood waiting while Jackie did her thing.

"We still have questions," Muldoon said.

"Sorry, detective. I'm shutting it down." She faced Beck again. "You'll have to stay in here tonight, but I'll get you arraigned tomorrow afternoon. Are you able to post bond?"

He nodded. All that damned modeling money earning interest in his mutual funds account would come in handy. The irony of using it for bail hit him all over again – all the years growing up in his criminal family and staying clean hadn't done a damn bit of good.

A shout came from the hallway and Beck's heart dropped to the floor.

Byron Lockhart appeared in the open doorway, his face twisted with rage, his jacket askew. More shouts rang out, footsteps pounding as someone chased after him.

"You fucking bastard," Lockhart said. "You killed my wife."

Then he reared back and sent a fist at Beck's face.

"What the...?" Jackie stood in stunned shock as a handcuffed Beck stumbled back from the cheap shot the FBI director had just thrown.

"Grab him!" she yelled. "What the hell is wrong with you guys letting him in here?"

Even handcuffed, Beck's big body moved to a fighting stance and his hands came up to protect his head.

Before Lockhart could throw another punch, Muldoon bear-hugged him from behind, dragging him backward.

"You killed her!" Lockhart screamed.

The only good thing about this whole setup was that the Director of the FBI had just been recorded punching a suspect. One of his own damned agents at that.

The press would pounce on this like catnip.

"Sir!" Brasich rushed into the room. "Calm down."

Unwilling to risk the Director coming unhinged, Jackie moved in front of Beck. Growing up with three older brothers, she'd diffused more than a few smackdowns.

She jabbed a finger at Muldoon, then Brasich. "I should have both your badges. In fact, we may sue the District for this. Throw the department into that lawsuit too. Why not?" She angled back to Beck. "Prepare to be a very rich man. We're taking everyone down."

Of all the wacky things she'd seen, this one topped it. If she wasn't so damned giddy over the colossal screw-up of a supposedly grieving husband anywhere near the murder suspect, she might rail about the injustice of it all. She'd bury them with this little ditty.

Muldoon held the back of Lockhart's suit coat while nudging him to the door, but...wait. How perfect was this?

"Director Lockhart," Jackie said, "where were *you* this evening?"

Brasich whirled on her. "Knock it off, counselor."

Not in this lifetime, pal. She waggled a hand between Brasich and Lockhart. "You guys had him in here for questioning, right? I mean, *hello*." She clunked herself on the head. "This makes total sense. With a highly public – and nasty –

divorce going on, of course he'd be your first suspect. Oh, and let's not forget their joint holdings. Lots of money at stake for the good director."

She cocked her head at Lockhart. He wanted to say something. She saw it in the purple glow of his cheeks. Years of trial work had taught her to read the signs. And if her experience taught her anything, with just a gentle poke, the Director would explode on her. Well, bring it on.

"From what I've heard," she said. "Director Lockhart is a jealous man. One with a beautiful wife. Oh, excuse me, *estranged* wife." She gestured to Beck. "And here we have the pinnacle of sexuality, absolute eye candy of a man who went out with Annabelle this evening. A man she *bid* on at an auction." She let out a snort. "Heck, I don't blame you for being upset. I mean, are any of us doubting what Annabelle had in mind for Mr. Pearson? I can tell you from the female perspective," she faced Beck, made a spectacle of checking him out from head to toe. "*I* have no doubt."

Oh, wow. She was pushing it here. Even for her, smartass of the century. This little stunt might finally land her in front of the bar association. But, well, she supposed the horse had already left the barn so she might as well play it out.

She stepped in Lockhart's path, completely invading his personal space while she locked onto his fiery blue eyes. "Did you kill your wife?"

He paused for a long few seconds, his jaw flexing hard. "Fuck. You."

The room fell silent. Even the detectives were struck mute and that didn't happen everyday. At least not in Jackie's life. If nothing else, she'd take pride in that.

Finally, Brasich snapped to and grabbed her by the elbow. "That's it." He hauled her out of the way while Muldoon shoved Lockhart out.

"No problem," Jackie said. She glanced up at the video camera mounted on the wall. "It's all recorded anyway."

She turned to Beck whose right cheek had already swelled. "Are you all right?"

He nodded. "I'm fine."

"Brasich," Jackie said, "please provide my client with an ice pack. And, given the department's complete lack of control when it comes to protecting Mr. Pearson, I want him in a private cell tonight, with a guard. No one goes near him. And get him a damned shirt." Now she invaded his space. "If anything happens to him, I'll put your ass in a sling."

4

Ten minutes later, the interrogation room door opened and Brasich handed Jackie the ice pack she'd asked for. After this whole cluster, one would think the detectives might want to hop on aiding their recently attacked prisoner. Go figure.

"Thank you," she said.

No sense in pissing the guy off any more than she had to. Brasich nodded then closed the door again, leaving Jackie and Beck alone. She waved her handcuffed client to a chair, waited for him to sit then passed him the ice.

He lifted the pack to his face, wincing at the contact. "Damn, he popped me good."

"It doesn't look...horrible. Sorry about the cuffs. I'll see if I can get them taken off."

"Forget it, not worth the fight. Let's pick our battles. Besides, they'll be taking them off to process me."

Jackie nodded. "You're the client, assuming you're hiring me. Or did you want me to call *Fleming*?"

A reward came by way of a quirking smile from Beck. The

man was under arrest for murder and still managed to find humor in her twisted joke.

And what was she doing? The easier question – the one with a simple answer that didn't require her already battered and exhausted brain to think – was what *wasn't* she doing? Which would be telling Beck she'd get him arraigned, but he needed to square up another attorney. One he didn't have a personal history with.

One he hadn't put his extremely male and private part inside.

Total mess.

He tossed the ice pack on the table and dropped his hands to his lap. "After the show you just put on, I'm hiring you. You're not afraid to push. Or piss people off."

"Oh, heck no. Where's the fun otherwise?"

"You realize I'm pretty much screwed, right?"

Jackie clucked her tongue. "With that attitude, you sure are. Listen up, glamour boy, you're not going down for this. We're barely two hours in and I already have a laundry list of screw-ups. As soon as I get you situated, I'll leak that I've been retained by you. Believe me, my phone will blow up with press inquiries. At which point, I will joyfully give them a literal blow by blow of what went on here tonight."

"No, I'm not trying this thing in the media."

Of course not. She'd win it on skill and good investigative work. The press could help though. Jackie slid into the chair opposite Beck and set her hands on top of the table. The camera, no doubt, recorded everything so she'd keep this brief. "That's not my intention, but you know how this works. The prosecution will use the press. They'll feed them little bits of circumstantial evidence that will make you look guilty before you even see a courtroom. We have to get ahead of that."

"I agree, but find another way. For Christ sake's, Jackie, I'm an

FBI agent who's been accused of killing the FBI Director's wife. My career with the Bureau is over, which means, if I'm not locked up, I'll be looking for a new job soon. Who's gonna hire me?"

She held up her hands. "Whoa. Settle down. We're on step one and you're pushing ahead to ten-thousand. It's way too early to speculate. We don't even know for sure what evidence they have. Let me do my thing. You, of all people, know I will tear their case apart. I have an excellent investigator and a brilliant – and highly aggressive – junior partner. We're good. Really good. So, when you're acquitted, don't worry, a lot of people will hire you. Don't give up on me, glamour boy. I've got this."

He blew out a hard breath and shook his head. "I'm not giving up, believe me, but I'm a realist and this," he held up his handcuffed hands, "doesn't look good."

The door opened and Muldoon jerked his chin. "Let's go, Pearson."

Jackie shot out of her chair. "Private cell?"

"Yes, counselor. It's just short of a suite at the Ritz."

"With a guard?"

Muldoon rolled his eyes. "As much as it pisses me off, yes. He's not getting hurt on my watch."

Jackie grinned, all I'm-a-sarcastic-bitch. "Well, at least not *again*, right?"

That may have been a cheap shot, but they deserved it. Lockhart should never have been allowed near her client.

Muldoon didn't bother answering. What could he say? He knew she was right. He stood in the doorway, waiting for Beck who – bless him – took his time getting to his feet.

Jackie set one hand on his arm, her fingers not making it around the rock hard biceps. "You'll be fine tonight. I'll have you out tomorrow."

"Thank you. I apologize for my bad manners earlier."

"Not wanting me for your lawyer? Forget it."

"Not that. The remark about your dating life. That was low and uncalled for."

She waved it off, laughing. "But not far from the truth."

He stepped into the hallway, but paused. "One more thing."

Jackie moved next to him. "What is it?"

He leaned in, got right next to her ear, and his warm breath tickled her skin, sending tiny electrifying shocks right to her core.

"Don't," he said, "call me glamour boy."

Two hundred and fifty thousand dollars bail. Jesus, he was worth more as a murder suspect than as an upstanding FBI agent.

An FBI agent with a dozen commendations in his personnel folder and a near-perfect close record for finding the missing. Of course the one he never found was related to the Donlin case. Before he'd been allowed on Taylor's team, he'd had to prove himself with criminal investigations. He'd found it easy to understand the perps and figure out ways to bring them down. Only Jackie DelRay had stood in his way, claiming there wasn't sufficient evidence.

Taylor hadn't seen it as a failure, liking the way Beck had pursued the conviction and gone over Jackie's head to do so. Taylor liked aggressive agents on her team. After the showdown at the precinct, Beck now understood why Jackie had gone defensive lineman on him and he'd loved it. Byron Lockhart was no small man and he'd obviously been on a tear. While Beck couldn't blame him, he had to admit disappointment that the Director immediately jumped to the same conclusion the cops had   that Beck was guilty. What he hadn't expected was that Jackie DelRay, all 5'6"of her, would jump in front of Lockhart's 6'2" bulky frame and defend him.

Crazy woman.

At least she'd gotten him out on bail. Most murder suspects

in DC sat in jail until their hearings, but not him. Not even with the circumstances of the high-profile victim and all that went along with Beck being a strong flight risk. As an agent, he had vast resources and the knowledge and skills to disappear in a heartbeat.

He actually did have a bag ready to go in his closet. Every good agent did. Not because they anticipated going on the run, but due to the fact they could be called up at any moment to fly across the country on an assignment.

Gingerly touching his bruised cheek as he opened the door to his place, he called out for Tink. It had been storming for the past few hours and she was probably hiding under the bed. A muffled meow echoed from the living room and he let out a small sigh of relief as the stray came running.

His phone was full of text messages and voicemails, but he needed a shower to wash off the jail stink. A nap and copious amounts of food were on the to-do list as well.

But first, he needed to do something normal, like feed his cat. He scratched her behind the ears as she weaved around his ankles, purring. Her happiness at seeing him was most likely due to the fact he'd missed feeding time, but he didn't care – being back at his home, taking care of the cat, was what his freaked-out brain needed more than anything.

Once Tink was well fed and showing her appreciation by rubbing against his ankles again, he prioritized what he needed to do: shower, shave, eat, call Taylor, call the other team members, since his caseload would need to be divided between them, and then he needed sleep. His new attorney had ordered him to stay in, keep his head down, and prepare for her to be all over his business like a tick on a coonhound.

Jackie had been the star of the show at the bail hearing, just like she had been during his interrogation and processing. Him being a law enforcement agent, her cutting, efficient manner mostly made him insane. Today? On his behalf, she'd been a rockstar who'd told him to keep his mouth shut and follow her lead. Not something he was used to being told, but he kind of liked it. He could see the judge liked her and Jackie was efficient but respectful. They were in and out in minutes.

Ball busters usually turned him off. He wasn't a profiler, but he knew most were simply overcompensating. Jackie was a different animal. She knew her stuff and her confidence made her a true force of nature, not just a bunch of bravado hiding an insecure woman. He'd sensed that in her the first time he'd met her and nothing had changed.

The fact he'd been assaulted by Lockhart had helped him land bail, thanks to Jackie's ability to spin anything and everything her way.

She was so damn sexy he got a hard-on just thinking about her smart mouth and those dangerous curves. Her body was born for tight skirts and heels. After going into private practice, she had to be making plenty of money and should have been carrying designer handbags, not creased up, old leather briefcases. No other woman had ever irritated him more in his career, or made him hornier. Her breasts alone were a thing of beauty, not to mention her legs.

He enjoyed fantasizing that she secretly wore sexy lingerie under those conservative suits. Red? Hot pink? Or was she more of a satin girl? Back in the day, on their one spring break together, it had been lace.

Lots of it.

While he continued his dance with normalcy, he kept images of being in prison out of his mind by putting his hot attorney in his own personal photo shoot, full of sexy pouts and daring displays of cleavage.

Ah, yes. Jackie DelRay was a sex kitten in all his fantasies.

Even if he hated her.

After cleaning up and stuffing his face, he started in on the calls he needed to make.

Of course, everyone on the team already knew – not much escaped the hallowed halls of the FBI – and he had actual threats from several of them because they also knew Jackie was his lawyer and he was out on bail. They all wanted to know why hadn't he called them straight away. Why was he letting DelRay anywhere near him? Had she kidnapped him? Was he delusional? He was likely to end up with one or all on his doorstep in short order if he didn't make contact.

First, he called Taylor who answered on the first ring. "What the hell is going on?" she barked at him.

"Hi, boss. How's your vacation?"

"I leave you in charge of the group and you end up arrested for murder? When Janiece called and told me you were in jail, I figured you'd finally had enough of the Golden Boy and you forgot to call me to help you bury the body."

Said Golden Boy was a profiler named Leo Wellington whom no one in their cold case unit liked but had to tolerate. Leo liked to steal cases from them right before they were about to find a missing child or bring a criminal to justice so he could ride their coattails and appear to be the best agent inside the FBI. In reality, he used everyone else's hard work to pad his successful close rate, as well as his ego. They'd often joked about offing him, but the weasel wasn't worth the jail time. "You know I live to make your life easier, but I'm afraid you have to keep working with Leo for now."

"Tell me what happened."

Tink curled up next to him as he ticked off the high points like it was someone else's case. He had to figure out who would take care of the cat if he ended up in prison.

"Don't worry, I'm fine," he told Taylor after he'd filled her in on the details, knowing full well she was probably already on her way to the airport, cutting her vacation short. "I've got everything under control."

"Liar. I'll be there in three hours, four tops, depending on the crap-hole weather you've got there in DC. They're already rerouting planes because of the storms from what I understand. Are you sure about DelRay? I can get you someone else. Justice Greystone knows everyone and between him, me, and the Schock sisters, we can find you the best lawyer on the east coast."

"I'm good. DelRay, as you know, is a pit bull. Pretty sure I already have the best lawyer, but thanks. And don't cut your vacation short. Mad Dog will never let me live it down and I don't need him bitching at me all the time."

His doorbell rang and Beck looked up. Had the press already figured out where he lived? Was Byron making a follow-up play? Was it possible his trench coat fantasy about Jackie was possibly coming true? The one where she was buck-naked underneath?

"Look, I've gotta go. I love you and I'm in good hands. I'll make sure my current cases are distributed among the others. I won't let any balls drop, I promise."

"Forget about delegating your cases, Beck. Janiece can handle it. Whatever you do, stay out of Lockhart's line of fire, okay? I'll be there by tonight and we'll make a plan of attack."

She hung up and his doorbell dinged again. Tossing the phone on the couch, he patted Tink's head and went to see who was beating up his doorbell.

It wasn't the press or Lockhart. Unfortunately, it wasn't Jackie in a sexy trench coat either.

He opened the door, knowing he was about to take the same beating his doorbell just had. "Sydney. Grey. What are you two doing here? I'm guessing it's not a personal invite to the next bachelor auction."

Sydney narrowed her eyes and motioned for him to get out of her way. "Quit being flippant. Why do you think we're here?"

He really had no idea, except oh, yeah, Annabelle's donation was probably an issue for Syd now that the woman was dead.

God, he was tired. Totally blown. At this rate, prison might actually be the only way to solve his sleep deprivation problem. But he opened the door wide and waved them in. "Come on in. No point in standing out there in the rain."

They both stepped inside, Sydney looking like she might just rip him a new one. "I don't even want to know how you got yourself into this situation, but if you need help, we're here for you."

Okay, not what he'd expected. "You're not mad?"

"Of course I'm mad." She pointed a finger at him, and yep, here it came. "Do you know how long it took Fallyn to talk me into doing a bachelor auction in the first place? Months! I hated the idea."

Fallyn Pasche was known as the Washington fixer – she knew how to cover up scandals and promote causes she felt were worthy of her time.

Syd tapped her foot. "But I caved and then it took months for us to design it, even with Caroline and Mitch's help. I had to grovel at people's feet and do all kinds of social media nonsense that I absolutely hate. But I did it, and everything went great. We raised thousands for the shelter, and I thought, *gee, Sydney, maybe it was all worth it*, and then bam!" She smacked her hands together, the sharp sound echoing in the room. "My biggest donor ends up murdered and her bachelor is the prime suspect."

Hoo, baby. The fire sizzling in her eyes and the smoke coming from her ears made Beck take a step back. "Can I get you guys something? Coffee? Hot tea? I have a really nice organic chai."

"This is not a social call," Grey said. "In case you haven't figured that out."

The defensive lineman in Beck rose to the surface, but he'd

learned a long time ago it was better to appear calm, cool, and collected no matter the odds. "I'm sorry this reflects negatively on St. Agnes. If there's anything I can do…"

Sydney took a step toward him, her coat dripping water on his floor. She curled a handful of his shirt in her fingers. "I'm sorry you're going through this. It's horrible. And, I want to be mad at you, but I can't seem to manage it. Not with what you're facing. But know this, hotshot, when your name is cleared, you will be doing many, many hours of community service at the shelter. *Hours and hours.* Your ass is mine." She gripped the shirt harder. "Do you understand?"

He raised his hands in submission. At least she seemed to believe he was innocent. "Whatever I can do to make this right, I'll do it."

She huffed slightly, expecting a fight. When he didn't give it to her, she released him and stepped back, resuming her place next to Grey who, if Beck wasn't mistaken, might be smiling.

"Good," Syd said. "Glad that's settled."

Beck met Grey's eyes. "I didn't kill Annabelle and whoever did is still out there."

Grey nodded. "Any ideas on our perp?"

Our perp? Hmm. "Only the most obvious one."

"Lockhart?"

Beck shrugged. "I know almost nothing about Annabelle, but with the divorce, he's the first person I'd take a hard look at."

Grey cocked his chin at Beck's face. "He give you that?"

Touching his cheek, Beck noted the swelling had gone down considerably. "Harvard may have prepared him for leading the FBI, but he hits like a Volunteer."

Sydney frowned. "A volunteer?"

"The Tennessee Volunteers, ma'am. The Tide sends them packing every year."

Syd rolled her eyes. "I have no idea what you're talking about, but okay."

Grey smirked. "You're in good hands with Jackie DelRay. My team will help in any way we can, but I expect a cigar when you're cleared."

Cigars were a tradition with Crimson players every time they beat Tennessee. Beck held out a hand. Here was a man who understood tradition. "You got it."

They shook and Grey hustled Sydney out into the rain. Beck headed to bed, sending off a few texts to his FBI teammates to let them know he was okay and for them to stay far away from him. Byron would no doubt be breathing down all their necks.

Tink snuggled beside him and he stroked her fur, wondering again who would take care of her if he ended up in prison. Another thing to add to his to-do list – find a home for the stray.

Jackie unlocked her law office door – so much for taking the day off – at 11:00 a.m. First Beck's arraignment and now a stop here. She flipped the lights on, reached behind the potted tree that hid the security system panel and punched in the code. After the beep-beep indicated the system was off, she bypassed the receptionist's desk and headed down the narrow hall to her office.

As office space went, this wasn't a bad set-up. Three large offices, a conference room and a roomy waiting area. All painted an earthy brown her mother had insisted on. Mom had great taste, but before paint went on the walls Jackie couldn't picture it. Too dark and gloomy, she'd thought. Eventually, she'd given in and had been forced to admit her mother was right.

Her mother wasn't a litigator for nothing.

Jackie walked the last few feet to her office, taking in the silence she'd be forever thankful for. Normally, the office energy ran high. Between the phone's ringing and Josh hollering to her from his office, it was a rare moment in stillness.

Giving everyone a day off had been the right call. She was so damned tired, she wasn't sure she could deal with her mouthy crew today. Bad enough she'd summoned Chessie in for a quick meeting.

Him, she couldn't avoid. Not when she'd just landed Beck's high-profile case that would surely drag her client through the news cycle for the next few days. What she needed now was for the President to botch something, a famous actor to leave his wife, or a smallpox outbreak. Anything to lure DC reporters from the murder of the FBI director's estranged wife.

And the man accused of said murder happened to be a hunky special agent the victim *won* in an auction. This thing had tabloid fodder *and* bad TV movie written all over it.

Sighing, Jackie kicked open her office door and smacked the wall switch. The desk lamp and the larger one in the corner flashed on, spraying the room in muted light. No industrial, overhead glare here. In the beginning, it had been yet another of her mother's ideas. As the nights dragged on, and fatigue, more often than not, pressed in, Jackie had come to appreciate the soft lighting.

She tossed her briefcase on the corner of the desk and dropped into her chair to survey the stacks of folders, mail, and trade magazines smothering the top. That last trial had eaten up her time, and day after day, her desk became more of a war zone. Under her crystal paperweight, the one from her mother that was heavy enough to crack a skull, sat a stack of hand-written notes from her assistant. Yep, plenty to do.

"Jackie?" Chessie's gravelly voice boomed from the reception area.

"My office," she called.

A second later he appeared in the doorway. He wore a black suit with a pink pocket square. Now that he worked the private sector and could afford it, Chessie enjoyed a vast wardrobe. He also held a white envelope in his hand.

"Nice hanky," she said.

He entered, giving the once-over to the roomy button-down top and ponytail she'd changed into after the arraignment. "Your hair is up. I like it."

"Thanks. Too tired to do much else with it. Between the jeans and ponytail, it's a good thing my mother isn't here."

The ultimate powersuit woman, Mom would kill her for wearing such casual attire to the office.

Chessie dropped the envelope on top of a stack of mail and sat in one of her upholstered guest chairs. "You look tired. More than usual anyway."

Wonderful. A real charmer this one. "Thanks so much, Chess. What's this envelope?"

"You *must* be tired since you missed it on the floor by the entrance. I thought you might have dropped it."

"Not me."

"Someone slid it under the door, maybe?"

Interesting. She picked it up, used it to point at Chessie. "Maybe Josh dropped it. Thanks for coming in. I wanted to get you started on this new case."

"Annabelle Lockhart? You landed it?"

"Bet your butt I did. What are your buddies saying?"

"Not much. Which means, they don't like Pearson for this. Too convenient."

"That's what I thought. Maybe he's the patsy."

Chessie shrugged. "What do you need from me?"

"The usual. Get into her closets. See what she's into. Any enemies – aside from her very powerful husband. Maybe they have a fetish or two the good director doesn't want exposed." Jackie flicked the envelope again. "Do your thing."

The investigator pushed out of his chair. "Will do. Anything else I can do for you?"

A wicked smile split Chessie's face and Jackie rolled her eyes. Had to love her throwback of an investigator. She really shouldn't encourage him, but she couldn't help it. She loved the guy. Sue her.

"No," she said. "I'm all set. Let me know what you find."

Chessie left and once again the office fell into blissful silence. The stack of mail on her desk loomed large. Maybe she'd take an hour and sort through it. It had always relaxed her, sharpened her senses. Something, in her current condition, she desperately needed. She'd start with the white envelope in her hand. The front was blank so she flipped it over. No return address on the back either. Probably one of those introductory offer things the phone company constantly left for them.

She reached into her desk drawer, grabbed the letter opener and sliced away, finding a folded sheet of letter-sized paper. She slid it out and patience running short, flapped the page open.

A full color photo.

Printed right on the page and with no caption or note. What the heck?

Assuming the note could have fallen out, she held the envelope open again, finding nothing before checking the desktop and finally the floor.

And then it happened. That weird snaking feeling that curled up her neck, indicating that – oh, yes – something extremely fascinating was about to happen. Jackleen DelRay, defense attorney on the rise, could live her entire existence on that feeling.

Flattening the page on her desk, she studied the photo where three men in tuxedos, all toasting with amber-filled rock glasses, flashed costly smiles. They had a look about them. Privilege with more than a hint of cockiness.

Was that...? The man on the left possessed dark features indicative of Greek or maybe Italian descent, but the one next to him? He was all classic WASPy blond hair and fair skin.

Skin that she'd seen just hours ago.

Byron Lockhart.

A whoosh of air left her and Jackie sat back. Damn, she shouldn't have touched that photo. If she hadn't been so fatigued, so completely brain-fried, she'd have considered the possibility that an anonymous envelope might contain evidence. Clearly, this was a message. What that was, she didn't know, *yet*.

But the questions, those babies fired like rockets from her brain. Who were the other men in the photo and what did they mean to Lockhart?

More than that, why was this photo on her desk, and who the hell shoved it under her door?

Beck's phone blared, jarring him out of a dream about quicksand sucking him into an abyss.

What the...? He came up on an elbow and reached for the cell before his eyes were open.

Which only resulted in him knocking it to the floor.

Swearing, he almost let the call go to voicemail instead of chasing the phone, sleep already trying to drag him back down, but he'd put his *do not disturb* on for everyone but Jackie.

Pushing out of bed, he reached for the damn thing, knowing Jackie would only keep calling until he answered and it might be something important.

"'Lo?"

It was dark in the room, stripes of light squeaking through the edges of the blinds. Still daytime.

"I just got into my office." Jackie said.

"Good for you."

"And found a strange envelope."

His voice was rough and he cleared his throat. "And that required calling me?"

"You need to get over here."

Fighting a yawn, he pushed to his feet. "Why? What's up with this envelope?"

"There was a picture inside. Three men at some black-tie event."

Wow, fascinating. "What does that have to do with me?"

"One of the people in the photo is Byron Lockhart."

"And? Is he holding a knife to his wife's neck? Because I really don't get why this is more important than my beauty rest."

"That's just it. I don't either, but it *is*. My investigator found it by the front door of my office."

"Okay."

"So, Special Agent Pearson, I'd like to know who slid this photo under my door, presumably overnight. Or at least early this morning. Any ideas?"

Well, when she put it that way. "Are you safe? Doors locked?"

"Of course."

"Anything stolen?"

"No. The alarm was on. No one entered. Quit worrying about my safety and get your butt over here. We need to figure this out."

"Do you have a weapon?"

"Relax, Special Agent. I can take care of myself."

His jaw tightened. "Are. You. Armed?"

"I'm sitting here with my Glock 19 pointed at the door. And trust me, I know how to load more than the dishwasher and washing machine. Anyone comes through it, they'll get lead in their balls."

"Good girl." Damn. Brains, body, and that mouth.

"Don't ever refer to me as girl again, unless you want me to return to calling you glamour boy."

"Point taken. I'll be there in twenty. Don't shoot me, 'kay?"

She just laughed before hanging up.

5

Overcast skies left a gray gloom blanketing the still wet streets as Beck found a parking spot a few blocks from DelRay & Associates. Construction across the street had turned the whole block into a mess.

His windshield wipers flapped annoyingly, the rain slowing to a soft mist. He turned them off, peering around to make sure no one had followed him. He'd had a reporter show up on his doorstep right after he'd gotten Jackie's phone call. Another had been on the first's heels. Word was out, and he'd be headline material on the eleven o'clock news, sure as shit.

Man, the world could sure go ass over apple cart in twenty-four hours.

It hadn't been hard to ditch the press, but he felt sort of guilty leaving Tink. They weren't supposed to trespass, but everyone knew reporters would do anything for a story.

Get to Jackie.

Shutting off the car, he glanced down the street. No one waited on the concrete steps to ambush him, so he locked up and jogged down the street. Who had left Jackie the photo of Byron Lockhart and what did it mean?

Lockhart wasn't stupid. He wasn't an emotional guy either. From his reaction at the station, Beck wondered if the show had been authentic or if the Director was a damn fine actor.

Because he wasn't the only one thinking Byron made a better suspect. Jackie had immediately latched on to the idea.

Beck took the stairs two at a time and found the front door locked. Good. He knocked twice.

"DelRay," he called, making sure she knew it was him.

A buzzer sounded followed by the clunk of a disengaging lock. He entered the office, locked the door behind him, and glanced around. The place was certainly more upscale than he'd expected, considering Jackie could barely dress herself. "I'm here."

"Last office on the right," she called.

The soft lighting and fancy paintings were a nice touch. *She must have had a designer.*

He had no trouble finding her door with the brass name-plate, *Jackleen DelRay, Attorney.*

The door was cracked an inch, and he pushed it all the way open, only to pull up short. Jackie stood at her desk with her shirt off, her generous breasts spilling over the edges of a sports bra and jiggling with abandon as she scrubbed at a shirt lying on the blotter.

She glanced up and didn't even flinch, continuing to scrub furiously. "I spilled coffee. Figured you'd give me grief if I didn't at least attempt to clean it up."

Beck stood in the doorway, unable to blink or even look away. He remembered those luscious mounds, how they'd felt in his hands, how her skin had tasted under his tongue. Everything in him, including the not-so-small mini-Beck inside his pants, screamed for him to get her under him again.

Bam, right there on the desk. He'd brush the heaps of files and that girly Glock off to the side and free those puppies from the tight nylon bursting at the seams.

But this wasn't Jackie DelRay, law student from the University of Pennsylvania, ready to go for broke on top of her big cherry desk. This was former Assistant United States Attorney DelRay, a mature, confident, successful woman who was now his lawyer.

So screwed.

Or not screwed, actually, he laughingly thought.

Knowing her, this little exhibition was payback. She wasn't seriously flashing those ginormous boobs at him because she'd spilled coffee. She was reminding him of what they'd shared twelve years ago and all the regret that came with it.

Mission accomplished.

Mini-Beck pressed against his zipper, as hard and unforgiving as Jackie the pit bull. Digging deep for a shred of sensibility, he wheeled around and turned his back to her. "Please put your shirt on."

He heard a soft laugh. "Oh, come on. My bathing suit has less material. Besides, it's not like you haven't seen this before."

"I'm serious, Jackie. You're my lawyer. I can't be ogling you, no matter how much I want to."

Another chuckle, then the sound of soft footsteps before something slapped against his back. "Here, put your eyes on this while I fix my shirt."

He glanced back to where she held a photo and a pair of latex gloves. Too bad his gaze strayed to her breasts, because once more she was too much temptation for him after the past twenty-four hours had brought him so low. "You're evil, but you know that, don't you?"

She tried to appear innocent, but jutted out her chest anyway. "Me? What did I do?"

She knew exactly what she was doing. "I'm only a man, Jackie."

"You are indeed. I've been known to bring a man to his knees if necessary. That doesn't make me evil."

"Keep talking like that and flaunting your rack at me and you'll find yourself on your back begging me to make you come. You remember what that feels like, don't you?"

Something changed in her eyes, like she might actually be considering it. Mini-Beck cheered.

He reached out and fingered a lock of hair that had pulled loose from her ponytail. His thumb brushed her clavicle and she sucked in a soft breath. "I don't have much to lose at this point. Might as well enjoy myself."

She didn't pull away. "We had this conversation. I told you I'd get you off."

"You better put your shirt on or you'll be getting me off in more ways than one."

Her chin came up, eyes sparking with challenge.

"Is that a threat or a promise, Agent Pearson?"

Was she really doing this right now?

Two could play that game.

He caressed the line of her throat, dropped his finger to run it down her cleavage. Another intake of breath made her chest rise. "You know from past experience, I don't make threats, and I *am* a man of my word."

The photo and gloves hit the floor and she launched herself at him, arms going around his neck as he caught her in his arms. Her legs fit perfectly around his waist and he carried her to the desk, ready to make his fantasy a reality.

Their lips met, the kiss as hot and feral as she was. Files flew off the desk, the gun skittered to the edge—and whoopsie daisy, Beck reached out and caught it before it went over. He wedged himself between Jackie's legs and she moaned.

He kissed her long and deep, sucking at her tongue, then biting her bottom lip. Her hands were all over his back, his shoulders, pulling at his short hair as she bucked her hips under him.

His hands got their wish and he filled both with her

glorious breasts. Dipping his head, he kissed, licked, and sucked at her skin, first the naked mounds above the cups of the bra, then her nipples through the thin fabric.

"God, yes," Jackie said as if he'd asked for permission. "More. Harder."

"Happy to accommodate."

And then, from somewhere behind him, he heard a throat being cleared. "Um, Jackie?"

Jackie jerked and let out an "eep", shoving at Beck to get him off her. His two-hundred and forty pounds kept her pinned, and he glanced over his shoulder, ready to kill whoever the asshole was in the doorway. "What the fuck do you want?"

"Hi, I'm Josh," the kid said. "Is Jackie okay?"

Seriously?

The woman in question squirmed out from under him and slapped him on the shoulder as if he were in trouble. "Josh! What are you doing here?"

"I came to wrap up the paperwork on the Brengle case. I heard about"—he motioned at Beck, a confused frown creasing his face—"your new client. I was going to call and see if you needed any help, but it looks like you, um, have things under control. You do, right?"

"Of course," Jackie said, quickly pulling on her shirt. Her fingers shook as she started buttoning it and she was breathing like she'd just run a mile sprint.

Beck chuckled, adjusting his pants and woody before picking up the fallen picture from the floor. "Jackie always has things under control."

Jackie moved toward the door, motioning Josh away. Her shirt was askew from the uneven button job. "Everything's good. We were just, uh, reviewing some details."

Beck waved the photo, a wide grin splitting his face. "Yep. Details."

She hustled Josh into the hallway and semi-closed the door

behind her. Lowering her voice, she must have given the kid an earful before she blew back in and leaned on the door with a look of pure embarrassment on her face. "That's my junior partner."

Jackie DelRay embarrassed? This was one for the books. "He needs to work on his timing."

She made a face and pointed to the photo. "Check out the lineup and tell me if you recognize anyone besides Byron."

His gaze stayed on her curvy ass as she walked to the desk, her jeans stretched tight across her butt cheeks. His fingers itched to cup them, but she loved playing cat-and-mouse games with him and he needed to take a step back from all of this.

He really did.

So why did that suck so effing much?

Rubbing his forehead with one hand, he forced his gaze to the floor. He was a fool to let her under his skin, but sometimes it felt damn good to do something so bad.

She'll be the death of me.

All the work of leaving his past behind and rising above what he'd come from. All the hours of pressing to be the best he could, instead of the worst. His intelligence could have helped his family's criminal enterprise considerably, but instead, he'd made it his mission to help people his family might have actually played a part in hurting.

So no matter how bad he wanted Jackie – and forget that his career with the Bureau was probably over – he couldn't let a few hours of sex sabotage his life.

Because falling for his attorney would do that. She had no more intention of creating a long-term relationship with him than she did with a dormouse and he'd already fallen for her once. Big, big mistake. If he did it again, she'd use him, chew him up, spit him out, and break his heart.

Losing that would be worse than losing his job.

Jackie snapped her fingers at him. "Earth to Beck. Where did you just go?"

"Where do you think?" he groused, taking a seat in a blue upholstered chair across from her. He studied the picture, squinted. "Byron looks like a kid in this photo. This must have been taken twenty years ago or more."

"The Director is fifty-three, so twenty years ago, he would have been thirty-three. Hardly a kid."

"Running the FBI has aged him considerably."

"Power can do that." Jackie rocked her office chair, noticing her misbuttoned shirt and starting to redo it. "What about the others?"

Beck studied the photo again but the soft lighting made it a challenge to see details and the photo was grainy. Jackie had a desk lamp, so he pushed out of the chair and went around to her side to turn it on.

The brighter light didn't help much, Jackie leaning forward to study the photo with him. She pointed a finger at one of the men who stood in the background, his head half turned as if he really didn't want his picture taken. "Does that guy look familiar? I swear I know him."

Beck zeroed in on the guy. He stood in a group with a bunch of other partygoers, a shadow falling over him. "Wait, is that...?"

Twenty years had aged him too. And farther behind him, Beck saw another indistinct figure. A woman staring at the man. She was behind a fancy column, only part of her face showing, but the look on it made him think she was totally crushing on the guy.

"Who?" Jackie demanded at Beck's pause. "Who is he?"

Beck straightened, setting the photo on the desk. "We need help with this."

"What do you mean? What kind of help?"

"I have a feeling I know who left this for you but the reason why might be a problem. Especially now."

"Stop being evasive. Who the hell is that guy and what does it have to do with your case?"

"That"—Beck tapped the woman's half-hidden face — "is Annabelle Lockhart. And that" — he tapped the man's face, forever frozen in time—"is currently the President of the United States."

Jackie pushed through the front door of her flat with Beck following. She'd lived in the first floor unit of the Georgetown brownstone for five years now and despite the rising rent, had no intention of leaving. Minutes from her office, the location served her well.

Like now.

As much as she hated to waste time coming home to change, her shirt was a dead loss. She bypassed the living room and adjoining kitchen/dining area on her way to the bedroom. Moving fast, she took off her trashed shirt and tossed it into the basket on the floor of the laundry room. Really, it was just a closet big enough for a stackable washer/dryer, but it saved her from making trips to the laundromat.

"I'll just be a second," she said. "Help yourself to whatever. Not that you'll find any food. Or, well, much of anything. There's some energy drinks in the fridge if you need it."

"Do you know what that stuff does to your body?"

The derision in Beck's voice would bring a lesser woman down. Her? Not so much.

"Listen, His Holiness the Dalai Lama, some of us are just regular people. We eat carbs and – heaven forbid – sweets. And when we haven't slept in days because we're springing hot FBI agents from lockup, we need a boost."

She entered her bedroom, moving straight to the closet where she grabbed a pair of casual slacks and a pullover that wouldn't wrinkle the second she put it on. Belt. Most times she'd skip it and just pull the shirt over her slacks, but with Mr. Vogue in tow, she needed to be put together.

"Ha!" Beck said. "When you have a heart attack from your crappy diet, don't blame me."

"Ha!" She jammed her feet into a pair of leopard print flats. At least her shoes would match this time. "I take full responsibility for my heathen ways."

She crossed the hall to the bathroom, took one look in the mirror and nearly cried. Between the pale skin, dark circles and her thick hair bursting free of her ponytail – and not in that cute way women purposely did – she looked like an escapee from a mental institution. Changes had to be made. Big changes.

Ones that would leave her feeling rested and not constantly in a rush that limited time spent on her appearance.

Sleep.

That's all she needed. A good eight or fifty hours.

Dealing with her hair first, she tugged on her ponytail holder, ran a brush through the long, in-need-of-a-trim strands, and twirled them into a chignon. No muss, no fuss. Her mother would be proud that some of her lessons still stuck.

Makeup came next. She'd need an entire team to fix her, but she could triage it. While dabbing concealer over the dark circles around her eyes, she contemplated Beck's case.

"Hey, hot stuff," she called, "who is it we're going to see?"

"He's a former profiler. Left the Bureau a few years ago."

After announcing one of the men in the photo was none other than the pre-politics president, Beck had phoned his boss, Taylor. They'd agreed to bring in Justice Greystone, and by the hero worship in Taylor's voice, the guy had to be something special. Or at least an FBI agent's version of it.

Jackie slapped on a little liner, narrowly avoiding stabbing herself in the eye. "And we're going to see him why?"

"He knows people. A lot of people."

Dang it. Smudged it. This was why she hated makeup. She snatched a small sponge from her toiletry bag and worked it across her eyelid to smooth out her mistake. Good enough. "Who does he work for now?"

"I have no idea."

A quick swipe of lipstick finished her mini-makeover and she popped back into the hallway where Beck stood leaning against the wall. She gestured for him to follow her to her office. "Wow," he said. "Look at you. I like your hair."

Go, Jackie. Maybe there was hope for her yet. "Thank you. Justice Greystone. Is he a spook?"

"Former Fed. He recently helped Taylor find her missing sister after nearly twenty years."

Jackie flipped the office light on and the three lamps illuminated the muted gray walls and white tray ceiling. She turned back. "Seriously?"

"Yeah."

"Alrighty then. I like him already. Let me grab my notes and we'll head out."

Whoever this Justice Greystone was, if he had contacts at the FBI – or anywhere else – who might help them identify the third man in the photo, Jackie was all for it.

She swung around her desk leaving Beck standing just inside the doorway beside the Italian, ultra-modern white sofa that cost her way more than any sane person should pay. But, oh, that leather. So soft.

Beck's perusal of the room stopped at the scraped oak bookshelves stuffed with her novels and legal books.

He let out a low whistle and she cocked her head. "What?"

"It's...nice," he said. "Bright and airy. Clean lines. Good energy."

"Thank you, I think. You seem surprised."

He met her gaze and held it. "I am."

Why did men have to be so honest? Idiots. The bunch of

them. "What did you expect? A cardboard box as my desk and a couple bean bag chairs? I spend most of my life in this room. I want it nice."

At some point she'd have to ruminate over why her desire to have a nice office was met with such shock. Then again, most of Beck's interaction with her, aside from that one crazy, lust-filled night – hell, even then maybe – revealed her to be...intense.

Tough.

Hard.

Dammit. Why did being good at her job mean she was a bitch? She was about to ask Mr. Wonderful that very question, had even opened her mouth and yet...no. Why bother? Asking would lead to a conversation. A personal one where maybe they'd confide in each other. Connect.

And she couldn't have that. No way. Not with the secrets she held. She'd already been torn up once by him. Of course, he didn't know that and she wouldn't risk him seeing anything but pit bull Jackie. Being a strong-willed man, he'd avoid an emotional connection with her. In her experience, alphas couldn't handle her. Not with their need to prove their manliness. Somehow, it all came down to her not being needy enough. And when the fuck did *that* become such a bad thing?

She looked away. Had to. The man was just too damned beautiful and she was a woman sorely lacking male attention. As evidenced by the fact she'd thrown herself at him and then succumbed to the humiliation of her partner finding her half naked in their client's arms.

Lord, Jackie.

She set her hand on the lone folder atop her desk. Unlike her law office, she preferred an uncluttered space at home. Here, even when working, she strived for peace. A break from the chaos that came with criminal defense work.

She ran her finger under the edge of the folder and flipped it open revealing...nothing.

Wait.

What the hell? She'd left an entire page of notes in there.

She stepped back, checked under the desk.

Beck came closer, his movements swift. "What is it?"

"After your arraignment I came home and made notes. I left them in this folder. They're gone."

"You sure?"

"Yes. I took a fresh folder from the drawer, wrote your name on it and shoved the notes in. Done."

"The paper isn't in your briefcase?"

Men. Unbelievable. "No, Beck." She held her hands out, spreading her fingers wide. "Why would I put notes in a folder and then not take the folder? I know what I did. The notes were in here."

A sound, something in the hallway, brought her gaze up. Having lived here for so long, she knew it's habits. The clunk of a pipe, the hum of the air conditioner, the rattle of the hot water heater, all of it a safety blanket for her mind.

That sound? The swish?

New.

Moving on instinct, she walked to the doorway. "Did you hear that?"

"What?"

If she knew, she wouldn't have asked. She stepped into the hall and peered right, checking the back door. Maybe an animal outside?

She waited a full second. Silence. Whatever it was, it was gone now.

Swish.

Or not.

She spun back and found a man dressed in jeans and a black long-sleeved T-shirt that covered every inch of his thick arms. He wore a baseball cap pulled low, almost covering his dark brows, but his eyes shifted. Left, right, left, right. She recognized the panic. Had seen it hundreds of times on defendants. That squirrelly anxiety inherent with guilt.

Tingles and a weird numbness shot down her arms, freezing them at her sides. Her self-defense instructor warned her about this. About paralyzing fear.

The intruder lunged, shoving her sideways. She slammed into the wall, cracking the side of her head before bouncing back and colliding with Beck, who locked onto her arms. Somehow, he was still moving while keeping her upright. "You okay?"

She nodded. He released her and took off, giving chase as the man unbolted her back door and slipped through.

6

———————

"*L*ock the door!" Beck yelled at Jackie as he sprinted out the back door after the intruder.

He hoped Jackie was all right because he was not —*not, by God*—letting this guy get away.

It was raining again and he was instantly drenched as he boogied down the alley. The smell of wet asphalt wafted up from the pavement and the ripe odor of garbage invaded his nostrils as he passed several giant bins.

The guy was all in black, including the cap on his head. He slipped as he ran around the corner but didn't go down, grabbing the edge of the building as he skidded.

Gloves. The guy was wearing gloves, which meant there would be no fingerprints.

Beck lowered his body slightly as he rounded the same corner, keeping extra weight on his left foot so he wouldn't slip.

He slowed when he hit the cross street, his vision blurry from the rain. *Where'd the guy go?*

The sidewalk was empty and brownstones crowded the entire block. No way the guy got down to the other end that fast.

His brain ticked off what he knew about the perp:

Approximately 5′9″, close to two hundred pounds.

Familiar with breaking and entering and not leaving fingerprints behind, but not stealthy on escapes.

Took Jackie's notes on the case.

Was this Annabelle's killer?

Movement to the right caught his eye. *There you are.*

The man burst from a shadowed doorway and cut across the street, trying to avoid the streetlights and almost succeeding. Illumination from an oncoming car foiled his plan.

Beck jetted after him. A heavy fog had risen, coating the streets. A horn sounded as Beck launched himself from between two parked cars and nearly got clipped. Reflexes to the rescue, he bolted up and over the hood and slid across to the opposite side, just missing another car from the other direction, and spurring a fresh round of horns and squealing brakes.

DC drivers were vocal and he heard a cacophony of swearing behind him. He paid it no heed, and ran harder as his quarry led him down another street at full speed.

His wet pants stuck to his legs and he wiped water from his face as he sprinted. Whoever this was, he wasn't stealthy enough to get out of Jackie's place without being seen, but was doing a damn good job at hauling ass. If Beck wasn't careful, he'd lose him before he could yell "FBI".

Was he FBI anymore? There had been no clarification from the higher-ups yet. Assistant Director Cunningham had been incommunicado. Taylor had been told nothing, just that Beck was on temporary suspension and to dole out his cases to the others on their team.

Right now, none of that mattered.

Get him.

The guy hung a right and disappeared. Beck dodged a couple hustling down the sidewalk with umbrellas and a couple of teenagers hanging out on the street corner.

Another ten yards and he found himself in front of a small park, but the man had disappeared once more, shadows swallowing him. Beck surveilled the scene in all directions, but nothing moved. The man had to be inside.

Where could a bulky guy hide?

Dogwoods and maples, losing their autumn-colored leaves, lined the square playland, a few on each end with trunks big enough to hide behind. A copse of Virginia sweetspire that really needed to be trimmed ran the length of the jogging path, and a semi-enclosed plastic castle from which a slide emerged sat flush in the center.

Not the trees—easy to slip behind but too exposed from multiple directions.

Not the castle—time consuming to climb the small steps and barely big enough for a two-hundred pound guy to squeeze into.

The sweetspire it is.

He had no clue if the perp was armed or not. For a moment, he wished he had his gun, but the element of surprise was better than any weapon.

The reddish color of the sweetspire leaves turned a silvery black under the muted lights. As Beck moved slowly among the shadows, he saw not one footprint in the mud, but several.

Gotcha.

Just like he'd guessed, the tracks led straight to the bushes and jogging track.

Coming at them straight on would give him away, so he snuck behind a set of swings and worked his way along the jogging path, using the trees as cover. Mud stuck to his shoes as the rain fell hard enough to disguise his footsteps.

Three feet away, a bush jiggled and Beck stopped in his tracks. The shadows were deep here, and his clothing, like the perp's, was dark, helping him blend in.

One slow step, then another, brought him closer. The

clouds parted for a moment, a sliver of moon bleeding through. That light glinted off the guy's watch and Beck took a deep breath, muscles coiling, ready to jump and take the man down.

Brrrng.

The sound of Beck's phone cut through the heavy night air like a warm knife through cold butter.

Ah, shit. In the excitement of the chase, he hadn't turned off his phone.

The man jerked his head around, saw Beck, and leaped for the jogging path. Beck tore off after him, but an instant later, the man raised a gun.

Bangbangbang.

The bullets went wide, hitting the leaves of a tree. Beck ducked behind a maple just as his phone went off once more.

Brrrng.

Question answered about the perp being armed. Luckily, he hadn't shot at Beck on the street or innocent people might have gotten hurt.

The man ran again, shoes squeaking on the asphalt. Beck started after him, grabbing his phone to turn off the ringer.

Ally McBeal showed on the screen. His nickname for Jackie.

"Jesus Christ in a cardigan sweater," Beck mumbled. He hit the answer bubble on the screen. "Hey, are you okay?"

"Did you catch him?"

The normal edge was in her voice, the knock against the wall must not have hurt her hard DelRay head. "No I didn't, thanks to you."

"What?"

"I was about to apprehend him when you called. The phone gave away my hiding place."

"Didn't you turn off your ringer?" Exasperation made her voice tight. "You let him get away?"

Was she serious? Beck steeled himself from raising his voice and rubbed his forehead. The guy was long gone, Beck once more alone, wet, and muddy. "Yes, I *let* him get away. On purpose, just to annoy you."

A long pause and then, "I'm sorry. It's been a long couple of days."

Beck started walking back toward her place. "Call the cops and report the break-in. We'll give them the best description we can, but this guy is in the wind for now. Can you duplicate your notes? Did he take anything else?"

"Nothing else is missing. I went through the whole place. I don't want the cops in on this. The intruder obviously is tied to your case, and with the players involved, I don't know who we can trust in law enforcement. I have a friend who can ask around on the down low and find out who might be sabotaging us. I'll give him—"

Her abrupt stop made Beck pick up his pace. "Jackie?"

He heard a crash in the background and his heart sped up with his feet. "Jackie!"

"I'm all right," she said, but sounded out of breath. "Just lost my balance for a bit and... Crap."

Beck started sprinting for the second time that night. "Are you dizzy? Nauseous?"

"My vision is a little blurry. I have a massive headache at the moment, thanks to that POS."

"Sit down and stay put. Don't hang up. I'm almost back to your place. I'll take you to the ER."

"I don't do emergency rooms, Pearson. An ice bag and some aspirin and I'll be right as rain."

A minute later, her brownstone was in sight, and she continued to chatter about her toughness. *Blah, blah, blah.* DelRays don't this. DelRays never do that. DelRays are the baddest of the bad. Was she trying to convince him or herself?

Cars clogged the street, thanks to a stoplight. He didn't hesitate, skirting bumpers and running through puddles. "Unlock your front door."

He climbed the steps and she let him in, the phone still held to her ear. "How can you be soaking wet from head to toe and still look this good?"

Disconnecting his phone, he set it on the small table just inside her door, and took hers. After shutting and locking the door behind him, he grabbed her and pulled her to the light. "Let me see your head."

"You're dripping all over my floor."

"Shut up and let me look at you."

She slapped at his hand. "I told you, I'm—"

One second she was jerking her head away and the next, her hand was clawing at him as she tipped sideways.

He caught her, scooping her up and carrying her to the sofa. "You might have a concussion." He'd had a few of those in his football days. "Trust me, they're nothing to mess with."

She huffed and argued — big surprise there — but he could be just as bullheaded as she was. He checked her pupils and breathed a sigh of relief that neither was dilated or looked disproportionate to the other. There was a bump on her head, but she claimed she wasn't dizzy or nauseous. "You really should see a doctor."

"No way. I need to call Chessie, and then we need to see this Greystone fellow."

"Do you really think I won't hog-tie you and drag you to the ER?"

Her eyes narrowed and he saw the wheels turning in her head. The lawyer rose to the surface, ready to cut a deal. "If I get sick, you can take me to the ER, but otherwise, we proceed as planned. I want to know where the photo came from and why. It might give us a clue as to who broke in here and stole my notes."

Always negotiating. Maybe it was time to cut his own deal. "I need to go back to my place and get out of these clothes. I also need to feed my cat. You come with me and stay there tonight so I can keep an eye on you and your head. I can have Grey meet us there to discuss the case."

"You have a cat?"

Of all the... "Either you stay at my place or I stay here. I'm not leaving you alone."

"You think that guy might come back, don't you?"

"I'm more concerned that you have a concussion and no amount of willpower will keep you upright if that's the case."

She drew in a deep breath and looked around as if seeing her place with a new perspective. Having someone break into your home could do that to you, especially if they assaulted you along the way.

"It's normal to feel scared after being attacked in your home," Beck told her. "Your root chakra is all out of whack."

Her gaze came back to him, a deep frown creasing her forehead. "I'm not scared, just a little unnerved, and what the hell is a root chakra?"

He patted her cheek gently. "Go pack a bag and I'll explain in the car."

Surprisingly, she didn't argue, rising and heading for her bedroom instead.

Jackie's skull may have been disintegrating. One small piece at a time. A bit here, a bit there, all scattered along the way like a trail of crumbs.

At least, that's how it felt as she made her way up the walk to Beck's porch. She stopped and gripped the iron handrail of the classic rowhome. Before her were—one, two, three—seven steps. Seven. The man might be trying to kill her. She stared up at the oversized front door. It was stained a deep black and offset by stark white trim on all sides. Neat and tidy. Just like it's owner.

Of course, His Holiness looked back just as she swayed

left and three of him danced in her vision. He tipped side-ways, his body curving into an arch and Jackie's stomach seized.

If she puked on his porch, a concussion wouldn't matter. Maybe she'd get lucky and die from the humiliation.

"Whoa." He locked onto her arm, holding her upright. "What's happening? Are you passing out?"

His fingers drenched her arm in warmth and she met his gaze, remembering the first time he'd touched her in a dive bar while on spring break in Ft. Lauderdale. How, after all these years, could she still feel that pull?

"No," she said. "The headache is wearing me out. I just need to rest for a few minutes."

"What you need is a hospital."

Again with the hospital nonsense. "Blah, blah. I'll make you a deal. If I don't feel better after some sleep, I'll go to the hospital. There. Happy?"

"Ecstatic. Are you good until I can get the door open?"

"Yes. Go."

Because, really, she didn't want all this hovering. And care-taking. It made her feel...weak and worse, cared for. She couldn't have that. Not from him.

Her *client*.

Remember that. Don't screw this up.

She blinked a few times and plural-Beck went back to singular. Fatigue. That's all this was. After months on a brutal case and now a surprise new one that included His Holiness the Dalai Lama, no wonder she was off her game.

Beck unlocked the door, pushed it open and turned back, clearly ready to sweep her up in his arms again and play the hero.

Good for him. Only, she didn't need a hero. In her line of work she dealt with all sorts of people. Most of them criminals. Lowest of the low. Not a hero to be found. Criminal work hardened her. How could it not? If she got emotional about cases – *clients* – she'd have been committed long ago.

She waved him away. "I can do it myself."

He backed away, snapping his hands high in the air. "Of course you can."

Now he wanted to get snippy? "Don't start. You're hovering. It's – "

"I'm trying to help you. But, hey, you wanna do it yourself, go for it."

He stepped through the door and waved her in, punching in a code for his security system. "Guest bedroom is upstairs, first door on the right. I'll put your bag in there. Help yourself to the bathroom. Tink is no doubt pissed off and hiding under my bed. She won't bother you."

With that, he left her in the entryway, his big feet silently moving up the hardwood staircase. A lot of men would make a statement by clomping up those stairs. Beck? He was the annoying sort that kept cool despite his anger. And make no mistake, if his rigid back was any indicator, the man was highly irritated.

Dammit. *Why do I do this?* Why did everything have to be a battle? She'd blame her family for that one. Debaters, every one of them. Every meal, even holidays, turned into a deliberation on everything from food stamps to Mickey Mouse. Even Dad, Mr. Low Key, couldn't resist a good argument.

"Beck?"

At the top of the stairs, he flipped a light switch, illuminating the upper hallway. "What?"

"I'm sorry. I'm…" she held out her hand, let it drop. "I'm used to being alone. Doing things myself."

"Sure, I get it, but that doesn't mean you can't let people help you."

Ha. In her family it did. As much as they loved each other – and they did – someone always walked away battered. She liked to joke that all the early training made her a good litigator.

In court, she excelled, but it was hell in the bedroom.

And the kitchen.

And anywhere else she might entertain a man.

She reached for the handrail, holding on as she climbed the steps. Beck stood at the top, but a weird tension filled the space between them.

Oh, this man. "You're dying to walk back down and help me, aren't you?"

"Yep, totally killing me, but I'm not risking you tearing my balls off. I like my nuts."

That made her laugh. An honest-to-God, from the gut one. "I recall liking them too."

Dammit. Her smart mouth, once again, leading the charge.

Too late. She glanced up, found Beck's eyes on her in a way that turned her core into a pit of hot lava.

Time for a little distraction from thoughts of an exceptional night of screwing that had almost derailed both their futures.

She reached the top of the steps. "Thank you," she said.

"For what?"

"For making me laugh. That hasn't happened a lot recently."

"Maybe you should change that."

Still focused on her, he stepped back an inch, giving her room on the landing, but not enough that she could miss his solid presence, the bulk of him that made her want to step just a little closer and...

She tipped her head up and the urge to run her fingers over his perfect cheekbones made her itch. T-R-O-U-B-L-E. But, Lord, being this close to him stirred her up. Made her want to turn into that bad girl she'd been on day one with Beck. "Maybe," she said, looking straight into his eyes, "I should."

Bam, bam, bam.

They both flinched at the iron fist banging on the front door. Way to kill a mood. *What am I doing?*

Beck jerked his chin. "That's Justice."

"Is he King Kong?"

"Sometimes, yeah." He hustled into the first bedroom and set her bag down. "Let me answer that before he blows his stack. Take your time." He jogged down the steps, his big body more graceful than a man his size should be. "Take it easy, Greystone! Before you knock my door down."

Men. Such animals. Jackie grabbed her toiletry bag from her suitcase and made her way to the bathroom. She flipped on the light, stared into the mirror and sighed. With her pallor, she might as well have been a corpse.

If Mom were here, she'd offer up that motherly advice she was so good at. *Drink more water, get on a regular sleep schedule and for the love of God, wear the right makeup.*

All of which, Jackie was sorely lacking at the moment. Yes, changes were definitely in order.

A spray tan wouldn't hurt either.

After freshening up, as much as she could anyway, she slipped into a fresh outfit of yoga pants and a long-sleeved top and made her way back to the living room where a tall man in a suit that screamed 'federal agent' stood looking over the shoulder of a thinner man sitting on the sofa. The skinny guy wore jeans and a wrinkled T-shirt with one of the Harry Potter characters on the front. He pounded away on a laptop, barely sparing her a glance.

"Hello," Jackie said, extending her hand to the taller man. "I'm Jackie DelRay."

"Ms. DelRay, nice to meet you." He smacked the skinny guy on the shoulder. "This rude guy is Teeg. Apparently, he never learned to stand when meeting people."

Teeg swung his head up, but didn't stop typing. "Huh?"

"This is Jackie DelRay," Grey said. "Beck's attorney."

"Oh, hi. Sorry. I'm in the middle of something here."

Beck pointed to the spot next to Teeg and Jackie sat, thankful to be off her feet. Her vision continued to mess with her, but the three ibuprofens she'd slammed had kicked in, taking the edge off the headache.

"You look better," Beck said.

His stare unnerved her, tempted her to straighten her clothes – or maybe remove them. If memory served, they'd been good at removing each other's.

"I *feel* better."

Apparently satisfied with her answer, he nodded. "I thought Grey might be the one who left the photo for you, but he says no. That leaves us with three people to investigate." He held up one finger. "We've got the guy *in* the photo with Lockhart and the prez." Another went up. "The person who *left* the photo." A third. "And the guy who broke into your house."

Grey touched her shoulder, drawing her attention. "Did you recognize the man who attacked you? Anything at all?"

"No. I've never seen him before." She gestured to the laptop. "What are we working on here?"

All three men paused. Beck finally took the lead. "The photo of Byron and the President. Teeg is running it through facial recognition software to see if we can figure out who the third man is."

Facial recognition. Uh-huh. "Is it the FBI's system?"

"Uh, no," Grey said. "This one is still in development and has a little...extra pop, you might say, versus the Bureau's version. We're beta testing."

Okay. Who the hell were these guys? The whole scenario had a *Men In Black* vibe.

"I see."

She glanced at Beck who gave her the slightest of head shakes. Clearly, he didn't want her making inquiries.

"I scanned the photo," Beck said. "Teeg is running it now. So far no hits."

"Does the system scan criminal files?"

"Yes," Grey said. "Also government databases, nationwide DMV files, and a bunch of other stuff, including banking records. If the guy has a state issued driver's license, we'll find him."

"*Really?*"

"Eh," Teeg waggled one hand. "The system uses 3D technology to identify different features. It can scan facial surface, eye sockets, the nose, etc. But the picture is old and grainy. Might be a stretch to match it to a current photo. We'll see though."

He pounded a few more keystrokes and then set the laptop on the coffee table. "This'll be a few minutes."

"Thanks, Teeg," Grey pulled a folded sheet of paper from his inside suit pocket and handed it to Beck. "This is for you, from Syd. It's the attendee list from the auction."

Beck perused it while Grey abandoned his spot behind the couch for one of the side chairs. "Mitch Monroe is on his way. He'll provide security for you for tonight. Give you both a chance to rest. I've got Tony Gerard scheduled for tomorrow."

Security? Now they needed babysitters? She angled back, peering up at Beck "Is that necessary? You have a security system."

"We don't know who that guy was that broke into your place. He could be Annabelle's killer. Whoever he was, he knows you're my lawyer. If he were a random perp, he would have stolen more than the notes from my case."

Grey leaned forward, resting his elbows on his knees. "What was on the notes?"

"Nothing critical. The bail amount, charges, etc. Nothing they couldn't find with a little digging. He may not have known that though. He was probably looking for something the real killer could use to further implicate Beck. Nothing in those notes would do that. The good news is attorney/client privilege hasn't been breached."

Teeg's laptop dinged and all eyes zoomed to it.

Grey hopped up and moved back to his spot behind Teeg. The poor kid had two tense, beefy guys literally looking over his shoulder.

"You got a hit," Grey said.

"Something."

Teeg clicked and a photo of a middle-aged man, maybe late 40s, popped up on his screen. Underneath the photo was a name.

"Dikko Travathian." Teeg glanced at Jackie. "Ring any bells?"

"Not a one."

He cracked his knuckles. "All right. Let's see who Dikko is."

"Travathian," Beck said. "Hang on."

Jackie glanced back at him. "Do you recognize the name?"

"Boom."

What, boom? "Don't hold out on us now. Whatcha got?"

Beck waved the sheet of paper. "There's a Rachael Travathian on here. She was the guest of Annabelle Lockhart."

"Oh, now that's interesting."

"Hang on." Teeg's fingers worked the keyboard and after a quick internet search gave them the basics, Teeg held his hands out. "Okay, peeps, I guess what we need to figure out is why the CEO of a company that produces combat helmets for the Department of Defense was hanging out with the Director of the FBI and, oh, right, the future President of the United States."

7

After an hour of queries into Dikko Travathian and coming up with zero links to Byron and President Murphy, Jackie looked like she was about to fall flat on her face. Mitch Monroe had arrived and introductions had been made. The flippant former agent, who Beck didn't particularly like, wore a solid black T-shirt with a saying on it that seemed slightly inappropriate, given the subject matter... *Never mistake my silence for weakness. No one plans a murder out loud.* He paced the floor like he wanted to be anywhere but there.

Makes two of us.

Teeg was packing up to head out, needing whatever high-tech equipment he had at Grey's to dig for Travathian on the deep web. Beck gave Grey a hand signal indicating it was time for them to wrap things up as well, and Grey nodded, his gaze bouncing over to Jackie who had her head in her hands. The whole time, Beck had itched to pull her close and massage her temples and shoulders, but he'd kept his hands to himself.

As soon as Grey and Teeg bailed, though, all bets were off.

"There's nothing else we can do tonight," Grey said, standing and following Teeg to the front door. "Teeg will keep digging, and you two get some rest. I'll be in touch as soon as we have something. Meanwhile, we still have a couple of unknown subjects floating around, any of which could be the killer, so watch your backsides."

Goodbyes were said and Beck showed them out, Mitch heading around the house to do a perimeter check.

As soon as Beck turned back to Jackie, he saw she was watching him with those luscious dark eyes of hers. Studying, evaluating. Between the two of them, they spent half their time together trying to read each other.

"What?" he asked, setting the alarm.

"You didn't have to chase them off. I'm fine."

Right. She was dead on her feet. "You don't have to be so tough all the time, Jackie. Besides, like Grey said, there was nothing else they could do here tonight. How's the head?"

"Not bad, but my neck is stiff. Guess when the guy slammed me into the wall, it did more than give me a bump on the head."

"You need some sleep."

"I'm too jittery. This whole thing has me off my game."

"I have just the cure."

One brow arched and she grinned. "I bet you do."

Typical Jackie, using a joke to defuse the suddenly more intimate situation.

She shifted slightly and the grin was replaced by a grimace. "Guess not. Okay then. As long as it's not illegal drugs, I guess I'm game."

The breath in his lungs froze. "You think I do drugs?"

Her hands rose in a defensive gesture. "I was joking, Beck. You're too much of a health nut to mess with that stuff."

His chest unclenched and he turned away. "Sorry. Touchy subject."

"Oh?"

He went to the gas fireplace and flipped the switch. No way was he getting into the story of his childhood. Soft flames materialized and gave the room an instant warmth. He killed the overhead lights and switched on his salt lamp and the LED water fountain in the corner. Next came the music; he selected his favorite track featuring Tibetan singing bowls, and adjusted the volume through his sound system. "I'll be right back."

Although she didn't appear to have a concussion, he wasn't taking any chances by giving her alcohol. Digging through his pantry, he pulled out the ingredients to make homemade hot chocolate.

While the almond milk warmed and the organic chocolate melted in a pan, he found his rolled up Thai mat in the hall closet and his favorite massage oil under the bathroom sink. He took both into the living room.

"What's that?" Jackie asked.

Shoving the coffee table out of the way, he set the oil on it and unrolled the padded mat. A couple pillows from the sofa joined the mat. Jackie was in yoga pants and a loose t-shirt, which would work just fine for what he had in mind. "You'll see."

The cocoa was ready when he got back to the kitchen and he doled out two cups' worth, bringing them back to the living room and handing one to her.

She peered at it, wary. "Smells good. What is it?"

"You've never had hot cocoa before?"

"Of course, but knowing you, this doesn't have a drop of Frangelico, Kahlua, or Bailey's."

"No alcohol for you for twenty-four hours until we're sure you don't have a concussion." He held the cup closer to her nose. "Try a sip. You don't need liquor to make it delicious."

"How will chocolate help? It has caffeine in it."

He sipped his and it was damn good. "I only used a small amount of my organic estate dark chocolate for richness, and I mixed in white chocolate to round out the flavor. White chocolate, which isn't technically chocolate, has no caffeine. The sensuousness of the warm milk and the chocolate blend is guaranteed to calm your jitters."

"Who are you, Martha Stewart?" Hesitantly, she took the cup and sipped. Took a second taste. Then a third. Her lids fluttered closed and she sighed. "Holy cow."

"Good?"

"Mmm. So good." She licked her lips and mini-Beck swelled.

He could literally see the tightness in her upper body fade. The creases around her mouth relaxed.

And he was only getting started.

She tilted her head back against the couch and peered at him through slitted eyes. "You made this, then? From scratch?"

"I'm a man of many talents."

"So I'm learning."

There it was again—that flash of heat they'd shared on the stairs. The sizzle and pop that had caught them in its clutches back in college and then again at her office earlier. All she ever had to do was look at him as she was now, and he wanted to get down on his knees and show her all the ways he could make her come.

All he had to do back then was touch her—that favorite spot he discovered on the back of her neck, right under her hairline—and she would melt.

Looked like some of that sexual chemistry was still there. Hell it *all* was.

They continued to play with their drinks, neither wanting to stop what might be happening, yet both knowing that acting on sexual attraction was a very bad decision. Client-attorney hanky-panky was a no-no in everyone's book.

Beck had made it his life's mission to kick bad decisions to the curb the moment they showed up. He'd seen all the bad choices his parents, siblings, and the dozens of perps he'd arrested over the years had made, and no sir. That was not for him. He liked life simple and straightforward.

But right now, he was facing prison if the woman in front of him—looking like she was ready to dribble her cocoa all over him and lick him clean—didn't clear his name of murder.

Sometimes, it didn't pay to be the good guy.

She drank the rest of her cocoa and set the cup on the table, stood, and put her hands on her hips. Her toe kicked at the mat. "Whatever you're planning, let's get on with it."

He smiled to himself, mentally reviewing all the things he wanted to do that would make her toes curl. Setting his cup aside, he grabbed the massage oil.

Good decisions only, he reminded himself. *Wise choices.*

Yeah, right. Nothing about bringing Jackie here, where she was so close and a little bit vulnerable, was smart on his part, yet how could he not? She needed someone to take care of her.

She'd been through a lot since she'd taken on his case and banging her senseless wasn't the polite thing to do since she was about to save his ass from prison. Didn't stop him from wanting to though. "A little massage, a little Reiki," he assured her—or maybe himself. He couldn't quite tell. "You're going to love it."

"Whatever." She flapped a hand in the air. "I trust you."

"Since when?" he teased, genuinely surprised.

She cocked a thumb over her shoulder at the table. "Since the cocoa. It's a miracle drug. I feel better than I have in days."

"Wait 'til you see what I can do with my hands."

Her gaze snapped to his. "I remember all too well what you can do with them."

He knelt on the edge of the mat and rearranged the pillows. Patted the soft cotton. "Lie down and close your eyes."

Sighing, she acquiesced.

Boy, oh boy, that sigh. Beck wanted to hear that again.

Once he had her comfortable, he started at her feet.

Rubbing oil into the palms of his hands, he took a couple deep breaths to center himself and keep from exploding just from the sight of Jackie at his mercy. Her dark hair was spread out over the pillow, the yoga pants outlining her sexy legs, and the loose T-shirt did nothing to hide her big, beautiful breasts.

Taking her feet in his hands, he pressed the tips of his thumbs gently into her arches and made the Cho Ku Rei sign in his mind. When he felt the muscles there release, he let go and shook out her legs. Her lower body loosened and he worked his palms up her shins and down her calves, kneading the tight muscles into submission.

"Oh my God," she murmured. He started on the front of her hips, pressing on the hip bones. "My legs feel so much lighter."

Her femoral pulses were strong and equal. He hovered over her, keeping the pressure light but firm. "Your *qi* was blocked above the knees on both sides. Probably due to those horrendous shoes you wear. We're getting the energy flowing again along your meridians. Once I clear your aura, I'll balance your chakras."

One eye peeled open slowly. "Once again, I have no idea what you're saying, but if it feels this good, I don't care. What is that root chakra thingie you were talking about earlier?"

He eased off her hips and sat back on his heels. The position was entirely sexual when he had Jackie underneath him, and mini-Beck sprang to life once more.

"You have seven in-body chakras, going from the base of the spine up to the top of your head." Lightly, he tapped her pelvic area. "The root chakra is your base, your foundation, and it governs survival, so when someone threatens your life, violates your home, or steals your possessions, it can knock the energy off balance there, like an earthquake weakens an entire structure."

"Sounds like a bunch of woo-woo stuff."

Americans usually didn't trust anything outside of traditional Western medicine. While that had its place, Beck believed Eastern medicines had a lot of proven benefits too. "You took a double whammy when that guy attacked you — he broke into your home, stole your notes, and banged you into the wall, causing a bump to your head and physical pain." He touched the swollen lump near her temple. "This area is governed by your third eye chakra. Your physical eyes had trouble focusing earlier, right? You felt dizzy? Well, the third eye chakra, located inside the center of your head, was knocked out of balance as well. A little massage, some Reiki, and a good night's sleep, and we'll have your energy stabilized and you'll feel like kicking ass again."

"I like the sound of that."

Hovering over her, he stared for a moment at her lips, considered tasting them. *I bet they taste like chocolate.*

As if she read his mind, she lifted a hand and slid her fingers up his arm and over his shoulder. Her nails tickled along his jawline. "Thank you for taking my mind off...you know."

The intruder. Yeah, he knew. "It's really too bad you have ethics because I'd love to kiss the shit out of you right now."

She chuckled, her gaze going to his lips. "Ditto."

Leaning down, he dropped a kiss on her jaw, brushed another across her cheek. "You make me crazy, DelRay."

"My plan all along." She didn't push him away, didn't balk about him being her client or ethics. Her fingers wound in his hair and kept him from pulling away. Her voice was soft, provocative. The woman could make a million dollars running an 800-sexy-voice hotline. "I still think about that night. In Ft. Lauderdale – "

He didn't let her finish, giving in for one sweet, heavenly moment as he took her mouth with his. Her already parted lips gave him full access and his tongue dove in.

Yep, chocolate.

And *Jackie*. That sexy, mystical taste that drove him flippin' nuts every time.

She tugged at him, but he kept his body suspended over hers, not giving in all the way, because there was definitely no turning back then.

Damned if he did, and damned if he didn't, but one thing was for sure, he wasn't about to seduce her and have her regret it in the morning.

After he'd kissed her senseless, he broke away and moved off her. Which was the stupidest thing he'd ever done, but also the smartest. Shifting to the side, he scrubbed his face and listened to her complain.

"Right," she said. "We should stop."

"Massage. Let's stick with that."

When she started to rise, he gently kept her prone and shushed her further grievances. They didn't last long, her common sense kicking in.

"How'd you get the scar on your chin?" he asked her.

"Ha! Not my most shining moment. I was twelve and challenged my brother to a bike race. I was sure I could beat him."

"What happened?"

"We were in full speed and I didn't see the chunk of broken road. My front tire hit it and down I went." She touched the scar. "Six stitches and I lost the damned race. Cal never lets me forget that."

After a minute, she relaxed, closing her eyes. He worked on her arms, then her shoulders and neck. She *oohed* and *ahhed* and he moved to kneel at the top of her head, laying his hands at her temples, then hovering over her forehead and eyes while he channeled energy.

"Do I want to know how you learned all this about chakras and *qi*?" Jackie asked. "Are your parents hippies or Buddhists or something?"

Not quite. "I had a couple of injuries in college. Banged me up good and I ended up needing several surgeries. When the physical therapy and pain killers weren't enough, I looked for some alternatives—*non-drug* alternatives. Holistic medicine saved my bacon. A few years ago, I took training to deepen my understanding of how energy healing works."

"I figured it was just so you could pick up women, 'cuz let me tell you, this is some trick."

"That, too." He chuckled. Her eyes were closed but she was smiling, and he could just enjoy her beauty for once without it feeling like a sparring match. He was definitely going to need a cold shower after this. "Guess you know my secrets now."

"Not all of them, but I will eventually." Her eyes opened and she stared up at him. One of her hands grabbed his and tugged it downward. "I think my root chakra needs more work."

"Damn it, Jackie. You get me started again and I won't be able to stop this time."

Their eyes met and he could see the war going on behind hers. She wanted him, she didn't want him. Another reason she made him nuts.

He tried to pull his hand away but she didn't let go. "You will regret this come morning."

He had to shift quickly as she dragged his hand to her hip, then lower. "I know. It just feels...good."

Yeah, it did.

Like he'd told her at the office, he was only a man. He didn't pull away and instead, slid his hand between her legs.

He kneaded the sensitive spot there and she moaned, arching under his hand. "You sure about this?" he asked. "Cause I mean it when I say that once I get started, your root chakra may never be the same."

"God, I hope so."

He kissed her, she kissed him back, and yep, all bets were off.

"Are you two fucking nuts?"

Beck and Jackie jumped apart, Beck instantly coming to his feet in a defensive posture, ready to take on the intruder.

But it wasn't any old intruder.

Although Beck wasn't entirely sure he still wasn't going to kill the man.

Mitch Monroe stood near the kitchen, leaning against the doorjamb and eating a half-peeled banana. "What is all this, Pearson? You seducing your lawyer?"

Beck straightened, crossed the space to Mitch, and got in his face. "What the hell are you doing in here? You're supposed to be standing guard outside."

"I had to take a leak, and I was hungry."

"How did you get past the security system?"

"Obviously, Grey forgot to inform you I have mad skills." Mitch glanced around Beck at Jackie, then dragged him deeper into the kitchen and started opening and closing cabinets until he found the mugs. He snagged one and poured the last of the cocoa on the stove into it. "I'm disappointed you didn't offer me some hot chocolate."

From the corner of his eye, Beck saw Jackie climbing the stairs to the second floor. *Damn it.* "In case it didn't dawn on you, Mitch, you're interrupting something here."

Mitch lowered his voice and shot a glance toward the stairs where Jackie had disappeared. "Good thing I did too. What's the matter with you, trying to boff your lawyer? Don't you know better? If the press gets wind you two are screwing, it could ruin her, not to mention any sympathy you might get from a jury if this thing goes to trial, because believe me, everyone will know about it. Sexual misconduct with a client will land her ass in front of the state ethics committee before you can say, 'root chakra'."

How long had he been standing there? Beck leaned against the counter and rubbed his head. *Fuck.* "I'm so screwed."

Mitch raised the mug and walked past him on his way to

the back door. "Welcome to the club. Now go numb your nuts in a cold shower and keep your hands off the woman who's going to keep you out of prison, you idjit."

The back door slammed and Beck made a mental note to change his security code first thing in the morning.

Driving rain pelted the roof as Jackie made her way into the kitchen where the glorious aroma of cooking meat poked her senses awake. Barely seven-thirty and Beck was organized enough to start breakfast.

Of course the man could cook. This was Beck with the magic hands.

She stepped into the kitchen, found him standing at the stove, freshly showered and wearing jeans and a polo shirt that fit his body in all the ways they should. Which meant perfection. Something the female part of her couldn't deny.

The other, the *smart* part, nagged about Jackie being his lawyer. One who'd been bad last night. Really bad.

Thankfully, Mitch Monroe had broken up the *massage* before Jackie had completely lost her mind and let lust rule the evening.

It would have been easy to just let go. To experience Beck again and maybe recapture some of the intense connection they'd shared twelve years earlier. So much had happened since then and they weren't horny college students anymore.

Different time. Different place. And now they had to face each other after they'd almost bumped privates the night before. How to handle it, she hadn't decided. Pretending it never happened could be an option.

So not her style, but her priority needed to be winning Beck's case. If she did that, he'd be free. And maybe, just maybe, after that they'd...

No. She wouldn't go there. Thinking about a future with Beck meant distractions and she owed him being at the top of her game.

One step at a time.

She'd have to remember that.

"Good morning." She crossed her arms and leaned against the door frame. "Smells great in here."

Beck swiveled away from the stove, pausing for a few seconds as he took in her body language. "Morning." He waved the spatula in his hand. "I...uh...figured you could use a good meal."

Only five feet separated them, but a weird tension crowded the small space. Beck's kitchen wasn't big enough for them and all their baggage. No kitchen would be.

What am I doing? Smart Jackie again.

Lonely Jackie blew out a breath.

"Sounds good," she said. "Can I help?"

His gaze moved down her body, over her blouse and slacks that comprised her work uniform. The only thing missing was her blazer. She'd draped that over the back of the couch after coming downstairs.

Beck gestured with the spatula. "You can do toast. Bread is in the drawer."

Thankful for something to do, she went to work at the toaster.

"Jackie, we should—"

Refusing to face him, she held up her hand. "I know. Just... not yet. Please. We'll talk about it later."

Someone tapped lightly on the back door and Jackie said a silent thank you for the timely interruption. Beck peered out the window over the sink.

"Great," he said.

"Who is it?"

"Monroe." He moved to the door, popped the lock and went back to the stove.

Monroe pushed through, bringing that crazy zinging energy with him. She'd only met the man once, but he tended to electrify a room, and not necessarily in a good way.

"Hi, Mitch," she said. "You're still here."

"Yeah." He pointed at Beck. "You got problems."

He'd just figured that out?

"Tell me something I don't know."

Mitch waggled his thumb. "I am. Company out front. Reporters. A lot of 'em."

"Shit."

Dammit. She'd anticipated press inquiries via the phone, but a camp-out? So soon? She punched the cancel button on the toaster and headed for the front window. The blinds were still closed and rather than alert them of her presence—how the hell would she explain that when they hadn't seen her walk in?—she peeped through them.

News vans lined both sides of the street while vehicles dodged reporters sheltered under umbrellas and cameramen jockeying for any opening that would best their competitor. Bodies and various equipment crammed the sidewalk from two doors down in either direction. Someone was interviewing a woman on a porch across the street.

Jackie let go of the blind, turned back and found Beck in the kitchen doorway.

"How bad is it?"

"I've seen worse."

Then again, her perspective, given the sensational case she'd just won, might be skewed.

Beck huffed. "That bad, huh? Maybe we can sneak out the back? Have someone pick us up on the next block."

Not a chance. "We're not running. It sends the wrong message. I'd rather face it and maybe get ahead of the prosecution." She pointed to the door and met his eye. "We're going to walk out there and I'll do the talking. Got it?"

Even if he didn't understand it, too bad. At this point, nothing good could come of him making a statement. Something she hoped, given his law enforcement experience, he'd accept.

"Yes, ma'am," he said.

Excellent. A smart man. But she'd known that about him from the first night she'd met him. It was, in fact, one of the traits that drew her to him. Her ultimate downfall when it came to Beck.

Back in the kitchen Mitch had helped himself to bacon and the toast she'd walked away from. "Mitch," she said, "can you help us? When we open the front door, they'll swarm. You can go out first and create a path for us to get to the car."

Mitch shrugged. "Sure. I'm good at being the muscle." He turned to Beck, offered a sarcastic grin. "Anything for you, buddy."

"Fuck off, Monroe. But, thank you."

"You're welcome. This bacon is good. Maple?"

Beck sighed.

"Save the bacon," Jackie said. "I want to get outside and deal with these reporters. Get our message out there before the other side does. Let me get myself together and we'll do this."

She left the kitchen and grabbed her blazer from the sofa on her way to the powder room where she'd check her hair and lipstick. More than that, she needed a few minutes of quiet to get her thoughts in order.

These moments didn't happen often. The ones where a slight slip of the tongue could send a case shooting off in another direction. Or get her client a life sentence.

Focus.

"Stick to what you know," she whispered to her reflection. "You've got this."

She slid her shoulders back, Marianna DelRay style, and drew air through her nose. Taking a second to center herself, she visualized the front door opening, the rush of reporters, the bursting lights, all of it enough to trigger her nerves if she hadn't been here before.

Shark Jackie.

"I've got this."

After one last tug on her blazer sleeves, she turned, threw the door open and marched into the living room where Monroe and Beck waited. Beck held her briefcase in one hand and an umbrella in the other. He handed over her briefcase while Monroe moved to the door.

One hand on the knob, he paused and looked back. "You both ready?"

Beck nodded.

"Let's go," Jackie said.

Monroe swung the door open and a commotion erupted from outside. Shouting voices, the slap of feet on wet pavement, someone swearing, all of it creating chaos. Beck quickly popped the umbrella up and Jackie held it while he locked the door. Monroe led the charge, hustling to Beck's car sitting in the driveway.

"Mr. Pearson," Connie Butler from the NBC affiliate yelled, "what do you have to say about the blood found on your coat sleeve?"

Crap. The blood evidence. Damned cops already starting with leaks to the press.

Might as well deal with that bit of nastiness straight away.

Jackie halted in the middle of the front walk, apparently surprising Beck who kept moving. Fat, pounding drops of rain pelted her—there went her carefully primped hair—for a few seconds before Beck realized he'd left her behind. He retreated, once again sheltering her from the deluge. Still, her hair, the armor she'd sprayed in place, was trashed. *Forget it.* She'd do this looking ratty. The message would still be clear.

"Ms. Delray," someone said, "have you been here all night?"

You've got this.

Shark Jackie faced one of the cameras, her practiced sly grin in place. "You folks aren't nearly as inconspicuous as you'd like to think. I spotted you on my way over and slipped through the back door. And, Connie, to answer your question, Mr. Pearson has nothing to hide. The blood on his sleeve included. It's public knowledge Mr. Pearson spent time with the victim the night she died due to a charity event. She cut her hand on broken glass and Mr. Pearson rendered basic first aid to stop the bleeding. *That's* how the blood got there. Think about it. If Mr. Pearson committed this crime, he'd have blood all over that jacket. Not just a few drops on the sleeve. If the prosecution intends on trying my client for murder, they'd better present more than easily explainable evidence."

Another round of shouts sounded, an absolute bombing of questions mixing with the slap of pounding rain, but Jackie was done. She'd given them their sound bite, managing to call out the opposition for leaking evidence. When she went to court, she'd rail about it, maybe get them a scolding from the judge to start things off right.

One thing was for sure. Based on the number of people currently on Beck's front lawn, they had a heater of a case. Normally Jackie's dream come true.

Not this time. This time, all eyes were on them. On her. Which meant being a whole lot more careful when it came to the personal nature of her relationship with the accused.

8

"*Wow.*"

Jackie sat in the passenger seat of Chessie's Caddie, her eyes glued to a stately brick Colonial as they pulled around the curving driveway.

She'd known the home values in Potomac were no joke, but this baby had to be at the higher end of the scale.

"I bet it's 10,000 square feet," she said.

"Close, 9,600. I checked the stats before I picked you up. Six bedrooms, five bathrooms and a guest house around back."

A low whistle sounded from the back seat where Beck had squeezed himself to the floorboard. He hadn't been happy about being left out, but they couldn't be dragging the murder suspect along on interviews.

Plus, after the Reiki-gone-wrong fiasco the evening before, his hands all over her – *all* over – she needed him out of her range of sight. And not distracting her.

Even looking at him challenged her. Physically and emotionally. Her out-of-character and completely sponta-neous hookup with him twelve years ago taught her hard lessons. The first being that a casual sexual encounter changed her life. She couldn't allow herself to be that careless. Or vulnerable.

Particularly with Beck and the flood of lust he sparked in her. Proving his innocence meant his lawyer – namely her – needed to be focused.

Not horny.

When it came to this interview with Rachael Travathian, the best Jackie could do was compromise and allow him to listen in via the microphone tucked into her jacket pocket. Annabelle had no family they could talk to, outside of Byron, so the next step was to check out Dikko under the guise of talking to Annabelle's friend. A friend who just happened to be at the same bachelor auction.

Chessie pulled around to the front, forgoing the side area with the three-car garage and a wide expanse for parking. A flashy red sports car – possibly a Ferrari, but what did Jackie know? – sat in front of one of the garage bays.

"Nice ride," Chessie said.

"Any idea what they paid for this house?"

"It was listed for five mill three years ago. I'll dig around and see what the actual selling price was."

"That's okay. I was just curious."

Decorative clusters of columns accented the covered porch, each with four posts that gave the home an elegant, intimidating feel.

Maybe that's what the Travathians wanted. For anyone who entered their world to feel the full brunt of their wealth. And try to keep up.

The front door opened and a woman wearing a maid's uniform – unbelievable – stood in the entry staring out at the strange car in the driveway.

"Jesus," Chessie said. "The help answering the door? It's like a scene from *Gone With the Wind*."

Beck let out a snort and Jackie fought the urge to look back.

"Beck, stay in here, out of sight. God help us if anyone walks up and checks out this car."

Jackie exited, adjusting her jacket sleeves before turning back for her briefcase. "Hello," she called. "My name is Jackie DelRay. I'm here to see Mrs. Travathian. I called earlier."

"Yes, she's expecting you."

Chessie made his way around the car and motioned Jackie ahead. They climbed the brick stairs where large pots of overflowing flowers greeted them. The pots alone had to be $500. Selling helmets to the government must have been profitable.

I'm in the wrong line of work.

The woman ushered them into the first room on the left. Not quite a living room, but large enough to fit an upholstered sofa with two giant wing backed chairs. Her mother's house had a room like this. Mom called it the quick-stay room. Cozy enough to entertain a few guests she didn't necessarily want staying and close enough to the front door to shuttle them out in a hurry.

"May I get you anything?" The woman asked. "Coffee? Water?"

"I'm fine. Thank you."

"I'm good," Chessie added.

"Please have a seat. Madam will be with you in a moment." The woman offered a little bow before taking her leave and Jackie fought the eyeroll. How effing pretentious could these people be? And this poor woman had to put up with this nonsense.

"Frankly, my dear," Chessie muttered, "I don't give a damn."

She nudged him with her elbow. "No kidding. Still, knock it off with the *Gone with the Wind* crap."

He pointed to the sofa. "Let's take the sofa."

"Why?"

"From there we can see the door. Psychological advantage. She can't see what's coming behind her."

Power play. Excellent. "I do love you, Chesley."

Before Chessie could unleash one of his smartass comments, a tall woman, maybe early forties, with sleek auburn hair and glowing skin, entered. The glow may have been courtesy of her expertly applied makeup because up close, her shadowed eyes indicated a lack of sleep.

They stood and she held her hand out.

"Hello. I'm Rachael."

"I'm Jackie DelRay. This is my associate, Chesley."

Early in her career, Jackie learned referring to her investigator as an associate provided a better chance of loosening lips. People tended to clam up at his actual title.

"Please, sit." Rachael smoothed her pristine pencil skirt, giving them a view of her ample cleavage under the extra undone button on her blouse.

Hopefully, Chessie wouldn't need oxygen after this. Jackie glanced at him and his smirk was more nice-try-lady than lust.

Rachael eased into the chair and did some minor wardrobe adjusting before settling in for their chat.

"Thank you for seeing us," Jackie said.

"Of course. You said it was about Annabelle." She set her hand on her chest, closed her eyes and breathed deep. "I still can't believe it. We were just together."

Maybe she did have a little Scarlett O'Hara in her. Jackie waited for her to open her eyes, but when the woman continued to sit in some sort of grief-inflicted meditative state, Jackie forged ahead. "I understand you attended the charity auction with Annabelle."

Rachael's eyes fluttered open, focusing on Chessie as she dragged her hand down her chest and across one breast. Oh, she liked to rile men up, didn't she? Some women were like that. Jackie had never been one of them. She was lucky not to have spinach in her teeth.

"I did," Rachael said. "We were friends and enjoyed doing things like that together."

"How did you meet?"

Might as well clarify that, in case they'd been friends prior to marrying their spouses.

"Our husbands. They were in the military together. They've remained friends all these years."

"I see."

Chessie shifted in his seat, drawing Rachael's attention. "Did Annabelle seem upset at the auction? Anything bothering her?"

"Nothing out of the ordinary. The divorce was taking its toll. They were fighting a lot."

"About?"

"Money, of course."

Of course. "They were having trouble coming to a settlement?"

"Yes. I never asked for particulars. So crass. But she did mention there were issues related to jointly-owned stock."

A chime sounded and Jackie glanced to the hallway.

"That's the garage door," Rachael said. "My husband is home."

"Hon?" a man called.

Beck better have stayed down and out of sight when Travathian pulled up the drive. Then again, if he'd checked out the Caddie and seen Beck, he wouldn't be coming in the side door. He'd be busting in the front.

Maybe they'd get lucky and have a two-fer with Mr. Dikko Travathian *and* his wife.

"In here, baby."

Seconds later, a man strutted into the room and Jackie instantly recognized his dark features from the photos they'd found on the internet.

"I didn't realize we were expecting guests," he said to Rachael.

"Darling," she said "this is Jackie DelRay and her associate, Chesley. They're investigating Annabelle's murder."

When Jackie and Chessie made a move to stand, he held his hand up. "Not necessary." He shook their hands. "I'm Dikko Travathian. You from homicide?"

Uh, no. "I'm an attorney," Jackie said. "Beckett Pearson is my client."

The temperature in the room dropped twenty degrees, but the Travathians, well, these people were no slouches. Rachael pushed her shoulders back.

"I..." Rachael cleared her throat. "I assumed you were from the prosecutor's office. You didn't specify."

True. When Jackie had called, all she'd said was she was a lawyer. She just hadn't mentioned for whom.

And really, she had no answer for the socialite.

Mr. Travathian cleared his throat. "Doesn't matter. How can you defend that son of a bitch?"

Ah, the cocktail party question, as it was known in the world of defense attorneys. "Mr. Travathian, if you were unjustly accused of a crime, wouldn't you want an attorney?"

"Whatever," he said.

Jackie unbuckled the front clasp of her briefcase and retrieved a copy of the photo of Byron, Dikko, and the President. "Mr. Travathian, do you remember where this was taken?"

He snatched the picture from her. "Jesus. I haven't seen this in years. Yeah, I remember. It was a get-together."

"Pretty fancy since you're all in tuxedos."

"A fundraiser, for Senator Adams, if I remember right."

"I understand you and Director Lockhart were already friends, but what about the President? Did you know him as well?"

"Nah. Met him that day. Byron introduced us. They served

together too. Murphy was his commanding officer. Ironic, no? The whole Commander in Chief thing?"

That was one word for it.

"Are you friends?"

"The President?" He shrugged. "Before he took office, we saw each other on occasion. What does that have to do with Annabelle's murder?"

The blare of a ringtone filled the space and Travathian unclipped his cell from his waist holder. He checked the screen. "I gotta take this." He glanced at his wife, then back to Jackie. "We're done here."

Following orders, Rachael popped out of her chair. "I'll see you out."

Jackie clucked her tongue at Chessie. "Meeting is over, I guess."

"You guessed right," Travathian said.

Smartass. He disappeared down the long hallway, ducking into a side room while his wife swung the front door open.

"You know," she said, her tone clipped and more than a little pissy, "you should have told me who you were. I hope this isn't the way you normally do business."

"Mrs. Travathian, I'm doing my job. I have a client to protect."

Rachael peered down the hallway, then leaned closer. "You're client is a mur-der-er. He killed my friend. I feel like I'm betraying Annabelle's memory just talking to you."

"Mr. Pearson didn't kill her."

"Oh, come on. He was the last one with her. It's obvious. She probably refused his advances and..." she shivered and brought her hand to her mouth. "I can't even *think* about it. About what she went through."

Throughout her years as a prosecutor Jackie had seen just about every phase of grief. Anger being one of them. As much as Jackie believed Beck to be innocent, Mrs. Travathian had lost her friend. And Beck, reasonably so, was a suspect.

She needed to smooth things with Rachael. At least enough where she might be able to call on the woman again for information.

Jackie touched the woman's arm. "I am very sorry for your loss. This can't be easy. If I've made it any more difficult, well, I apologize for that also."

Always one to run for it when it came to emotions, Chessie jerked a thumb outside. "I'll, uh, wait in the car."

Rachael stepped back, placing one hand on the door. "You should go. I can't talk about this anymore. There's nothing to say. He killed her. And...and..."

Tears blurted from her eyes and guilt slammed Jackie. Dammit.

"I'm sorry."

"You keep saying that, and I believe you." Rachael hiccupped. "I do, but it won't bring her back. I miss her so much and you're trying to free her killer."

"I want to find her killer as much as you do. My guy is not him. Don't you want to be sure? Not wonder in ten years if the right man is behind bars?"

"Of course. I'll do anything to make sure of that."

"Good. Then we're on the same page."

Rachael swiped at her tears and glanced back down the hall.

"I'll go," Jackie said. "I don't want to cause a problem for you."

"Thank you. My husband is...protective."

"I'm sure he is."

Jackie stepped onto the porch.

"Ms. DelRay?"

"Yes?"

"I want to find her killer too. Even if that means talking to you again."

"You're willing to do that?"

Her eyes darted toward the room where Dikko had disappeared and she lowered her voice. "I'll do whatever it takes to help find Annabelle's killer."

They picked up gyros at a mom-and-pop deli not far from the Travathian mansion and Chessie headed to Jackie's place. The aroma of onions, meat, and tzatziki filled the car, and Beck's knees hit the back of Jackie's seat even though she'd pulled it all the way forward.

Aside from their brief exchange that morning, she'd been totally incommunicado about what had passed between them the previous night at his place, back to all-business once more. He couldn't blame her, but this rollercoaster of lust and flirting was taking its toll. He'd tossed in his big bed all night, knowing she was just down the hall. Poor Tink had finally gotten tired of his restlessness and slept under the bed.

Jackie had a lot on the line with him and his case, and so far, their leads for finding the real killer weren't panning out. She had Chessie work his contacts regarding Annabelle's case, but he'd claimed there had been no updates outside of the leaked test results from Beck's jacket. Annabelle's blood was confirmed. The police were convinced he was the killer. They weren't wasting precious man hours searching for anyone else, and even if they had other leads, they weren't sharing the information with Jackie.

Beck's phone buzzed. He shoved aside one of the blue-and-white striped bags and fished it out of his pocket. Taylor.

"Hey, boss. What's up?"

"I'm back." Her voice was strained. "We need to talk."

"I'm on the road right now. Can I call you back in a few minutes?"

"Now would be better."

Since the press had been camped on his doorstep, she'd probably heard about the blood test results. He'd prepared her for this, but she still sounded shook up. "I've got it under control, Taylor. I know it looks bad, but—"

"It doesn't just *look* bad, Beck." She gave a heavy sigh. He could see her in his mind's eye, fiddling with the ponytail she usually wore. When she got stressed, she liked to twirl the ends around her fingers. "It *is* bad. Lockhart just gave me a heads-up. You're officially suspended come tomorrow morning. The email will go out to everyone at 8 am."

His gut did a slide toward his knees, even though it was no surprise. Being an agent was everything to him. Still, it was important not to let Taylor know he was sinking deep. "We expected this, Taylor."

"Doesn't matter. Everyone knows you didn't kill Annabelle." Obviously, 'everyone' didn't include the police. "Byron's just looking for a scapegoat because his ego's bruised that Annabelle bought you at the bachelor auction. Has your attorney found any leads on the real killer?"

"We're working on it." Taylor had plenty on her plate and he didn't want her worrying about him. "I'm sorry my caseload is getting dumped on you and the others. You should put in a request for Tilda LeMars from Leo's group. I worked with her on the Sanderson case. She's good with investigations as well as behavioral analysis."

"Quit worrying about me and the team. We'll be fine. And you know it will be a cold day in hell before I ask the Golden Boy to lend me one of his profilers."

"I'll wrap this up as fast as I can, but you probably should..." He couldn't bring himself to say it, so he had to force the words out. "Plan for the worst."

"Bullshit. I don't do worst-case scenarios and you know it. I'm going to work with Grey and see what we can do, okay? There's got to be something."

As they rounded the corner onto Jackie's street, Chessie said, "Whoa," under his breath, and Beck seconded that with a, "Cripes. What does she want?"

Taylor asked what was going on and Beck told her he had to go. He hung up and shoved the phone back in his pocket. *Fucking A.*

Across from Jackie's house, taking up two parking spaces, was a large red, white, and blue van with WJTA 7 News and a picture of a camera painted on the side. The local affiliate covered the greater DC area. The brunette who manned the eleven o'clock news desk, Debra Johansen, leaned against the rear doors, staring at a cell phone. Like a wolf catching scent of its prey, her head came up when she noticed their car.

"I know what she wants," Jackie said, a hint of rebellion in her tone. She unsnapped her seatbelt and rolled her shoulders back. "After this morning, she wants a follow-up sound bite, and I'm going to give it to her."

Chessie snickered, but Beck made a fist, crinkling the top of the bags in his lap. His privacy had always been important to him and he cringed at the thought of Jackie—once again—putting herself out there for target practice. "You've already chased off reporters. Johansen's going to try and trip you up, Jackie. Just ignore her."

She leaned slightly forward in her seat and motioned Chessie to pull up behind the van. "Don't sweat it. I've handled Debra before. We can use her as much as she wants to use us."

Chessie eased the car to a stop, invading the reporter's space with the bumper. She straightened, a look of surprise on her face, and took a step back.

Beck put a hand on Jackie's shoulder, anchoring her to the seat. "I'll handle Debra. You hold the food."

He smacked the three blue and white bags into her lap and left her gaping as he bailed from the back seat.

Debra sent a threatening look at Chessie and his bumper, then turned her wolf eyes on Beck. "Agent Pearson—or should I say, *Mr.* Pearson, since I hear you're suspended from the FBI. I'm doing a feature story tomorrow on our *True Crime* segment about Annabelle Lockhart's murder. Would you like to give a quote? We could sit down together and I could get your side of the things."

She'd already heard about his suspension? How the hell had that happened? "It's still Agent Pearson at the moment, and no, I'm not giving you a quote or an interview, so please don't harass my attorney by parking outside her home all night. You're wasting your time."

Her ruby-red lips parted and showed teeth far too white to be natural. "I was sure you'd want to discuss your side of things and help our viewers understand your family, but I guess you don't care about them, do you?"

His gut did that downward slide again and he sent her a quizzical look. "My family?"

A car door slammed behind him as Debra withdrew a folded paper from inside her coat. "I received an email with a whole lot of juicy information on their criminal histories. Several of them have long rap sheets, and a couple are wanted by the very organization you work for, isn't that correct?"

Everything in him joined his stomach down at his ankles. He felt Jackie closing in, and a healthy dose of anger shot up his spine.

This was one of the reasons his privacy had always been important, and why he'd distanced himself from his parents and siblings, and how ironic — he suddenly felt protective of them. "Who is the email from?"

"That's enough," Jackie said. "Back in the car, Beck."

Debra ignored Jackie. "It's from a free hotmail account that was apparently deleted right after the email was sent. The person used a fictitious name. Guess they wanted to stay anonymous, especially seeing as how you're still walking the streets."

Setting hands on hips so he didn't snatch the paper from her, he called up his Bureau face and gave her a smirk. "An anonymous emailer? You really expect me to believe that? Come on, Debbie. You went digging and came up with some dirt on my family — big deal. At least own up to the fact you have no legitimate outside source for your information. And I don't buy for a minute that you want your viewers to understand my family, so save it."

The smile flatlined. "I can assure you, the email is—"

He didn't let her finish. "Let me guess, you're getting older and your fan base has declined, so you're hoping to jumpstart your flailing career with a shocking story that has nothing to do with the truth and everything to do with ratings." Her face blanched. *Bingo.* "Newsflash, you're not getting promoted to that prime six o'clock slot, regardless of the scandal you try to create over Annabelle's death, and I'm sure as shit not helping you drag her family or mine through the mud. You want to be a respected investigative reporter? Go find a real story that isn't handed to you on a silver platter. And lay off the sugar and carbs. You're aging prematurely but a healthier diet will help slow the wrinkles."

Turning away from the woman's shocked face, he took Jackie's elbow and helped her across the street. Chessie locked the car with a *bleepbleep* and jogged to catch up with them.

Once inside, they all shed their coats. Jackie peeked out the window. "Well, I should yell at you for pissing off a reporter, but nice job taking her down a notch. She's leaving." She turned and circled a finger at Beck. "Way to use the aging card. Ouch. You know where to hit a girl where it hurts."

"It wasn't a card." He headed to the kitchen table where

Chessie was digging into his bag. Anger sizzled and popped in his veins. First the news about his suspension, and then a reporter ready to reveal the ugly truth about his family on the Capitol's nightly news. He wanted to punch something to release his pressure valve, but doing so in front of Jackie and Chessie would let them see how much Debra had gotten to him. How much the news of his suspension had gotten to him. "It's Behavioral Analysis 101. We don't just learn how to shoot a gun at the Academy, you know. We learn how to read people and figure out their motivations as well."

Jackie grabbed sodas from her fridge and handed them out. "Is it true? What she said about your family?"

"Unfortunately, yes." He unwrapped his gyro, picked up a tomato slice that fell out, and made work of rearranging the meat and onions. The embarrassment that discussing his family invoked surfaced. "Doesn't affect the case."

"Kind of does," Chessie said around a mouthful. "Paints you as having the potential for criminal activity."

Beck chewed a bite, the flavor flat on his tongue. Chessie was right, but damn it. The implications of his family's business aside, he had a spotless record. All these years of hiding the facts about them...was it all for nothing?

He set down his sandwich, sipped his soda. Snuck a glance at Jackie.

Yep, he could tell by the look in her eyes, she wanted— needed—to know.

"Drug paraphernalia." He glanced between Jackie and Chessie, neither of them missing a beat as they continued to chow down, eyes on him as he admitted the truth. "My family was into drugs, but they made money selling paraphernalia. Pipes, tubing, Bunsen burners, you name it. Instead of Legos and building blocks, my siblings and I were raised sorting and bagging that stuff to be sold. There's a lot of money to be made in the drug world without dealing them."

Chessie made an affirmative grunt. "It's a profitable service industry with less hard time if you're arrested."

"They expanded during slow times," Beck said. "Stealing from neighbors, identity theft, heading to the nearest chain-store and 'accidentally' falling so they could sue. You name it, they've probably used it as a way to make money."

Jackie nodded, digging into her salad. "Who do you think sent the email?"

That was it? No judgments? No pity? Beck sat forward and picked up his sandwich again.

"My family's run-ins with the law are public record. Debra went digging and wants to make out she has an independent source." A thought occurred. "Unless..."

"Unless what?" Jackie's fork halted midway to her mouth.

Beck put down his sandwich, his anger morphing into a red-hot cloud of disbelief. Instead of profiling the reporter, he should be profiling the Director of the FBI. "Lockhart is sending out the official notice about my suspension first thing in the morning. That's what Taylor called about. Byron notified her today so she could get her ducks in a row to break it to the team before the information goes wide. No one else should know, but Debra did."

Chessie shrugged. "She got a source at the Bureau?"

Beck shoved his chair back, no longer hungry. "Of course she does. Byron Lockhart. He put her on to the story about my family as well as telling her about my suspension."

"So he's lining up his ducks," Jackie said. "He either believes you *are* the murderer, or—"

"He's deflecting and framing me to look like it." Beck hopped up from the chair and paced away, pulling out his phone.

"Who are you calling?" Jackie asked.

The man he needed answered on the first ring. "Grey?" Beck asked. "I need to borrow Teeg again."

"I'm glad you called. Is your attorney nearby?"

"Yeah." He pressed a button and set the phone on the table amidst the food. "You're on speaker. What is it?"

"Teeg pulled tax returns for Travathian International. They netted 200 million last year and did over 100 million in the first two quarters of this year, most of it in government contracts for helmets."

Beck let out a low whistle. That was a lot of money. "Good old Dick knows Byron Lockhart, and Rachael claims she and Annabelle were good friends, which holds weight since they were at the auction together. Is it possible Byron helped Dick get those government contracts?"

"Might be worth looking into."

Jackie grabbed her phone and appeared to be making notes to herself, her fingers flying over the keys.

"Lockhart is still gunning for me," Beck told Grey, "and he's getting more creative. If anyone had the means, motive, and opportunity to kill Annabelle, it was him, but he's using his power and status to frame me. I need to find out if he's leaking information to reporters about this case, and I'd like to turn the tables on him. Dig into his closets and make him squirm. Can Teeg look into his finances? I want to see if there's anything that looks like bribe money or gifts to the Lockharts for helping Dick secure those contracts."

Chessie grunted a laugh. "Dick. I like it."

The sound of paper being shuffled came over the line from Grey's end. "I already took the liberty of having Teeg pull Byron's tax returns. He was an early investor in Dikko's company twenty years ago, and in fact, didn't sell off those shares until right before he ended up in the director's chair."

That got Jackie's attention. Her head snapped up. "Dikko never mentioned that."

Teeg, who must have been close to Grey, piped up. "Lockhart made a cool ten million from it."

Damn. The Director was a millionaire? Who knew? He must have been squirreling it away, since he sure didn't act like a rich man.

"Was Annabelle going to see any of that in the divorce?" Beck asked.

"Haven't dug into the divorce proceedings yet," Grey said. "But I'll put Mitch on it and see what we can find."

Beck was suddenly ravenously hungry again. "Thanks, Grey. I'll be in touch."

"One more thing."

"Yeah?"

"Taylor hired Pasche & Associates to handle your PR. Expect a call from Fallyn tonight."

PR? Jesus, what was his life coming to? "Can she handle nosy reporters who want to expose my family's criminal histories?"

Fallyn Pasche was known around DC as the scandal lady. She hadn't met a crisis she couldn't resolve.

"I believe that's right up her alley," Grey said. "Is there a particular reporter leading the charge?"

Beck filled him in on Debra Johansen and the story she was after. "Obviously, the FBI did an extensive background check on me before they let me into the Academy so the higher-ups know all about my family's criminal enterprises. I think Lockhart leaked the information to Johansen, and possibly others, to continue his smear campaign against me and set me up. The story breaks tomorrow."

"I'll call Fallyn and let her know. I suspect she'll eat Miss Johansen alive."

Beck disconnected, feeling his anger subside a bit. Jackie started handing out orders before he could sit down.

"Finish up, Chessie. We're going back to talk to Dikko. Then tomorrow, I want you to look into Annabelle's relationships—family, friends, coworkers, the whole ball of wax. Beck, you talk to Ms. Pasche and stop that reporter completely or find a way to spin that story, got it?"

Beck picked up his sandwich. The last thing he wanted to do was talk to Fallyn Pasche, but it *was* his family and he had to do what he could to protect them from this.

He didn't want to get hurt by their life choices yet again, especially with something as huge as a murder case hanging over his head, but he also didn't want reporters sniffing around and making their lives hell either. He'd given them plenty of grief over the years to clean up their acts, but the press would be merciless and go after them for no other reason than to sensationalize a story.

Beck bit into his sandwich. Once again, right or wrong, he had to protect his family.

9

*B*efore heading back to Travathian's to rip that conniving weasel a new one, Jackie and Chessie detoured to Byron Lockhart's condo, a cushy place on the Potomac where the doorman informed them the Director was unavailable.

Forever.

Wasn't he just the smartass?

His refusal to cooperate didn't shock her. She had, in fact, planned on it. Which didn't stop her from leaving Lockhart a message about speaking with him regarding his wife's murder.

And their impending divorce.

Especially since the deceased had no next of kin.

She left out the part about him leaking Beck's personal information to the press. Eventually, the bloodhounds would have sniffed that out anyway. All Lockhart had done was give them a head start.

"Now," she said to Chessie as they strode along the sidewalk on the way to the parking garage, "we're on part two of this mission."

"How's about I drop you at the office? I'll handle Travathian."

Ha. Good one. Not a chance. She wanted to tear that guy to shreds. In or out of a courtroom.

"No," she said. "I'm going."

Chessie did a hard stop in the middle of the sidewalk. The sun glinted off the streaks of silver in his dark hair, and that, combined with a pissed-off-Dad vibe, brought Jackie to a halt beside him. "Problem?"

"What are you doing?"

"Aside from walking to your car?"

One of Chessie's eyebrows hitched. "Cut the crap. You know what I'm talking about."

Beck. That's what he was talking about. And Jackie's sudden interest in accompanying her investigator while he kicked a bunch of tires. She met his stare, but kept any other body language to a minimum. The problem with Chessie was how good he was at his job. Which made lying to him nearly impossible. "Last I checked," she said, "I'm defending my client."

Slowly, his head moved back and forth. Back and forth. He wasn't buying it. Leave it to her to hire smart people whose Spidey-sense never failed.

"All due respect," he said, "I'm calling bullshit. When have you ever gone with me to question people? Why now?"

"It's an important case."

"So was the Senator."

Damned Chessie. The stare-down continued while Jackie sorted possible arguments. Chatter from a young couple walking toward them broke the tension and Jackie stepped back, allowing them to move through.

All the while, Chessie kept his eyes pinned to her. The man had spent a career weeding out liars – or breaking them. Over the years he'd perfected the art of asking questions that may have seemed random but were part of a carefully crafted interrogation. Eventually, he'd trip the suspect up and force an admission. Precisely why, when he'd retired from the force, Jackie snatched him up before another savvy attorney could. Now, he worked for her and only her.

"I know you," he said. "This case seems different. Like you have more than a professional history with him."

She sure did.

"Jackie," Chessie said, "are you doing this guy?"

Of course. Right to sex. Men.

She made a show of huffing out a breath, her feigned exasperation evident. "First of all, that's none of your business. Second, no, I'm not *doing* him."

Not yet anyway.

"All right. Then what? And don't give me a runaround. If we're gonna clear this guy, I need to know what questions to ask. The more I have the better. Is it something with his family? We know *his* record is clean. The feds wouldn't have hired him otherwise. I'm ruling out a drug problem. He's too into that holistic shit for that. And, if he hired you, at your hourly rate, he must have money."

He held up a finger. "Family." Another finger went up. "Drugs." Third finger. "Money. They're all out. You know what that leaves."

Chessie had a theory. In his opinion, all crimes stemmed from family squabbles, drugs, money, or sex. And, damn him, she'd built a career on all of it so his theory was sound.

"Sex," she said. "It leaves sex."

He touched the tip of her nose with his index finger and his gold bracelet jingled. "Bingo."

No way out. For three years Chessie had been her go-to investigator. Over that three years, they'd become friends as well as co-workers. They'd shared war stories, not to mention bottles of scotch, after grueling, mind-melting cases. She'd discussed with him her problems and insecurities, her dreams, her goal to be the top criminal attorney in DC. All of it laid bare for him.

In short, he *knew* her.

She tipped her head back, closed her eyes and a soft breeze tickled her face. Could she do this? Confide in him once more. Actually say it out loud when doing so would bring back painful memories. And secrets. Ones she'd never revealed. Not to her family, not to her girlfriends.

Not to Beck.

Maybe it was time. If nothing else, Chessie provided neutral territory. She opened her eyes, stared into her friend's dark eyes. *Do it.* "You're right. There's history with Beck."

"What kind?"

"We met in college. Spring break in Ft. Lauderdale. I was with some friends who were into the bar scene." She sighed. "That had never been my idea of fun. All I wanted was the beach, but I figured it was spring break so why not. I met Beck and well..."

"Shit," Chessie said. "You picked him up."

She gave him a half-hearted smile. "I like to think he picked me up."

And, oh, the man had rocked her world. She drifted back, dragging the memories from her vault. He'd worn jeans that night and a T-shirt and his body – dear Lord – no man had the right to look that good. It was the perfect V of broad shoulders and lean hips and there she was, a brainiac so focused on acing her LSATs that she'd been without male attention for months.

"One night stand," Chessie said, bringing her from her mind travel.

She shook her head. "More like a weekend stand."

The only one of her lifetime. Never before and never after. Especially after.

She couldn't say it had been worth it, but he'd brought out something in her. Something wild, passionate, and...freeing.

With him, she wasn't Marianna DelRay's kid. She didn't have to win every debate or prove she could tough it out.

She was simply a woman wanted by a man.

And, even now, she'd never quite gotten over him. "Afterward, we both went back to our lives. No exchanging numbers, no emails, just sex."

But they'd talked a lot. Gotten to know each other some in between doing *other* things.

Other things that had landed her in a heap of trouble. Dammit. She looked away, her eyes tracking the vehicles moving along the street. Anything that gave her time to let the humiliation pass before facing Chessie again. For years, she'd kept the six weeks after her fling with Beck to herself. Silently dealing with what would turn out to be a moment in her life that changed everything.

A moment that devastated her.

"So," Chessie pressed, "what happened then?"

She met her investigator's steady gaze. She should tell him. Just spill it and be done with it. Finally free herself of it. Three little words. So easy, yet so...what? Difficult? Heartbreaking? All of the above?

"I got – " she froze. The word stalled on her tongue, refusing to be freed. After all this time, telling anyone but Beck seemed a betrayal. One he didn't deserve.

"You got what?"

Pregnant.

"I got...back to school and never saw him again until five years later. I'd been promoted to violent crimes and was in court for a hearing when in walked Beck. Not for my case, but the one after mine. Imagine the shock when he strolled in."

"You weren't interested?"

Oh, she was. Had been ever since that weekend in Ft. Lauderdale. Heck, when the assistant state's attorney position in DC came open, she'd jumped at it, wondering if he'd ever fulfilled his dream of working at FBI headquarters.

"It's...complicated," she said. "And I didn't need complications. It didn't matter anyway. He came to my office one day wanting me to sign off on an arrest warrant. He'd been working a case, a murdered child, and had a suspect but not enough evidence. The case would never have stuck. Never. And I wasn't about to go into court and get my rear handed to me. I told him we needed more. That he didn't have it yet."

"Great," Chessie said. "We investigators love when prosecutors tell us we haven't done our jobs."

"That wasn't it. He'd done great work. It just wasn't enough and I wouldn't risk double jeopardy."

What Beck had given her amounted to a circumstantial case that wouldn't be enough to convince a jury. Not the full jury. Having a career prosecutor for a mother taught Jackie a determined stealth juror could sway the rest. And if they'd come back with a not guilty? Forget it. No second chances. Not on that case, with that same evidence. Acquittals meant freedom, otherwise known as double jeopardy. So, she'd sent Beck on his way.

"Which," Chessie said, "pissed him off."

"He went over my head to my boss, who stood by my assessment, which pissed Beck off even more. We were never able to charge the suspect. To say things were frigid with Beck would be an understatement. I believe he hated me for that."

Chessie waved a hand. "So this – you defending him, is what? You making it up to him?"

She shrugged. "Maybe."

In truth, she didn't know. This might be the Jackleen DelRay dream scenario. Another sensational case to catapult her to the top of her field *and* an opportunity to make things right with Beck.

"Chessie," she said, "I owe him."

. . .

An hour later Jackie found herself once again at Dikko Travathian's doorstep. This time armed with copies of his and Lockhart's tax returns for the year Byron cashed out of DTC – short for Dikko Travathian Corporation. How very original.

The front door opened and the uniform-clad housekeeper stood there, a welcoming smile plummeting when she realized who was calling.

Again.

"Hello," Jackie said, "we'd like to speak with Mr. Travathian."

"Please wait," the woman said.

She made a move to close the door, then paused, obviously not wanting to be rude. Rather than invite them in, she left the front door hanging open and disappeared somewhere behind it. A compromise for a flustered employee.

Craning his neck to see around the door, Chessie let out a snort. "I think she went into the room across from where we were this morning."

Having not been invited in, they stood on the doorstep while Chessie hummed his favorite Sinatra tune. He tended to do that when killing time. He was accustomed to waiting. Jackie? Not so much.

Annoyance had started to set in when Travathian swung into view. He wore track pants and a T-shirt with nary a wrinkle. Probably had the housekeeper iron them. His casual attire, however, was overrun by his stiff posture and locked jaw.

"We're back," Jackie chirped. "We have a few more questions."

"Which I won't answer."

Before Travathian could slam the door, Chessie set his hand on it. "Don't be too hasty."

The two men exchanged a look that screamed pissing match. Such shenanigans.

"Oh, Chessie," she waved a hand. "Let's forget this nonsense. I'll release the tax returns to WJTA. Maybe then Mr. Travathian will realize he should have spoken to us."

Jackie wasn't sure if the name drop of the local news affiliate or the phrase tax returns got Travathian's attention, but the man's slivered gaze moved to Chessie and back. "What are you babbling about?"

"WJTA. You know, the *news channel*. Imagine our shock when Debra Johansen was waiting outside my home earlier. She's digging around for information on Special Agent Pearson. It seems she's received a tip from an anonymous source. And given the, shall we say, personal nature of that information, I can narrow down the source. Or sourc-*es*."

"You think it was me? What the hell do I have to do with it?"

"I'm not sure, which is why I'm here. You failed to mention Byron Lockhart was an early investor in your company."

"You never asked."

Please. This guy couldn't be that dumb. Could he? Realistically, yes, he could. God knew she'd seen her share of idiots.

"Tsk-tsk-tsk," Jackie waggled one finger. "Given the contentious divorce between the Lockharts, obviously their wealth would factor in. Maybe they were fighting over money."

Chessie let out a long whistle. "She had to be taking his ass to the cleaners."

"I would," Jackie agreed. "All these years she'd been the upstanding FBI wife, left alone constantly while her husband quite literally tried to save our country. I'd imagine all that lost time is worth big bucks." She snapped her fingers. "You know, it would be *so* easy to prove in court. All I'd have to do is show Byron made a bundle from Mr. Travathian's company. Which, of course, might mean the Travathians being subpoenaed."

"Oh, yeah," Chessie agreed, "that's a given."

"Huh," she said. "Now that I think about it. I'm not sure we need to be here after all." She tugged on his sleeve, guiding him down the steps. "Let's leave Mr. Travathian alone, shall we?"

"You're bluffing," Travathian said. "You don't have my returns. How would you have gotten them?"

Now she had him. She squeezed Chessie's elbow and fought a smug smile before turning back. "Mr. Travathian, this is a murder case. Do you really think it matters how I did? Believe me, I can prove you and Mr. Lockhart were in business together. Byron made a bundle as a result. And if that fortune was at risk, I'd say we have motive for murder. So, unless you want your finances spewed to the entire DC area, you might want to answer my questions."

The look Travathian gave her should have knocked her into next year. Obviously, he didn't appreciate her machinations.

Too bad. Sometimes life sucked that way.

Travathian propped his hands on his hips, his fingers tapping. "What do you want to know?"

Better. Now they were getting somewhere. "How long were you partners?"

"He was my first investor. I needed seed money and he had cash from an inheritance. He gave me 50K to get off the ground."

"And then?"

"I brought in a spec ops guy with an idea for a safer, more lightweight helmet. We took it to market, landed a few big contracts with law enforcement agencies and started making money. It took years, but we got there."

"When did Lockhart cash out?"

Travathian didn't bother to think about it. "When he got promoted to assistant director. He had his eye on the top job. By then, we'd gone public and I was bidding on government contracts."

"Conflict of interest," Jackie said. "If you got the contract, he didn't want people thinking he greased the wheels."

The man didn't nod. He didn't shake her off either. He simply lifted his chin in a non-committal way that Jackie took as agreement.

"Look," he said, "it wasn't a big deal. He sold his shares. No harm. No foul."

At least until his estranged wife was murdered.

10

The eyes of the FBI's ten most wanted hung on the walls of headquarters, watching Beck as he made his way to Taylor's office first thing Monday morning. Security hadn't stopped him at the entrance, so apparently, he hadn't been labeled persona non grata yet.

The morning's young.

Taylor was speaking to him on his cell, chirping in his ear. "There's no need for you to come in."

The walls weren't the only thing watching him. "I think there is," he said. The eyes of other early morning employees grabbing coffee and making small talk on their way to various offices and cubbyholes weighed heavy on him. By now, most had heard about his weekend activities and were no doubt wondering if he was innocent or guilty. "I want to look the good director in the eye when he tells me I'm suspended."

Taylor's voice held a note of pride, even if she disagreed. "That's a terrible idea under the circumstances."

Beck took refuge in the elevator and hit the button to the floor he needed. "*Under the circumstances*, you and I both know Lockhart should be on suspension, considering he's a much more likely murder suspect than I am. I'm thinking of pressing charges against him for belting me at the station. Figured I'd tell him that in person when I hand over my service weapon."

"Beck..." Her sigh was heavy. "You're a good agent and everyone loves you. Hell, half the people in this building—men and women alike—want to make out with you, regardless of their sexual preference because you're that flippin' hot. And *nice*. This is an unfortunate blip in your life, but it's not the end of your career."

There was noise in the background and Taylor affected a more professional voice. "We'll find the killer and bring him to justice. You'll be back to work before you know it, but you need to be patient."

"Thanks for the vote of confidence." The elevator dinged and let him off. "The rousing speech is a nice touch too. Rah, rah. But I'm coming in so save your breath."

"Beck, I really don't think you should do that."

He opened her office door and swept in, a cup of her favorite chai tea in his hand. "Too late, I'm here." He grinned and disconnected. "Who else is going to bring you tea, Tay?"

Her face fell and she stiffened, eyes darting across the way and then back to him. "Beck...uh, Agent Pearson. You're here."

He pushed the door aside and saw Director Lockhart looking out the single window in the office, hands tucked in the pockets of suit pants. "Hello, Beck," he said without turning.

Tickticktick. The clock on the wall broke the awkward silence as Beck considered his options.

One, give Byron Lockhart a taste of his fist and let whatever happened happen.

Two, pretend the man didn't get under his skin, and turn in his ID and weapon without a fuss.

Three, raise hell and let the Director know he was messing with the wrong man.

As if Taylor sensed Beck leaning toward option three, she

jumped up from her chair and came around the desk. "This is an awkward situation, and I expect the two of you will handle it like civilized adult men, or I will make you both wish you hadn't ventured into my office today, got it?"

Oh, Taylor. Acting so tough. She was skilled in hand-to-hand, and nasty with a weapon, but she probably wasn't much more than 5'5" and a hundred and twenty pounds. No match for him, although he loved her for her gumption. Reminded him of another tough lady.

Beck patted Taylor's shoulder and took two steps toward the window, covertly hitting the button on his phone for his microphone app. "You have something to say to me, Director Lockhart?"

The man swiveled to look Beck in the eye, hands still in his pockets. At least it appeared he wasn't going to throw a punch this round. "You're suspended, and unlike Agent Sinclair here, I know what you did. I know you killed my wife. It's only a matter of time before you pay for it."

Beck set his jaw and tapped his hand against his leg still considering Option Three.

"Beck..." Taylor warned.

Beck waved the phone in her direction, letting her know he wasn't going to throw Lockhart out the window. "If you were anyone besides Director of the FBI, the cops would be all over you. Annabelle was your *estranged* wife and sounds to me like she was going to take you for a whole lot of money. You couldn't let that happen, could you?"

Lockhart's eyes narrowed. "The divorce papers weren't finalized. We were getting back together. Until you murdered her."

"Getting back together?" Beck smirked. "Is that why she was at the bachelor auction throwing a lot of money around to buy a date with me?"

Lockhart's hands emerged from his pockets. "You asshole. She was helping the shelter, that's all."

"Three thousand dollars. That's what she bid on me. Not too many people have that kind of fun money lying around. Was she still an investor in the Travathian Company? I hear you two made quite a killing investing in Dikko's business. Helmets for US soldiers, right?"

Lockhart reddened and he fisted his hands. "I have no idea what you're getting at."

"Sure you do." Beck sat on the edge of Taylor's desk, pretending a casualness he didn't feel. It wasn't the first time he'd interrogated a suspect he knew was guilty. "You helped Dikko land those government contracts, didn't you? And then you made millions off the stock when the time came to divest. Annabelle was there for the whole ride, and she knew you got Dikko in good with the DOD. She planned to take you to the cleaners, so you killed her, saving yourself a lot of money. And she took your secrets to the grave."

Taylor stepped closer to Beck, giving Lockhart the side-eye. "Is this true?"

"Of course, it's not," Lockhart growled. "Not the way he's making it out to be. There's a lot more to the story, and none of it was illegal or unethical."

Beck didn't argue, but gave the man a hard look. "Ten million dollars is a lot of money. People have killed for less."

A fist came up. Lockhart shook it at Beck. "I loved Annabelle and you took her away from me."

Go ahead, take the punch. All I need is for you to throw the first one.

Because if Lockhart started a fight, this time Beck was going to end it. "You keep telling yourself that, Director, but we all know the truth. You worked long hours and neglected her in your quest to become the Bureau's top dog. You did some underhanded wheeling and dealing along the way and she kept her mouth shut, but eventually, she wanted a warm body in her bed and you weren't around. You were the typical DC cliché, married to the job, but she realized she had some power too, having been the keeper of your secrets for all these years. She decided to bail on you, and you weren't about to let that happen."

The fist lowered but Lockhart moved closer, his dull brown eyes full of righteous venom. "You don't know anything about my marriage."

Taylor inserted herself between the two of them. "Director, please step back. Beck, stop stirring the pot. We are not holding a trial in my office, and if you'd both get control of your egos, you'd realize neither one of you is the killer and you're wasting precious time going at each other instead of figuring out who is."

Lockhart paced away, rubbing a hand over his face, and Taylor turned on Beck, giving him a *what the fuck* look. He set his phone, app still recording, on her desk and motioned with his head for her to move aside. She rolled her eyes but stepped back far enough for him to see Lockhart again. "Why'd you leak the news about my suspension to the press?"

Lockhart barely glanced at him, his attention pinned to view outside the window again. "I don't know what you're talking about."

Such a liar. "You and Taylor were the only ones who knew the suspension would happen first thing this morning, correct?"

"Yes," Taylor answered. She swiveled to look at the Director. "Weren't we?"

No answer.

Beck shook his head. "Taylor didn't call the news station to announce it, so it must have been you."

Taylor set hands on hips and glared at the Director. "You leaked Beck's suspension to a news station?"

Staring outside helped Lockhart keep his emotions under control, but Beck saw the muscles in his jaw working. "Any federal agent accused of murder is going to be suspended until the charges are dropped or the agent is found guilty," he ground out. "It was a bygone conclusion that I'm sure the press jumped on."

"You didn't answer the question." Taylor's voice had gone flat.

"He doesn't need to," Beck said. "WJTA is running a story tonight about my suspension along with the dirty, scandalous news about my family's criminal histories. I'll give you one guess where Debra Johansen got her facts."

"No." Taylor marched over and stared at Lockhart. "You didn't."

She knew about Beck's family and the history he'd fought so hard to overcome. Not everything, but most of it. Taylor always had his back and she'd been a good friend, helping him feel like he belonged on her team. Like he had family inside the Bureau's walls. Some days, she was more of a sister to him than any of his blood relations.

But that illusion crashed down on him with full force. He couldn't put her in this predicament, couldn't rely on the Bureau for the sense of security and belonging he'd always craved. After all this time, after all of his dedication, that was gone.

Beck tossed his ID on Taylor's desk and unstrapped his service weapon to lay next to it. "I thought you were better than that, Director. When you took your oath to this institution, I guess you didn't mean it when it came to fidelity and integrity."

Lockhart ground his jaw. "You're relieved of duty, Pearson. Get out before I call security and have you escorted from the building."

Pushing off Taylor's desk, Beck faced the man and shut off the recording app. "I'm going to find Annabelle's killer, with or without your help, but don't be surprised if there's some tit for tat with the press. Debra's going to love hearing my theories about you and your estranged wife, and a copy of your tax returns, including those questionable investments, might suddenly turn up in her inbox."

Lockhart's head snapped around. He closed the distance, finger coming up to point at Beck. "You better be careful who you're messing with, boy."

Boy. He hadn't been called that in a long time. His father often used the term, not like a normal father would with his son, but almost like a curse. A threat.

Tickticktick, the clock once again mocked the silence. Taylor didn't move, didn't say anything, but her eyes pleaded with Beck not to lose his cool.

The story of his life. *Stay cool. Use your head. Don't let emotions get in the way.*

What good had it done him? Everything about his life had been turned ass-over-gridiron because of Byron Lockhart.

Daddy always said good guys never win.

Beck had tried to prove him wrong.

Looks like Daddy was right after all.

Anger fired low. He got right in Lockhart's face, staring the man down. "You're the one who messed with the wrong guy. You've ruined my career, my reputation, and you brought my family into this. In other words, you stepped in a big o' pile of shit."

Taylor's hand landed on Beck's arm, which he hadn't even realized he'd lifted. He glanced down to see his hand curled in a fist.

Dropping it, he drew himself to full height. Lockhart took a step back.

"Don't be surprised to see me when you look in your rearview." He whirled and walked away before he wiped the floor with the man, but stopped in the doorway and gave Lockhart a cutthroat glare. "I'm gunning for you now, Director, and you're gonna wish you never laid eyes on me."

. . .

Jackie rode shotgun while Beck drove to Vienna, Virginia, a thirty minute ride from DC. Thirty minutes. For a meeting she'd been unaware of with people she didn't know. *Way to control a situation, girlfriend.*

"Beck, honestly, what are we doing here? We don't have time to screw around."

He made a left onto a tree-lined street leading toward the center of town. "We're not screwing around. My boss's boyfriend is a PI."

"I have a PI. A damned good one."

Beck sighed. "I realize that. We need all hands on deck though. And Matt's a good guy. Smart. He works for Schock Investigations."

Wait. Schock? She knew that name. Odd and so recognizable. Jackie focused on the trees flying by her window while her mind ticked back.

"The cold case broads."

Beck laughed. "Broads?"

"It's Chessie speak. They're the ones, right? One's a sculptor and the other is a...what?"

"Forensic psychologist."

Jackie snapped her fingers. "Yes!"

"Between Matt and the *broads* there's not much they can't accomplish. Taylor's hands are tied but she talked to Matt about my case and they've offered to help."

"Can you afford that?"

He took his eyes off the road, giving her a bored look. "Modeling was good to me."

"I guess so. Maybe I should raise my hourly rate."

"Maybe I should hire Fleming."

Of all the lowdown, rotten things to say. "You little bastard, spilling that kind of filth in this car."

Beck cracked up, his smile going full wattage and decimating the tension.

"Hey," he said, "you started it. And Fleming is a good guy."

"If you want someone to plead out, he's the master. A great negotiator. When it comes to the war of trial work," Jackie shook her head, "he's a preschooler. Plus, we're not pleading out. We're winning this thing."

Whatever it took, she'd clear Beck's name. And then, maybe, they'd be in a place where she could have a conversation with him about a baby who never got a chance at life.

He reached over, squeezed her arm and the heat from his fingers sent sparks rocketing up her arm. Every damned time the man touched her, it seemed her clothes begged to vaporize. Even that first night. That wild spring break where Jackie the good girl broke her cardinal rule about not sleeping with strangers.

Beck had been different. Confident, nice, and...well...beautiful. Back then his body had been a work of art. From what she'd seen of his bare chest the night of his arrest, the rest probably still was. How any woman could resist him was way outside of Jackie's intuitive boundaries. Then and now.

Except now, she'd learned the hard way that quick flings brought heartache. And each time she saw him she relived it. The lust, the happiness, the fun.

The guilt.

She had to tell him. Had to. Before, when he hated her and they barely spoke, it was easy to keep it to herself. So easy to justify. Now? Sitting in this car, alone with him, it wasn't.

"Thank you," he said.

Thank you? She'd lied to him by omission and he was thanking her?

She looked away, breaking the heavy eye contact for a view of a two-story historic house turned museum.

"Jackie?"

God, she didn't want to talk. To face him. "You shouldn't be thanking me."

"My ass. You're trying to keep me from life in prison. I'd say that requires a thanks."

If he only knew. Another stream of silence lingered and she shifted closer to the door, bumping the frame. Nowhere to run. Stuck. She couldn't hold the secret anymore and she sure as hell couldn't run from it.

Damned Beck. He should have just stayed hating her.

Tell him.

He eased to a stop at a light and the tension rolled in again, thick and heavy and Jackie couldn't look at him. Too much.

"Hey," he said, "what's going on with you? One second we were joking around and now you're pissed. I was kidding about Fleming."

Fleming. If only it was that easy. "It's not about Fleming."

"Then what?"

The light flashed green. Go signal. Tell him. Perfect opening.

A horn behind them sounded and he hit the gas. "Talk to me, Jackie."

Yes. *Talk to him.*

His GPS blared to life. *You have reached your destination...*

They sure had.

Beck pulled to the curb in front of a one-story office building where a painted sign mounted next to the front door read Schock Investigations in fancy scroll lettering.

"This is it," she said.

"Yeah." Beck checked his phone. "Everyone is inside, but they can wait. What's up?"

Panic built in her chest, robbing her air. She opened the door and inhaled, taking a long pull of fresh oxygen. How the hell did she tell a man he was almost a father? And that she'd kept it from him?

For twelve years.

She glanced at the building again. With all he faced and going into this meeting to discuss the murder charge against him, now sure wasn't the time to clue him in.

She turned back, pinned a smile in place. "It's nothing. We can discuss it later. Let's not keep everyone waiting."

"You sure?"

When it came to Beck, she wasn't sure of anything. "Come on. Let's see what these crack investigators of yours can do for us."

He led Jackie through the front door of Schock Investigations where a receptionist sat at an oversized desk made of natural wood. A nice touch in an otherwise small room containing a red loveseat and a chair bursting with upholstered sunflowers. The place definitely had a woman's touch.

"Hello," the receptionist said to Beck. "May I help you?"

Her tone was cool but her gaze? Total man-eater. Jackie didn't blame her. The vaporizing clothes theory. No sane woman could look at Beck and not want to ravage him.

"Beck Pearson and Jackie DelRay. Here to see Matt."

"Yes, they're all in the conference room."

The woman rose from her chair, her eyes nearly searing Beck's flesh as she waved him forward. Jackie's gut churned and she fought the fit of jealousy. This is why she didn't have relationships. She wasn't even *in* one and she wanted to cut a bitch.

"Unbelievable," she muttered.

Beck glanced back. "What?"

"Nothing. Thinking. Sorry."

The receptionist knocked on the third door on the right and a man yelled for her to enter. She held the door for them making a little more extended eye contact with Beck as he marched by. To his credit, he simply nodded and turned his attention to the others in the room.

The twisted part of Jackie wanted to announce to the

aggressive blonde that Beck was suspected of murder. Maybe *that* would back her off.

With the way he looked? Probably not.

"Hey, guys," Beck said.

He shook hands with a tall man. Presumably Matt.

"Jackie, meet Matt Stephens. And this is Meg and Charlie Schock. They own the agency."

After introductions were made, Beck pulled a chair out for Jackie and she slid into it. "Thank you all for seeing us."

Charlie nodded. "Of course. Beck helped us with a case recently. We want to repay the favor."

Standing in front of a gorgeous redhead, with blue eyes and an outfit so well accessorized, left Jackie feeling like a homeless person in her drab suit.

I need a wardrobe upgrade. Maybe try for silk blouses and slacks, like Charlie Schock.

Could she even pull off those styles? Might be worth experimenting with.

"Can we get you anything?" Meg asked.

For sisters, these two were an interesting pair. In direct opposition to her sister's elegance, Meg wore an old T-shirt complete with paint stains. If Jackie had daughters, that's what she'd want. Two women offering varying perspectives. She glanced at Beck, casually leaning back in his chair. Would their baby have been a girl he could spoil? Would he have even wanted their baby? Or would he have felt trapped?

She'd never know. The years and opportunity to see his reaction were gone.

He cocked his head and his mouth moved, but all Jackie heard was a whooshing sound.

Beck lifted a hand and snapped his fingers. "Earth calling."

Oh, God. She'd spaced out. The hotshot lawyer daydreaming in front of Beck's private investigators. Excellent first impression.

"I'm sorry," she said. "I was thinking."

His mouth curved into a sexy grin that once again inspired an urge for clothing evaporation. Damned man. So arrogant.

"Meg asked if you wanted a drink?"

Double vodka maybe. She faced her hosts. "Just water. Thanks."

A small refrigerator hummed in the corner and Meg retrieved three water bottles. Jackie reached for one of the glasses on the tray in the middle of the table and cracked a bottle open.

"Beck," Charlie said, "how about you bring us up to date?"

"We can do that," he said.

We. Not I. Jackie liked the sound of that.

It took him ten minutes to replay the events of the weekend, including a summation of his 'date' with Annabelle.

"Okay." Matt rose from his chair and moved to the giant whiteboard mounted on the wall. "Let's make a list of what we've got and I'll tell you what we found out this morning."

That sounded promising.

He snatched a marker from a bowl on the credenza and uncapped it. "We'll start with our suspects."

He wrote Beck's name on the board. "After leaving Annabelle's you went straight home?"

"Yeah. I was tired. I'd just spent an entire evening trying not to insult my boss's estranged wife while rebuffing her advances. That may not sound like rough duty, but believe me, it sucked."

"Were you home alone?" Meg asked.

"Yes. I set my burglar alarm though. The security company should have a record of that."

Charlie leaned forward and jotted a note. Under her notepad was a small stack of reports that Jackie assumed were for use in this meeting.

When she finished her note, she set her pen down. "Suspect

number two. The estranged husband. What do we know about him?"

"Well, they were in the middle of a knockdown, drag-out divorce. Based on what we've found out from their friends – the Travathians – money was an issue."

"Did Annabelle work?"

"Yes," Jackie said. "My investigator looked into that. She was a partner at a small accounting firm. She made $90,000 last year, but the firm is only in its third year and still growing. Mostly corporate audits and forensic accounting."

"What's the difference?"

The question came from Meg, and Jackie, having dealt with forensic accountants during trials, took it. "Audits will tell if there are any misstatements in the financials. Forensic accounting is more of a fraud investigation for use in lawsuits or criminal cases."

Meg nodded. "Okay. We'll assume she could support herself. It was just the splitting of the marital assets they were fighting over."

"Yes, and they had a lot of them," Jackie said. "Our esteemed FBI director was an early investor in Mr. Travathian's company. He sold his stock before being promoted and made a bundle."

Matt added a dollar sign under Byron's name. "Now that's interesting. Any idea when he cashed out?"

Jackie retrieved the copies of Byron's returns from her brief-case. "January 2015. That was before he became director, so we already figured out there was no conflict of interest. Why?"

Taking a cue from Matt, Charlie pushed the stack of reports from under her notepad to her sister, who shared with Beck and Jackie.

Matt tapped his marker on the table. "I pulled this report together. Grey told me about Travathian so I started digging. In February 2015, DTC settled a lawsuit."

Before Matt could finish, Jackie perused the report. She never was any good at waiting.

"Oh, wow," she said. "A fifty million dollar lawsuit for defective helmets?"

"Yeah. They were using a material that the Justice Department decertified for use in any helmets approved by the U.S. government. DTC was warned to stop using it, but they already had a warehouse full of helmets. Travathian had his number two guy falsify some financials that made it appear like they were taking a loss on those helmets, since presumably they couldn't use them."

Beck set his report down and focused on Matt. "Why do I feel a 'but' coming?"

"Because there is one."

Anticipating his answer, Jackie rifled ahead in the report, shuffling through the pages. Page three. Second paragraph from the bottom. "That son of a bitch," she said. "He took a loss on the helmets and sold them anyway."

"Shit," Beck said. "He put defective helmets on our soldiers?"

"He did. And he got caught. An Army private was taking target practice and thought putting one of the old helmets on top of a two-by-four might help him practice head shots. Two of his bullets penetrated the helmet."

"Jesus," Beck said. "Some of our guys could have been killed."

"Which is why the government sued. Since there were no casualties or deaths, Travathian's lawyers were able to settle the case and have the depositions sealed. And, politics being what it is, DTC formed a subsidiary company that, guess what?"

Oh, Jackie wasn't believing this one. She smacked the report on the table. "The government continued using him."

"Yes. Apparently, the fact that the holding company was DTC slipped through the cracks. They treated him as a new vendor. He at least had to prove his product was safe. Rigorous testing."

"And you know this how?"

Matt nodded at Charlie again and she handed over another stack of pages. "A deposition given by DTC's number two guy. He was spec ops and brought in by Travathian to help design the helmet."

"Wait," Jackie said. "I thought the case was sealed."

"Here's the pisser. I called the court reporting service used at the deposition. The case was initially temporarily sealed. When the parties came to a settlement agreement, no one asked the court to permanently seal the discovery materials."

Jackie smiled. "Which means anyone can access them."

"Yes, ma'am."

Beck held up a hand. "And the settlement was in February 2015?"

"Yep," Charlie said. "Guess who else cashed out of DTC stock?"

It was a fucking shame that Charlie Schock had left the FBI and joined forces with her sister. Good thing she had though, because Beck would definitely be holding his ass right now, looking like a fool if it weren't for her and Grey.

The back of his neck tingled as he saw the Cheshire cat grin Charlie shot him from across the table, that same heat he always felt when he was about to find a key to solve a case.

"Who else cashed out?" Beck asked, the answer already pinging against his temple like an ice pick. He sat forward, elbows on the conference table. The picture someone had slipped to Jackie sat between them, the men in the photo bringing it all home. "President Murphy? He was an investor too?"

The grin on Charlie's face grew, a fire in her eyes. She knew the feeling Beck was experiencing—that 'gotcha' moment. She'd been there plenty of times, digging up dirt on a perp and discovering the one fact that put her on the right path. "Bingo. There is definitely a link between Murphy, Lockhart, and Dikko Travathian, and it has nothing to do with friendship. Their paths go much deeper than that. Someone greased the wheels for Dikko and none of us need two guesses as to who."

"How much did Murphy make when he cashed out?" Jackie said. "Did he dump the stock before he took office?"

"There's where the problem lies," Charlie said. "Like Lockhart, it looks like Murphy cashed out before there was any conflict of interest."

"Ten million dollars?" Meg frowned at a page she then handed to Jackie. "That's a lot of money."

"And exactly the same as Lockhart," Jackie said. "He and Murphy were both early investors who cashed out at relatively the same time and made the same amount."

"And no doubt helped Dick get his contract accepted by the DOD," Matt added.

"But Travathian then got caught manufacturing defective helmets and Murphy and Lockhart bailed right before that was revealed. So maybe it wasn't all about conflict of interest." Jackie looked at Beck. "Insider trading?"

Beck sat back, totally deflated. "That's probably the least of it, and it doesn't help us figure out who killed Annabelle."

Charlie shrugged, not deflated at all. "Any lead is a good lead. These three have a suspicious relationship that revolves around a lot of power and money. Annabelle knew all three and if they were trying to cover up insider trading, conflict of interest, or defective products sold to the DOD, she might have been using it as a bargaining chip with Byron. Lockhart still looks good for her murder, in my opinion."

Meg sipped from her cup. "I never cared for that guy."

Charlie rolled her eyes. "You met him, like, once, Meg."

"I can tell a lot about a person in one meeting."

Beck didn't doubt it.

Jackie smiled down at the deposition notes as she continued to read. "Did you see this?"

She handed the paper to Beck, pointing at the section in question. "Rachael, Dikko's wife, is CEO of DTC."

Beck slapped the paper on the table. "Rachael knew about the defective helmets."

"Not only knew about them but let her husband set her up as head of the subsidiary that resold them." Jackie shook her head in disgust. Her dark eyes swung to Beck's. "Rachael and Annabelle were friends. Maybe Rachael confided in her. Annabelle knew there was fishy business going on. Maybe she threatened to expose Dikko."

They stared at each other for a moment, both processing, following all the threads and where they might lead when it came to motive for Annabelle's murder.

God, she was beautiful, Beck thought. Beautiful and so, so smart.

"We need proof and Rachael won't tell us squat. Looked to me like he ran the show. As soon as he showed up, she turned into the obedient wife," Beck said, fighting to keep his head in the game when all he wanted to do was find out why Jackie looked so sad behind those dark eyes of hers. "She's a dead end, regardless of her claim that she wants to see Annabelle's killer caught, especially if Dikko had a hand in the murder. She'll do whatever he says."

The room fell silent. Charlie looked around at everyone as if waiting for a lightbulb to go on over someone's head. "Who stood to lose the most if something was leaked? Dikko stood to lose his entire company if someone like Annabelle made waves or exposed the subsidiary company reselling the detective helmets. If there was any kind of collusion between Travathian, the Director of the FBI, and the President, Murphy could possibly lose the Oval, but it would take a shitload of evidence and the case would never make it past the Justice Department. Lockhart could lose his nice office much easier. I still say we have three strong leads. Every single one of these guys is a power player in Washington and none would go down without a fight, but I'm leaning toward Dikko and Lockhart being our two best suspects at this point."

Matt glanced at Beck. "What's your gut telling you, Pearson?"

"I agree with Charlie." Beck blew out a heavy sigh. "While I still like Lockhart for this, it's more personal bias than clear logic spurring me on, so I may be wrong about him. And the President may have been an early investor, but Murphy's had his sights set on the White House for a long time. Yes, the timing of the cash-out is suspicious, but out of all three, he has the fewest ties to Annabelle, and the biggest guns to protect him from someone like her. She wouldn't be a blip on his radar, I don't think, and if he needed to shut her up, discrediting her would be easier than murder."

"So you're thinking Dikko is our top suspect?" Meg asked.

Beck nodded. "I want it to be Lockhart, but something's telling me he actually did love Annabelle and was just as shocked as everyone else that she was murdered."

Jackie's finger slid down to the last line on the page. "The accounting firm DTC used is listed here. What if we look into them, see where it leads? I can also have Chessie dig around DTC and see if anything else turns up."

What could it hurt? Beck nodded, taking out his cell. He had two missed calls from Fallyn Pasche and a text. She'd handled Debra and the news feature, but she wanted him to call her back ASAP to discuss doing an official campaign to raise his popularity score. Popularity score? What the hell was that? He'd call her back after the meeting, once he and Jackie were back at his place. "You call them and I'll call Grey," he said to her. "I want Teeg to look deeper into Dikko, see if there's anything sketchy in his background, okay?"

Charlie grabbed her laptop. "I'll dig into Dikko. We don't need Greystone for that."

Beck hit a speed dial button. "No offense, and I appreciate any help you can offer, but Grey has resources we can't even imagine and a tech guru who scares me with the amount of stuff he can uncover."

Charlie snickered and started typing. "First one to come up with something good wins a fancy steak dinner, deal?"

Beck chuckled as the phone rang on Grey's end. "Deal."

11

On the way from Schock Investigations, Jackie put a call into Chessie requesting he research any high-profile cases Annabelle may have worked on recently. Maybe they'd get lucky and find an unhappy client somewhere who might be mad enough to commit murder. Chessie's research, coupled with Teeg attempting to hack into Annabelle's emails, left Jackie and Beck in a holding pattern. One that prompted Beck to announce his near starvation and a detour to his favorite watering hole.

He held the door open to what looked like a DC version of an old-time tavern and Jackie stepped over the threshold. Two steps in and she halted, her eyes scanning the handful of wooden booths along the wall, the battered bar with touches of gleaming brass and the vinyl barstools.

Dive bar.

Just like O'Hara's.

A vision of Beck, twelve years younger, all broad-shoul-dered and cocky, flashed. "Wow," she said.

Beck smiled at her. "Crazy, right?"

It sure was.

He grabbed her hand, dragging her down the narrow space between the booths and barstools. "Don't be fooled by the ambience. The food is great."

The way her stomach curled into a tight lump from the flood of memories swarming her, she wouldn't be able to choke anything down.

She stumbled along behind him, her ears ringing at the sound of the ancient jukebox and Tom Petty's *Free Fallin'*. She knew the feeling.

"Hey, Toby." Beck waved to the bartender.

"Beck, how's it going? Good to see you, dude."

The bartender waved him over to the service area. On numb legs, Jackie followed.

"What's up?" Beck asked.

"Nothing. I heard about that woman who got killed. That's bullshit, man. I know you didn't do it."

Beck reached across the bar and shook the man's hand. "Thanks. Appreciate that. We'll get it worked out." He turned back to Jackie. "Speaking of which, this is my attorney, Jackie. She's the best in DC."

And, oh, Beck was no fool. He knew the way to her heart. Even if he was sucking up, hearing such high praise – from him – gave her a rush.

She shook Toby's hand. "Don't listen to him. He's trying to get on my good side." Then she couldn't resist turning back to Beck with a smile. "Lucky for him, it's working."

The two of them stood at the bar, eyes locked for a long few seconds while Jackie's inner smart girl scolded her. Yes, it was wrong. It also wasn't causing her to shuffle Beck's case to another attorney. One who didn't have emotional entanglements with the client.

Beck pointed to the rear of the bar. "We're gonna grab this last booth."

Two men sitting at the bar did a half-turn, checking out the newcomers while Jackie's mind drifted again.

This place was a perfect replica of the bar where they'd first met before spending a lust-filled, wickedly fun night that turned into high drama.

Beck stopped in front of a booth and waved her in before taking the seat across from her. He snatched menus from the holder behind the napkin dispenser and handed her one.

Food. Right.

She gripped the menu – maybe a little too tight given the ache in her fingertips – and glanced around, taking in the neon beer signs lining the walls. T-shirts in every color hung from the dropped ceiling and the old wound to her heart, the Beck-wound, split open.

Why would he bring her here? To this place that made her think of what could have been?

Even that damned brass rail along the bar matched the one she'd been leaning against the first time she'd put eyes on Beck...

Memories of that night came in flashes. The crowd, the music, the jungle of packed-tight bodies and illicit behavior. Jackie inhaled and the stale air of the bar brought her to the smell of sweat, draft beer, and college students on the hunt for adventure. All part of spring break fun, Jackie had been assured. Up to that night, she hadn't been convinced, and had continued to contemplate it as she stood at the bar with the just-turned-21 guy trying to pick her up.

"Yeah," the guy had said. "Rough one last night. Puked my guts out all night."

Riveting conversationalist this one. "Wow. Are you okay?"

"Yeah. I drank a beer when I got up and felt better."

Excellent. Jackie glanced left through the crush separating

her from her girlfriends sitting in a booth along the wall. In the words of the great Quasimodo, sanctuary!

Jackie glanced down at her second-skin dress. No wonder this drunk wouldn't leave her alone. In an effort to get her out of her shorts and sleeveless tees the girls had taken her shopping, deciding she needed a stretchy black number that. as Gracie put it, showed off her tits and ass. The getup was beyond foreign but when she'd put it on, somehow she didn't mind. Being a girl who rode the fine line between thin and curvy, she might as well use her assets.

Plus, with her mother not around waxing on about how women shouldn't flaunt their bodies, Jackie needed to take advantage of the freedom. Just once.

Which led to Gracie pushing the makeover a step farther by attacking Jackie's normally pinned-up hair with a fat-barreled curling iron. Add in Jazz's makeup prowess and they had a Jackie makeover that attracted horny college boys. Like the one standing in front of her proclaiming love at first sight.

"Well," Jackie held up her barely-touched and thoroughly warm beer, "it was great talking to you, but I need to get back to my friends."

The drunk attempted a sexy grin. "Ah, come on. You can't leave me now."

Yes, actually, I can.

In fact, she might head right out the door to sit by the beach until the girls were ready to go.

Someone bumped her from behind and she angled back. A big guy, with dark wavy hair and blue eyes that slayed a girl, squeezed in.

"Sorry," he said. "Tryin' to get a beer."

Something snapped in her brain, sending her body on full hottie alert. She sucked in a hard breath, holding it a second and wondering if she might be drooling. Had he said something? Jackie wasn't sure. All she knew were his eyes were devastating. Summer sky blue and twinkling enough that she stood rooted in her spot, completely polarized. The snug-but-not-too-much T-shirt that clung to long-lean muscle didn't help. The man was...beautiful. In a totally masculine Greek God way.

"No problem," she said. "The place is a zoo."

"So," the drunk at the bar said, "about your friends."

Still dumbstruck, Jackie couldn't turn away from the big guy. Had she seen him somewhere before?

Zeus glanced over her shoulder at Horny-Boy, then brought his electric gaze back to her, leaning in enough to talk without screaming. "He bugging you?"

And, oh, oh, oh, he might even be nice. She leaned in, got a whiff of salty air from his shirt. "He's harmless but persistent. I'm trying to make my getaway without insulting him."

"Gotcha." Zeus looked over her shoulder again. "Dude," he said to Horny-Boy. "Thanks for keeping my girl company until I got here. Appreciate it."

Her hero. Jackie faced Horny-Boy and smiled. "Sorry," she said, "I didn't get a chance to tell you I was waiting for someone."

Horny-Boy took a long gander at the big guy outweighing him by at least fifty pounds. If this didn't get rid of him, Jackie would just leave and find a quiet spot somewhere outside to wait for her friends.

But, alas, Horny-Boy came to his drunken senses, rolled his eyes and left. So much for love at first sight.

Jackie laughed and turned back to Zeus. "Thank you."

"No problem."

The bartender shoved some bills in a tip cup then swung back to Zeus. "What can I get you?"

"A bucket of Coronas."

He pointed at Jackie's beer. "You need a fresh one?"

She set the beer on the bar. "No, thanks. I barely drank this one."

"Yeah, that stuff is crap. Let's get her a cranberry juice. Lots of ice. It's hot in here."

Cranberry juice. Clearly the man wasn't trying to get her drunk.

"I'm not a big drinker," she said.

He turned sideways giving her the full blast of his undivided attention and something low in her belly twinged. She'd been so caught up studying for the LSATs over the past year she'd opted out of dating. And anything else related to getting cozy with the male species. Now that she'd aced the test, her mind and body liked to remind her men weren't the enemy.

Most of the time.

"What's your name?" he asked.

"Jackie. Jackie DelRay."

Up north, she didn't like giving out her last name. Marianna DelRay had made quite a name for herself as a prosecutor-turned DA. Some loved her, others hated her. Talk about polarizing. For that reason, Jackie tended to keep her lineage on the down-low. In Florida no one knew them. Hopefully.

"I'm Beck," Zeus said. "Pearson. You here on spring break?"

"I am."

"Me too. I go to Alabama."

"I'm at UPenn Philly."

"Major?"

"Pre-law."

His face lit up. "No shit? I'm criminal justice."

How about that? Two strangers with a love of the law. She sipped her cranberry juice, thankful for the icy cold that took the harsh edge off the heat. "Where do you want to end up?"

"Hoping for Quantico."

Oh, wow. A Bureau man. "An FBI agent? That's cool."

"Yeah, I'd like to land in DC."

And on and on it went. Two hours of conversation and debates ranging from Kermit the Frog to their stances on capital punishment. He for, her against. Eventually, they migrated from the bar to a corner near the door that provided a break from the loud music and swelling voices.

Jackie leaned back against the wall. Beck wedged in beside her and his chest brushed her boobs sending all sorts of naughty thoughts streaming.

"Dickhead!" someone yelled.

Ten feet from them, a guy took a swing at one of Beck's buddies.

"Shit," he said. "I'll be right back. Do not move from this spot. It's the safest place."

Then he was gone, taking all that delicious muscle with him and diving into the middle of the fray where one of his friends had the drunk's shirt in his hands. Beck bullied his way into the middle of it, ducked a wide right from the instigator, who stumbled and fell over.

Beck heaved the guy up by the waistband and carried him outside to safety before a bunch of Alabama football players rearranged his body parts.

Jackie followed behind, waiting as Beck spoke to the cab driver. She tipped her head back, stared up at a perfect three-quarter moon while the ocean breeze settled her mind. Peace. This is what it felt like to not think, to not worry about exams, law school, and where she'd be in five years.

This was fun.

"Thanks, man," Beck said

She looked back down just as he slapped the cab's roof and turned back to her. He took one step and halted. His eyes raked over her body—damned stretchy dress—and for the first time all night a wave of self-consciousness buckled her shoulders.

He slapped a hand over his chest. "Have I mentioned you're beautiful?"

Oh, he was good. Fully understanding the man was probably a player – so what? – she stood a little taller. This was spring break and she intended to enjoy what was left of it. She stepped closer. "In fact, you haven't, but thank you. I got the 'Gracie special' before we left the motel. My friends call this amped-up Jackie." She glanced down, tugging on the stretchy fabric. "Usually I'm a shorts and tank-top girl."

Beck moved toward her. She met him halfway, got close enough to feel the heat of his body and the tingles started all over again. He set one hand on her hip.

"Something tells me," he said, meeting her eye and holding the stare. "I'd like that version too."

He nudged his chin toward the beach. "How about a walk? I'm kinda done screaming over noise so we can talk."

A walk. It sounded nice. Perfect in fact. But smart-Jackie, the girl who'd had it pounded into her to never—ever—go off with strange men, sent up a warning flare. "Have I mentioned," she said, "my mother is the DA in Philly?"

"Meaning, if I hurt you she'll come after me?"

"Exactly."

He cocked his head, then lifted one finger, running it down the side of her cheek and his touch set off an inferno that between the cool breeze and her body's response to his touch made her nipples go hard. Thank goodness for padded push-up bras or Beck would have quite a visual.

"I won't hurt you," he said. "First of all, that's not me. Not ever. And, if I intended anything illegal, immoral, or unethical, I wouldn't have spent the last two hours giving you the scoop on me. Second, it would do wonders for my FBI career, and third, I like you, Jackie. You're beautiful, smart, and challenge me intellectually. I've never had all of that in one package. Right now, I'm a really happy guy who doesn't want this night to end."

That tore it. Game over. Her nipples damned near blasted

through the padded bra so Jackie did the only thing she could. She slapped her hand over the back of his neck and kissed him, absolutely melted into him, feeling every curve of muscle as he wrapped his arms around her, pulling her in tight. He ran his tongue over her bottom lip and she let out a soft groan. A cabbie honked at them and Beck pulled back, grinning down at her.

"We're giving them a show," she said.

"What do you say? Should we move this to the beach?"

She met his gaze, that pretty blue she'd never forget and any doubts she'd had about Beck vanished. This broad-shouldered, intelligent, gorgeous jock made her laugh and then saved a dumb stranger from an ass-whupping. Maybe, just maybe, the good-girl, the one who'd been a virgin until 19, might, for the first time, fuck a man blind during a fling...

And she had.

They'd explored each other, laughed, and shared funny stories.

That had been twelve years ago, and now they sat, older and hopefully wiser, in yet another dive bar. Only this time, Jackie's haunting secrets came with her.

"It looks just like O'Hara's," she said. "Even the T-shirts."

"I know." Beck shoved the menu back in its holder. "I found it by accident when I first came to DC. The food's a bonus."

A young waitress – Lyndsey – wearing jeans, sneakers and a tight red tank top stepped up, greeted Beck like an old friend and took their drink order. Something on draft for Beck and water for Jackie. Although, a double-vodka wouldn't hurt right now.

He focused on her, cocking his head in that way of his that meant his thoughts were spinning. "We should talk about it. The thing that's bugging you."

No, they shouldn't. "What?"

"Don't play dumb. I *know,* Jackie."

Dear God. How could he? She hadn't told anyone. No. One. "Bugging me?"

"Yeah. Donlin."

A whoosh of air shot up her throat, but she held it, fighting the relief. She eased against the unforgiving backrest and felt the press of wood against her spine. "We *should* clear the air on that. You have no idea how much I wanted to sign off on the arrest warrant. You worked hard on that case. I knew it. There just wasn't enough physical evidence. And if we'd gone to trial and he'd gotten a not guilty, we'd have been screwed. No going back. Back then, from the prosecutor's table, I couldn't risk it."

"What about from the defense side?"

"The defense wants that case. It's winnable. It keeps a man out of prison."

"What about my case? Winnable?"

"Absolutely. Selfishly, I wouldn't mind going to trial here. We'd tear the prosecution apart. I don't think we'll get there though. We'll find who did this and the charges against you will be dropped."

"You seem pretty sure of that."

"I am." Beck may have been a lot of things – stubborn, insistent, *sexy* – but he wasn't a murderer. She leaned in. "As you know, I don't take losing cases."

"I'm surprised you wanted this one." He wagged a finger back and forth between them. "Given our history."

"I didn't, at first. Chessie called and told me they hadn't given you your phone call. I couldn't let you sit there without counsel. It's a huge case. My intention was to help you until your lawyer showed up."

"And what changed?"

She laughed, but it came out as more of a resigned sigh. "Um, I saw you."

And what our unborn child might have looked like.

"O-kay. What exactly does that mean?"

Caught between wanting to guard her secret, yet be free of it, Jackie peered down at the scarred wood of the table. *Tell him.* She should. Right now. Now that they'd formed a truce, keeping it from him would be unfair. "Beck, there's something I should tell you. About...Ft. Lauderdale."

He sat forward, propped his elbows on the table, setting his hands down. If she stretched her fingers just a little, bitty inch, she'd touch him. Feel that insane heat that came with him from the very start.

"Jackie, I'm sorry about how things with us ended. It shouldn't have happened."

"I know."

Boy, did she.

Before she could go on, the waitress delivered their drinks and Beck ordered a cobb salad. Having not even looked at the menu, Jackie did the same. If this pit in her stomach didn't evaporate, she wouldn't be eating anyway.

The waitress cleared out and Jackie faced Beck again. For years she'd wondered about him and the woman who'd shown up at the motel that morning. His former girlfriend who'd popped up to "surprise" him.

She'd certainly done that. Jackie had been in the bathroom, cleaning herself up after another round of rock-em, sock-em sexual ecstasy. She'd walked out and found Beck at the door speaking with a blonde who should have been on the cover of Cosmopolitan magazine. As beautiful as Beck was, she'd been his perfect match and Jackie felt...ordinary.

Plain.

She'd quickly excused herself and run back to her motel four blocks away where her friend entertained one of Beck's football buddies. Oh, they'd all made the perfect pairings for a weekend jaunt.

At least until Jackie knocked on her own door and got the full story about Beck's girlfriend.

"Whatever happened with her?" Jackie asked.

He shrugged. "Nothing happened. We talked for awhile and I sent her home. She hurt me."

"I know."

This surprised him. "You *know*?"

"Henry told me."

Beck shook his head. "Good old Henry with the big mouth. Haven't seen him in ten years and can't say I miss him always getting my ass in trouble."

"It wasn't his fault."

"Telling you my business? Really?"

"I was upset. I thought you were just another jerk looking to get laid."

That brought a half-smile to his lips, but nothing about it conveyed happiness. Regret, yes. Happiness? Far from it.

"I was," he said. "I liked you though. A lot."

"You had a situation to work out."

"I guess that's a tidy way to say it."

Jackie rolled her lips in. What a cluster. "I'm sorry, I don't know the right words here. And about...you know."

The pain ripped through Beck like a hot, serrated knife. Twelve years and he still hadn't come to terms with all the emotions Portia still evoked in him. Not that he cared for her anymore. Oh no, not at all. What she had done had screwed him up but good.

Lyndsey, having the world's worst timing, showed up with their food so Beck took a second to get his head together. After the whole can-I-get-you-anything routine, she scrambled off to the next table.

Needing something to do with his hands, Beck picked up

his fork. "She aborted my baby. There was nothing to work out. I told her that and sent her on her way. That was the last I talked to her."

He jammed the fork into his salad and shoved way too much into his mouth. The pain centered in his chest pulsed along with his heartbeat. What would have happened if Portia had listened to him rather than her snooty, upscale family who couldn't stand to look at him? Would his child be alive?

His life would certainly be different right now.

Grinding at the salad, he squashed the anger and sadness like he'd been doing since that day right before Christmas. "Portia told me she was pregnant at Thanksgiving. It happened the night of Homecoming. I made the winning touchdown in a tight game against Ole Miss. For the first time in my life, I was living the dream and Portia wanted to celebrate in a very memorable way."

Realizing he was bending the fork from the pressure, he deliberately set it down. "Unbeknownst to me, Portia had sabotaged us by going off the pill. She broke the news to me six weeks later, and I felt my future go up in a puff of smoke — my college career, done. No future with the NFL."

"Oh, Beck," Jackie said.

He didn't want her pity, knew he couldn't stop the way she was looking at him. "The crazy thing was—I was happy, Jackie. I was going to have a family. A *real* family. My own kid to take care of and love for the rest of his life. In that moment, with our combined futures a big, fat unknown, I finally had purpose. I was going to be a father, and everything I had to give up in order to marry Portia and raise our kid didn't matter one iota. No question, I would take being a father over being a football player."

He'd loved Portia back then—or at least he'd thought that's what it was—and he'd been ready and willing to take care of her and his kid, no doubt about it.

Across the table, Jackie sat completely still, staring at him with her sad eyes.

Bringing her here was a bad idea. He'd wanted to remind her of the fun they'd had on spring break back then, not dredge up how it had come to a screeching halt.

"Let it go," he told her. "That was a lifetime ago. I'm over it."

Disbelief carved tight lines around her mouth. "I know you well enough to know you'll never get over something like that."

"Look, my family is a goddamn mess, and while I hate what Portia did, maybe in the long run, it was better not to bring an innocent baby into that disaster. I just wish..."

She toyed with the handle of her spoon as his unsaid words hung in the air with dying notes of the jukebox song. "You wish you'd had some say in what happened."

He picked up his fork, set it down again and rubbed a hand down his face. God, he felt old right now. Old and worn out. "I told Portia I'd marry her. That I'd get a full-time job to support her and the baby. But her parents never believed I was good enough for her and convinced her that I would run out on her. I thought she knew me better than that, but I guess with my family being criminals and all, she was afraid to take the chance. In hindsight, a part of me can't blame her, but I also can't forgive her for killing my child. She told me on my birthday, after the deed was already done. She didn't really have any ambitions other than dreaming of having her own reality TV show. Mommy and Daddy convinced her I was a joke, so she got rid of our child." He couldn't keep the bitterness out of his voice. "Happy fucking birthday to me. Every year, it's a horrible reminder of what happened."

"Beck..."

Jackie's eyes had teared up and he immediately felt like an ass for going down that rabbit hole. No good came from talking about any of this—the past was the past. It couldn't be changed.

And he'd never been one for a pity party.

He reached over and took her hand. Her fingers felt cold and stiff, and he rubbed them, trying to get warmth back into the digits. "Portia's my past. I screwed up, got her pregnant, and then I wasn't the person she needed to feel safe and secure enough to bring our child into the world. When she showed up on spring break, what she really wanted was to hookup. That was all. She didn't suddenly come to her senses about what she'd thrown away, nor did she feel any guilt or sadness over what had happened. It made me realize all over again that she was never the person I thought she was."

"I'm sorry I ran out on you. I didn't know."

"Of course not, and then Henry had to be a douchebag and tell you selective bits and pieces of the sordid story. I don't blame you for running away, it's understandable." He shrugged. "I have a lot of regrets, Jackie, but I can't alter the past. We were all just stupid, young kids that weekend in Ft. Lauderdale. I'd like to think you and I have both moved on. More importantly, I'm hoping we have a future together after we bring Annabelle's killer to justice."

She detached her hand from his and sipped her water. Her fingers shook as she brushed them across her brow. "You know, I'm not feeling all that great. Do you think we can skip the rest of the meal and get out of here?"

Jackie skipping a good meal? Had he said something wrong? Tossing his napkin on the table, he pulled out his wallet. "Of course. I'll pay the check and we can head back to my place."

"Great." She jumped up, snatching her purse and holding it close to her stomach. "I'll be outside. I need some air."

Well, shit. "Jackie, are you o—"

But she was already gone, pushing her way through the people, now three deep at the bar. Beck watched her until she went out the front door. Once again, it seemed his past had put him in the doghouse, although he wasn't sure why.

He payed the check, went back and threw some bills on the table for a tip, and headed outside. He'd just hit the front side-walk when he saw Jackie climbing into a cab a couple yards down the block.

"Jackie!"

The door closed and the cab took off, leaving Beck standing on the sidewalk wondering what the fuck had just happened.

12

The cabbie had barely gotten to the curb before Jackie tossed a twenty over the seat and pushed open the door.

"Lady," he hollered over his shoulder, "your change!"

She couldn't worry about that right now. Just ahead, her front door stood waiting. She needed inside. Into her space. Her own little world where she could curl up and not think about the mess she'd created.

The fling, taking Beck's case, all of it so reckless. Given their history, she had no business anywhere near a criminal case involving Beckett Pearson.

The father of her lost baby.

A furious whooshing clogged her ears, knocking her off balance. Her body swayed left as the cement path leading to her front door tilted and curved. *Stop.*

That's what she needed. To stop, take a few deep breaths of the cooling night air and get herself together.

She stared down at her feet. Four of them.

Oh, goddamnit.

Years she'd been hanging on, holding all that grief over a

baby she'd never had the chance to know. She wanted to though. A little boy who could throw a football. Or a girl who could. How about that?

A ball of rage unfurled, right smack in the middle of her solar plexus and the burn shot in all directions.

Get inside. That's all she needed to do. Just move off the street and climb to her bed.

In the morning, she'd find Beck a new lawyer and get back to life on her own terms. Yes, that's what she'd do. Throw herself back into her work and put Beck behind her. Hanging on to the rail, she stumbled up the porch, dragged her keys from her purse and unlocked the door.

Her space. Her neat, ordinary, drama-free home.

"Jackie!"

Oh, no. No, no, no. Beck had followed her. Of course he did. That's the type of guy he was. A woman in distress? Absolute candy for Beck. Damn him and his hero complex.

Well, now she was done. She whipped around and there he was, all glorious muscles and fluid movement storming up her walkway and holy cow, the man was hotter than a two dollar pistol.

"What the hell?" he asked. "Are you sick or something?"

She was sick all right. Sick of carrying this goddamned guilt and pain. What kind of woman refuses to tell a man he was almost a father?

Backing into the house, she held up one hand. "I can't...talk right now."

Blowing that off, he hopped up on the porch and followed her right through the door. "What's wrong?" He latched onto her arm and steered her toward the sofa. "You're totally white. What hurts?"

Everything. Every nerve is decimated.

"Sit down," he said. "I'll make you tea. Do you have any chamomile?"

As if a fucking cup of *tea* would fix this? *I need him gone.*

She dropped to the couch and rubbed her palm up her forehead where a harsh throb exploded. "Beck, I'm fine. Please. Just...go."

He marched into the kitchen, started throwing open cabinets. "Clearly, you're not. Where's the tea?"

No tea.

Another giant and vast difference in the Jackie-Beck saga. She snorted and he glanced over the breakfast bar at her, his face a mix of hard angles. "What?"

Even from the distance, his eyes sparked. So, so blue. That color had stayed with her for twelve years. Even when he wasn't around she pictured Beck's eyes.

And wondered if their baby would have had them.

"What?" he repeated.

A swampy mess of heartache built, climbing higher and higher inside her. Pressure. In her throat. Everything was stuck. Right there. Stuck, stuck, stuck.

Can't do it.

Not anymore.

"Beck," she said, "I can't do this anymore."

"Do what?"

Was that all the man could say? For the love of God come up with something new.

She flapped her arms. "This! The lines are blurred. I should never have taken this case. Never. I knew it and did it anyway."

He came around the breakfast bar and headed for her.

No. If he sat down, he'd be too close. Jackie jumped up and they squared off in front of the sofa. She crossed her arms, pushed her shoulders back Marianna DelRay style. Battle ready.

Beck cocked his head, the investigator in him trying to decode her back-off message. "Okay," he said, "I have no idea what the fuck is going on. All I know is you freaked on me and ran off. Talk to me, Jackie."

"What's to talk about? I shouldn't have taken your case. It's a major conflict of interest."

"Because we had a thing years ago? Please. We've barely spoken a civil word in all that time."

"It's not that. Not entirely."

He stepped closer, reached his arms out and Jackie flinched.

"Whoa," he said, holding his hands up. "Do you think I'm going to *hit* you?"

"No! Of course not. You wouldn't. I just..."

He dropped his arms. "Tell me what's going on. Now."

Why did he have to be such a pain in the ass with all the questions? Always. Even on that first night, he'd asked her so damned many. Innocent, get-to-know-you ones that she'd loved because he was so focused on her. Genuinely curious and so...present. No wonder she'd broken every moral rule she had and fallen into bed with him.

And now he wanted to hold her? Definitely not the smart thing right now.

She shook her head, took a tiny step back.

"Jackie, come on. Please. Is this about family? Portia? Just fucking talk to me. I'm not going until you do."

She should leave him in her living room and just go to bed. With her luck he'd kick in her bedroom door. Well, terrific. *Let's do it.* She met his eye. "Fine. I'll talk. I don't want you to touch me."

His jaw dropped, but before he could speak she forged ahead. "I get all screwed up when you do. I get *reckless*, and you don't want that. Not when I'm trying to keep you out of prison. You can't have it both ways, Beck. Do you want me to love you or keep you out of jail?"

"Knock it off. You expect me to believe this is about love? Nice try." He leaned in a little, nearly touched her nose with his.

"Guess what, babe? I know you. I've watched you in court thousands of times. Times when you didn't even know I was there. When you're hiding something, you do that indignant, holier-than-thou thing that distracts the jury. Gets them thinking in another direction. That's you, the ultimate spin doctor."

He caught that? Shoot. Still, she huffed out a breath and rolled her eyes. "Thank you, doctor, for your diagnosis."

"And when you get busted, you turn to sarcasm. So tell me, Jackie, what exactly are you hiding? What don't you want me to know? Please tell me you haven't changed your mind about my innocence. You know I would never hurt anyone."

Here it was. Her opening. He had her cornered and yet, she didn't feel threatened. The man was magic. No wonder he was so good at his job.

All she knew was she couldn't do this anymore. Couldn't hold this secret. Not if she intended to keep him out of prison.

And maybe, just maybe have a life with him.

She reached for him, wrapping her icy fingers around his thick wrists, immediately feeling the warmth that always came with Beck. "I know you're innocent, but I'm..." She shook her head. "There's something I haven't known how to tell you."

He relaxed a fraction. Relief. "How about just spitting it out? It's not that hard."

Easy for him to say. Still, he'd given her the opening. She exhaled. One long breath before meeting his gaze again and holding it, praying he'd see what this had done to her. "It's about Ft. Lauderdale. That's why I got upset tonight. That bar, it was so...similar. It took me back and stirred up too many memories."

"We had fun."

"We did. And then I came home and thought about you. Wondered what you were doing. If you'd gotten back together with your ex-girlfriend. I put you out of my head. Dove back

160

into my studies and after a few weeks, I'd done a sufficient job of staying busy." She squeezed his wrists again. "Until I missed my period."

His head lopped forward. "You...what?"

"Pregnant, Beck. I was pregnant. With your baby."

Was. Baby. The words rang in Beck's head. A sharp, thick vibration as if someone had put him under a colossal bell and hit the thing with a sledgehammer.

He stepped back, breaking Jackie's hold on his wrists, his feet feeling completely disconnected from the floor. "My...*baby*?"

Jackie came at him, trying to hang on, trying to grab his other wrist. "I was going to tell you. Call you, but..."

No, no, no. This couldn't be happening. Not again.

He shook her off, ended up with his back against the wall. "But what? What the fuck, Jackie? What did you do?" The last words were whispered, his throat closing. His chest physically hurt as if his heart couldn't beat. "Please tell me you didn't..."

Tears spilled over her bottom lids. "No, no, I would never. I *lost* the baby, Beck. Almost the minute I realized I was pregnant, I miscarried."

Mother Nature had stepped in, or maybe God.

It should have been a relief.

It wasn't.

A sudden flash of memories that had never been created, never shared, rose in Beck's mind.

Jackie and a baby. *My baby.*

The grief hit hard as he saw them in his mind's eye. Him and Jackie building a life together, raising their child *together*. How cool could that scenario have been?

All the long, lonely days and nights of his life. The holidays.

He could have been living it with his family. With this woman right in front of him.

The grief and regret nearly sucked his breath away. His hand absently rubbed at the ache in his chest.

It all made sense now. Why she'd been acting so weird around him.

Why she'd really taken his case.

He cleared his throat, found his voice again. "Why didn't you tell me?"

She looked away, as if the lamp on the side table were suddenly more interesting than him. He expected her to turn away too, but she didn't.

She drew in a breath from somewhere around her toes, bringing it up, up, up, and then slowly let it out, shifting her gaze back to his.

Brave. Determined.

More tears streaked down her cheeks but she stood her ground right in front of him. "I don't have a good excuse. I didn't know you back then, and I wasn't sure if you and Portia were getting back together, and I... Like you said at the bar, we were all just kids. I didn't know what the hell to do, and well, either way, nothing I did would bring our baby back."

Our baby.

The way she said it, his heart broke all over again. *I'm not the only one who lost something invaluable here.*

The memory of her from back then flashed across his mind. She'd been pretty innocent but trying to act worldly and tough. It was one of the things that had attracted him to her. She hadn't been flouting herself like ninety-nine percent of the girls on spring break. She'd been grounded, funny, smart. She'd seduced his mind as well as his body, and it had knocked his socks off.

He pinched his eyes shut and rubbed them, imagining her back in Philly with her mom the DA, her life on track to become a successful lawyer in a family of them. To find out she was pregnant from a spring break fling, with him no less, had to have scared the hell out of her. Then to lose the baby before she'd even figured out what she was going to do? Yeah, he wasn't the only one who'd had his life changed forever by a baby who'd never had a chance to be born.

"You should have told me," he said, still struggling to get words out, "but I get it." He wiped tears off one of her cheeks. "I wasn't exactly prime daddy material, was I?"

Her eyes narrowed and she sniffed. "Stop. Right now. Portia, your family, and God knows who else, have done a number on your head. You don't think you're good enough for anyone, but that's not true. My God, you're"—she flapped a hand at him—"you're an FBI agent. You were a model. A football star. You're...*magic*."

"Back then, I wasn't an FBI agent, and you told me yourself, you hated jocks."

Her mouth trembled slightly as she tried to smirk. She dashed at the other cheek with the back of her hand, wiping away the wetness. "You've got nothing to prove, Beck. Not then and not now. I've spent the past twelve years wondering what it would be like to have had your child running around. Every time I see you, I wonder if he or she would have had your eyes, your intelligence, or your humor. I've ached for that—that little boy or girl."

All the pain vanished. Not the sadness; that was still flooding his system. But the gut-ripping pain of knowing he'd lost another child gave way to the realization that, even though it had been twelve years, Jackie was still hurting.

Right or wrong, she'd saved him that grief and pain and carried the secret all alone. All on her own. He didn't like that she'd kept him in the dark, but all this time? She'd been the one living with the burden of truth, and that truth sucked.

He tried so hard not to live in the past. It was a dark void of pain and regret, and mulling over it constantly did no good. Yet, here was Jackie, forever caught in what had happened that long ago weekend.

"Can I touch you now?" he asked quietly.

Her throat worked as she visibly swallowed. "If you do I'm going to lose all this grief and awfulness that I've been hanging onto all this time. I have to warn you, it's ugly."

He grabbed her then, pulling her into his arms and holding her tight. Rubbing her back, stroking her hair. "I'm so sorry. About all of it. I wish I could have been there for you then, but I'm here now. It's time to let it out, Jackie."

At first, she stayed rigid, fighting it. But then her chest hitched and her forehead banged into his chest, and the next thing he knew, things did indeed get ugly. The woman he loved – hell, he'd been in love with her since that weekend, if he were honest – finally caved and let go of her grief, melting into his arms.

13

For the first time in twelve years Jackie gave in. What was it about Beck that crawled inside her and flipped that pain-in-the-ass switch? The one that shut down every lesson her mother – DelRay University of Toughness President – taught her.

Right now, Mom would be appalled. As much as they adored each other, weakness had no place in Jackie's world.

Mom's not here.

Thank you very much, God of Lucky Breaks. There was only so much Jackie could handle and her mother thrown into this hot mess wouldn't help any of them.

Forget. That's all Jackie wanted, to just let it all go. Everything. The mistakes she'd made, the secrets she'd kept.

The failure.

Would it even be possible? With Beck, yes. She'd experienced that first hand in Ft. Lauderdale.

Stop. She pushed her reeling thoughts from her mind and nuzzled Beck's neck, inhaling his faded soapy scent that brought her back to a beach, salt air, and falling a little bit in love.

She'd never get that time – or her bad decisions – back. "I'm so sorry," she said.

"Sssh. There's nothing to be sorry for."

His voice was gentle, his breath warm against her ear and it sparked something long forgotten. Being with him like this was such a mistake. But...so good.

"I lost our baby," she said.

"Not your fault."

"I wanted a boy. One who would look like you and play ball too. Do everything like you. A Beck mini-me who'd bring me peace, love, and laughter. All the things I had with you for that little while." She shook her head. "It's a dream, I know. Too perfect. I don't care. I let myself believe it because we got robbed."

"I wish you'd have told me."

"I was going to. I swear. When I found out – I did one of those stick tests – I was alone in my apartment. I sat there on top of that stupid vanity while I waited for the results. When I saw the plus sign I was stunned. Condom gone wrong, I guess. I don't know, but something happened. I panicked at first. And then, the more I thought about it, the more I realized it was okay. Well, not okay, but meant to be. I had our baby inside me. A life. And I knew I'd keep him. Raising a child while in law school would be a challenge, but our baby needed me. I just had to wrap my mind around it for a couple days. When I did, I knew I couldn't keep it from you."

"So what happened?"

"You know me, I made a plan. I got your dorm number from Gracie. My friend that was with Henry that night."

"Did you call? I never got a message."

"I did, but Henry told me you were in New York on a modeling shoot. He gave me your cell number, but said you had a 4 a.m. call time the next day, so you were probably asleep. I told him I'd call you in the morning. I just wanted you to know.

166

Not because I wanted anything. I had everything I needed and wasn't about to force you to be in our lives, but you had a right to know. Then I woke up to bloody sheets. I went to the doctor and he told me our baby was gone."

All at once, it hit her. The rage, sadness, and relief of finally, finally telling the man he'd almost been a daddy, but wasn't.

Again.

A pounding fist rammed her chest and the pressure cracked something open. Her ribcage coming apart. Oh, she hated this. Despised the power it still had over her all these years.

Beck wrapped her in his arms again, squeezed her tight. "Ssshhh," he said. "You're okay. I promise, you are."

"I never told anyone. I swear. Chessie knows we slept together, but that's it. I had to tell him. All this time, I kept it to myself."

"Why?"

Well, that question might be truly offensive. What did he think? That she ran around telling everyone but him he'd almost been a father. "What do you mean, why? How the hell could I tell someone else when you didn't even know? It wasn't fair to you. And then, when I got the job in DC and you walked into court, what was I supposed to say. Guess what? You got me knocked up. How could I do that?" She gripped the back of his shirt. "I didn't know how to do it. And then you got mad at me about Donlin and there was no way I could tell you."

"It's...all right. I know now. Chessie knows we were together?"

"He damn near beat it out of me. He was concerned over my"–she rolled one hand–"emotional involvement. Like you, he's a good investigator. Reads people well. He knew something was up." She met his gaze and held it. "I lost your baby but I wasn't about to have you lose your freedom."

"You took my case because you couldn't have my baby?"

Ew. When he said it like that, it sounded bad. Really bad. But... "I failed you."

"You didn't."

"I did. As twisted as it sounds, that's how it feels to me. It's more than that, though. It was that time we had together. That one amazing spring break that let me relax and have fun. Not be so driven and focused. I lived a little that night. You made me feel things I'd never felt and I forgot all the pressure that came with being the only daughter of Marianna DelRay. It was a gift and I loved you for it. I will always love you for it."

Phew. All these years she'd kept her feelings, some she hadn't realized she'd had until Beck was arrested, under lock and key. Not letting anyone in. She should have talked to someone. A friend. A shrink. Whoever. Somehow, she couldn't. Couldn't let go of it. Maybe it was her excuse to stay focused. To build a career. No husband, no kids, but she had one hell of a career.

Did it make her pathetic or ambitious? Did it matter?

He kissed her.

And there was nothing soft about it. He simply hauled her into him and went to work. *No complaints, here.* She gave as good as she got and welcomed the kiss, bending into him, pressing every inch – *every* inch – against him. The hard swell of his erection told her exactly what Beck wanted and her mind ticked back twelve years. The short walk on the moonlit beach, their clasped hands swinging while they laughed over some dumb guy in the bar ready to take on a bunch of hulking Alabama jocks. As they walked, Beck told her about his dream of moving to DC.

Then he'd stopped walking, staring at her under the moonlight with the lapping waves of low tide behind them. When he dipped his head, she'd let it happen. Let his lips glide over hers until her body responded. Tingling breasts and hardening nipples that begged for his attention. The good girl turned sex kitten as her completely sober system let loose a burst of lust that startled and horrified her.

Just like now.

"God," she said, tearing her lips free. "Every time. I don't know what it is, but you make me crazy."

She moved in again, kissed him hard, driving her tongue into his mouth and rocking her hips into him, imagining that second, that incredible moment, after all these years, when he'd slide inside her.

It was all too much. The heat, the want, the passion. So long she'd been without. Searching for that skin-on-skin connection, that *closeness* she'd only ever experienced with him. A total stranger that took her places no lover ever had.

Beck.

Magic.

"Bedroom," he said, his mouth still on hers.

She backed up, bringing him with her, but at this rate it would take all night to get there. Not that she was in a hurry, but they had lost time to make up for.

He pulled his hand away, locked both of them around her biceps and set her back a step. "Fuck this."

"Huh?"

And then she was airborne, just flying through the air until she landed over his shoulder. He moved fast down the hallway.

"Take me, big boy."

He laughed and again she was back in Ft. Lauderdale, in that crappy motel room, cracking jokes to alleviate her nerves and making hunky Beck laugh.

From over his shoulder, she smacked him on the ass. "I love when you laugh at my jokes. It gets me hot."

"I remember."

He made the turn into the bedroom where the glow of a streetlight bullied its way through the blinds.

"Hang on," he said, gently lowering her to the bed.

Beck stepped back – *wait*.

"Watch the – "

Crap. Her Superman, her athletic hunk stumbled backward over the giant pile of dirty clothes she'd yet to wash. He caught himself on the tall dresser, landing on the chair near the door.

"Jesus, Jackie. Are you trying to kill me?"

"Sorry! It's my dirty clothes. I haven't had time to do laundry."

Still seated, he kicked off his shoes and went to work on the buttons of his shirt. A multi-tasker. Excellent.

"Well," he said, "you need to get organized. I can help with that."

"Honey, there's only one thing I want your help with right now."

Even in the dim light, his smile flashed and...oh, she couldn't stand it. She wiggled out of her slacks and not bothering with the buttons, tore her blouse over her head. She tossed it somewhere in the vicinity of her dirty clothes pile and Beck let out a sigh.

A lecture on proper care of her clothing was sure to come. "Don't start, glamour boy. The least you can do is give me an earth-mover of an orgasm before you yell at me."

He slipped out of his boxer briefs and stood and...*my, my, my.*

"Well, look at you," she said. "Still working out religiously, I see."

He moved closer, unhooking her bra and peeling it down her arms. Progress was halted when she wrapped her fingers around the full, hard length of him.

And stroked.

Beck tipped his head back and she locked her gaze on his throat and the throb of his pulse. Still stroking, she got up on her knees, ran her tongue along that spot on his neck and her mind flashed back again to the crappy motel mattress. The two of them falling onto it, laughing at the squeaky springs. Squeaking or not, they'd managed to make good use of that bed.

If she had her way, they'd do an even better job now.

She ran her free hand up his abs to his chest where his heart pounded against her palm. She paused and twirled her fingers into the fine chest hairs that added to the fun of touching him.

"I like touching you," she said.

She did. Every single inch of him.

His eyes darkened into that stormy blue she'd seen their first time together and Jackie's hands, already anticipating the replay of an incredible night, twitched. She was so ready for this.

"Jackie?"

"Yes?"

"I'm going to make you scream."

She held his gaze, returning the naughty smile, maybe even raising the screw-me-now factor. So fun, that. "Please do."

Gently, he nudged her back on the bed, crawling along next to her until they were both on their sides, facing each other, taking in the moment and in no particular rush.

Then he moved his hand over her, across her breasts where his gentle fingers brushed her nipples. She rolled to her back, giving him full access and he wasted no time replacing his fingers with his mouth. He sucked, gently at first, and then harder until she arched up.

"Mmm," he said, "some things never change."

He remembered. That first night, he'd discovered her highly sensitized nipples and drove her half mad by giving them extra attention. Tongue, teeth, lips, all of it sent her to one heck of an epic orgasm. Now, apparently, he intended a do-over.

But, God, it had been so long and what she wanted, needed, right now was him. Inside her.

She pulled free of his mouth and grabbed his cheeks, dotting kisses along his mouth and neck as she locked one leg around his hip.

"I want you," she said. "Now."

His hand went to her waist and he stroked his thumb over her belly button. "You in a hurry?"

After twelve years? He'd better believe it.

"I am. If I get my way, we'll have plenty of time to play after."

Then he was gone, rolling away from her taking all that luscious Beck sexuality and heat with him. He dug around in his pants, retrieving his wallet.

Condom.

After what he'd experienced with Portia, the man probably kept boxes of them around.

A minute later, he was beside her again, condom in place. "Sorry," he said.

"Don't apologize for being responsible. I love that about you."

She pushed her fingers through his hair, enjoying the silky feel while his own hands moved down her torso. Then lower.

And lower.

Where he plunged his finger into her finding out just exactly how much she wanted him.

She opened her legs and he stroked her. "Jesus, Jackie."

"Please." She grabbed his wrist. "Play later. Come inside me."

Without taking his eyes from her, he removed his hand and slowly slid over her, nestling his body – and extremely hard erection – between her legs. His weight pushed her into the mattress, wrapping all around her, once again giving her that feeling of safety and...peace.

Sanctuary.

Right here, with Beck.

He plunged into her, letting out a gasp.

"Oh, yes," she said.

He lifted himself and she clamped her hands over his rear, guiding him back, loving the feel of him, the connection she'd been without for so long.

Stroke after stroke, skin against skin, they moved together, their bodies remembering and rediscovering. She wanted everything. The old, the new, the unexplored. All of it with Beck.

He propped himself up on his elbows and brushed his lips against hers as he moved inside her. She opened her eyes, found him staring down at her and arched up again, grinding into him, forcing him to pick up the pace.

She knew what she wanted. Him. All day. All night.

"It was so good between us," she said. "So good."

"I know. I never had that before or ever again."

He rocked into her once more and her body went taut. A knot of tension spiraled in her core, rising higher and higher and she gripped his shoulders, digging her nails into hard muscle. Hanging on. *Not yet. Please, not yet.*

Years she'd dreamed of him and now she wanted it to last. And last.

But no, her body had other ideas. She swung her head sideways and slammed her eyes closed.

"Please don't stop," she said.

And he didn't, he drove into her, pumping his hips harder and harder and finally she opened her eyes, met his gaze and – oh, wow – her body bowed up as it gave itself over.

Still inside her, Beck hooked his arm around her waist, bringing her with him as he rolled to his back.

She knew what he wanted. They'd been here before. Sitting on top of him, she rocked her hips, driving him deeper inside. He threw one arm up over his eyes and her nipples tingled at the sight of all that perfect muscle.

Beck.

"You're beautiful," she said. "I could do this all night with you."

He moaned and bucked his hips again. "You just might. It's so good, Jackie."

"I know."

He dropped his arm, met her gaze and grabbed her hips, setting the pace he wanted. "Right there," he said. "You're gonna make me..."

He stopped talking, squeezed her hips hard and *come on, come on...yes...*cried out.

But he kept pumping his hips and guiding her over him as the orgasm tore into him. "So good."

Finally, he stopped moving and came to rest under her. Still joined, but needing the extra contact, Jackie collapsed forward, falling onto him. He brought his arms around her, gliding his long fingers over her back and sending sparks of warmth up her spine.

She rested her cheek against his chest where his heart slammed. They'd worked hard together.

Just like the first time.

"Jackie?"

She lifted her head and met his gaze. "Yes?"

"I missed you."

14

———

*B*eck, Matt, and Teeg sat around the conference table at Schock Sisters Investigations, all with laptops, plenty of hot coffee, and their respective love for digging into people's personal lives.

Beck downed his morning protein shake, following it with a big swig of coffee. Jackie's revelation the previous night, and the hours of love-making that followed, had him both wired and exhausted. He didn't want to let her out of his sight, but she was processing where their relationship had gone over the span of the last few hours and needed some time on her own. He was beginning to understand more about what made her tick and how she handled the curveballs life threw at her. Getting the secret about their unborn child off her chest had granted her some peace, but it had also resulted in them culminating their relationship. Again.

And this time, they weren't college kids on spring break. She was his attorney and he was her client. Her heart and body wanted him, but the ethical implications of their night of passion were bugging the shit out of her.

Beck's ability to compartmentalize things came in handy,

but this morning he wasn't sure he could. His chest cavity felt hollow when he thought about the children he'd lost. There was no going back, no fixing it, but he recognized a part of him needed closure. Once this was all over and they found Annabelle's killer, he needed to do some soul searching and try to find peace.

Jackie had gone to the office to check in with Josh on another case they were working and to talk to Chessie about the details he'd compiled about Annabelle's work and friends. While she did that, Beck and the other two at the table were digging beyond what Chessie could into Annabelle's digital world.

A window popped up on Beck's screen that looked like a link to Annabelle's cloud information and Teeg said, "You take Annabelle's business emails."

He hit a few keys and turned to Matt, "You've got her personal emails. Grey is tracing her phone records, and I'm on Dikko. He's adept at hiding his tracks, using a bunch of shell companies and switching up his contractors every few months, but he's no match for me."

Teeg was definitely a top of the line hacker. Beck's skills were less black hat and more basic FBI agent, but he did know how to work around passwords and break into certain encrypted files thanks to hours spent with the Bureau's computer forensics examiners.

Charlie Schock appeared in the doorway. "I owe you that steak dinner," she said to Beck. "Not because your kid here uncovered more than I did on Dick and the defective helmets, but Meg and I landed a new case and I don't have time to research Travathian."

Matt snickered and Beck knew Charlie was saving face. "I'll take you up on that soon."

Matt must have owned some genuine hacking skills, too, for Teeg to set him loose on breaking into Annabelle's personal emails. "She has three separate accounts," Matt said. "Gmail, AOL, and Yahoo. Why would she need that many?"

Good question. Beck did a quick browse in her work cloud. "Her accounting firm has one, but she has a subset email account for each client. This could take hours."

Teeg already had his headphones on and wasn't listening to Beck or Matt. They exchanged a look and Beck went back to work with a heavy sigh, starting a spreadsheet to track client names, dates, and the services Annabelle had provided.

The gods must have been smiling on him because his eye snagged on one of the client account files when he listed them out alphabetically. "Holy shit."

Matt looked up from his laptop. "Was is it?"

"DTC. Annabelle has an email file for them."

A quirk of Matt's brows suggested he dittoed the curse. "She handled something for DTC?"

Beck clicked on the folder and perused the email headings. "Apparently an audit of their books."

Scanning through a series of emails, he came to one between Annabelle and Rachael. "Ho boy. Looks like Annabelle ended their business arrangement just two days before she was killed."

"Does it say why?"

Beck shook his head. "The email is generic. Just a professional termination of services. No explanation, but she cc'd Dick on it."

Matt clicked away at his keyboard. "Let me look for recent emails in these private accounts and see if there's anything between the two of them that explains it in more depth."

While he did that, Beck called Jackie. She answered on the first ring. "Hey there. I'm glad you called. I'm meeting with Annabelle's partner, a Natalie Wong, at noon. Chessie says she started the accounting firm with Annabelle three years ago and they appear to have been close. Maybe she has insight into who would want to kill Annabelle. She probably knows Byron and the facts about the divorce. Maybe something about Dikko too."

"I'm betting she does. We just found an email that shows Annabelle was hired to audit DTC's records. She terminated the agreement two days before she was murdered, but the email doesn't say why. Maybe Wong knows."

"Ooh, interesting. I'll ask her about it and see how she reacts. We're meeting at O'Malley's. Figured she might be more open to talk if I bought her lunch. You want to join us?"

He glanced at his watch. "Sure. I'll keep digging here for a while and then I'll let you buy me lunch too."

He heard the smile in her voice. "Deal."

Two hours later, he had detailed information on many of Dikko's other subsidiaries that Teeg had uncovered, a dozen or so names to investigate from the client emails, and Matt was ready to look into six men that had exchanged risqué emails with Annabelle through a dating site. While Beck still felt that Dikko and Byron were the most likely suspects, there were plenty of stalkers who used dating sites to find their next victims. He thanked Matt and Teeg for their time and headed out to meet Jackie.

He was half a mile from O'Malley's when he saw a set of blue lights flashing in his rearview. What was this?

The white SUV with the Metro Police insignia rode his bumper until, begrudgingly, Beck picked a parking lot to pull into since there were no spaces on the street.

Resisting getting pinned in by the cop, Beck ignored the parking slots and stopped in the middle of the first row of the lot. He rolled down his window as the officer approached.

"Didn't you see my lights on, son?"

The man was dark-skinned and had small, deep-set eyes. Graying sideburns poked out from under his visored hat and

Beck noticed the single bar on his blue shirt sleeve. A pot belly hung over the man's belt.

"What can I help you with today, Officer...?"

The man didn't fill in his name. "You know the drill. License and registration. Insurance card, too."

Beck held his irritation in check. "Why did you pull me over?"

The man set his hands on his belt. "I said, license and registration, son."

He was about to argue when he thought of Jackie waiting for him at the restaurant. He was going to be late now as it was. Engaging in a pissing match with the cop might be more of a hassle than it was worth.

Keeping his mental mumblings to himself, he gathered the items the officer wanted and started to text Jackie while the man reviewed them.

"What are you doing?" the officer said, eyeing Beck's phone.

"I'm late for a lunch date with my attorney." He punched up the camera and aimed the phone at the man's badge, snapping a picture. "I'm letting her know what—or who, in this case, Officer Wendell—is holding me up."

The man shot him an annoyed smirk. "They told me you were a smartass, Pearson."

Beck searched the man's features. "I'm sorry, they?"

"The guys down at South. Told me you were a real piece of work."

South, as in Patrol Services South. The cops who'd arrested him had been from that precinct.

"And you just happened to see me driving by and decided to harass me?" He could smell a lawsuit coming when he told Jackie what the man had said.

"Let me tell you something, son..." He tossed Beck's credentials through the window and leaned down.

Oh this should be good. Like he'd done with Byron, Beck

turned on the recording app on his phone and held it discreetly near his leg.

"I don't like murderers roaming my streets," Wendell went on. "I heard about how you killed that woman and still managed to get bail because you're some high and mighty FBI agent. I made it a point to get your license number and the make and model of your car, so I could keep an eye out for you. I serve and protect. I strongly suggest you turn your ass around and get out of my side of town or you'll be getting familiar with North precinct today."

Was he serious? "You know, for a guy your age, you'd think you would have made more than lowly officer first class. You're barely above a recruit. No supervisory abilities. Out here pounding the pavement everyday. That's gotta play havoc with your solar plexus chakra. Could be why you're carrying extra weight in your belly. Might want to look into that, officer. Might help with your anger management issues too. Now, if you don't have a legitimate reason for stopping me, I'll be going."

Wendell had straightened at the mention of his status and now frowned like a bulldog, deep creases on either side of his mouth. "You watch yourself, Pearson."

Without waiting for the cop to say more, Beck put the car in drive and took off, leaving the man staring after him.

It shouldn't have bothered him, but it did. The pressure cooker inside him was hitting the red zone. He picked up his travel mug and threw it against the far windshield.

The laminated glass of the windshield held, but the ceramic travel mug wasn't so lucky. The impact caused it to explode, shrapnel hitting the dash and falling into the passenger seat. The remnants of his morning shake flew all over too, some landing on him and his phone.

Sucking shake off one of his fingers, he merged into traffic, once more headed to the restaurant. He needed to jump on his treadmill later to burn off steam. Even better, he could work off energy with Jackie.

Jackie sat at the table in O'Malley's, a trendy eatery in downtown DC that specialized in bratwursts of every variety. Anticipating the lunch rush, she'd shown up half an hour early to get a table and, well, center herself. As much as she could, anyway, with the chatter of voices echoing in the crowded restaurant. She probably should have picked a quieter place, but Natalie had been hesitant to meet and Jackie made the leap that a busy location where they could hide in plain sight might ease the tension.

The downfall was the noise. People coming and going, bumping her chair while they mostly screamed over the crowd. *Work with it.* She'd have to. Even after the emotional and, um, *erotic*, night with Beck left her with a whopper of a mental-fatigue hangover.

How she'd let herself get so deep in this, she couldn't quite grasp. From the beginning, despite all the nonsense she'd given herself about turning Beck over to another defense attorney, she'd recognized the conflict of interest. And yet, whether from her own feelings of failure when it came to losing the baby and possibly her own ambitions, she'd wanted the case.

Now she was in it. Failure would not be tolerated.

"Ms. DelRay?"

Jackie looked up from the menu she'd stopped reading ten minutes earlier and found a tall, dark-haired woman wearing a pleated, floral dress that said comfort more than chic.

"Yes," Jackie said. "Natalie?"

The woman nodded and Jackie stood to shake her hand. "Please, have a seat."

Before retaking her own seat, Jackie glanced at the door. No

Beck. He should have been here by now, considering this was his murder case. Where the hell was he?

Given Natalie's apprehension on the phone, Jackie couldn't wait on him. The woman might turn tail any second and Jackie couldn't risk losing whatever information Annabelle's partner could provide.

And, hello? Natalie turned out to be Annabelle's polar opposite. Where Annabelle had been petite and elegant, Natalie fit more into the category of big-boned and casual.

"Thank you for meeting me," Jackie said. "I'm sure this is a terrible time for you personally."

The woman worked the strap of her handbag, absently moving her fingers up and down then tugging. "It's so surreal. I saw her right before she left for that charity event. We'd just finished a meeting and she was excited to be heading out for the weekend."

Jackie thought about Josh, who wasn't her partner but had become an integral part of her law practice. If he were suddenly gone, she'd be...devastated. Personally and professionally.

Movement from the entrance drew Jackie's attention. Two men in suits. No Beck. Damn him. She'd have to start without him.

A young, college-aged waiter – Carl – stopped at the table, did his thing regarding the day's specials and took their drink order.

"If it's okay with you," Natalie said, "could we skip lunch? I want to help you, but I'm not sure what all I can tell you. And, I'm not comfortable helping the defense. Not if that guy killed Annabelle."

Jackie nodded. "I understand. If it makes you feel any better, I believe Mr. Pearson is being wrongly accused. I know I'm his attorney, but nothing is adding up. All I'm interested in right now is finding the real killer. You may think your information won't help, but you'd be surprised. Sometimes the smallest detail blows a case open."

"Like contaminated evidence?"

Jackie couldn't help it, she smiled. Apparently Natalie Wong watched the news.

"I checked you out," Natalie said. "Saw you just won that big case with the Senator."

"I'm good at my job. I've worked both sides of the aisle so my...perspective...I guess, is a bit different. I understand what the prosecution is trying to prove. It's my job to disprove it."

Carl dropped their drinks off and Jackie let him know she'd be getting a couple sandwiches to go. No sense tying up a table during lunch hour and shorting the kid on tips.

When Carl disappeared again, Natalie took a long sip of her diet soda, sucking on her straw like a lifeline.

This poor woman thought Jackie intended on grilling her. Jackie leaned in and met her gaze. "I promise I'll do right by you. As long as you're honest with me, we shouldn't have any issues."

Natalie set her glass down, fiddled with the straw for a few seconds, then nodded. "Thank you. Annabelle would want me to help. That's the only thing that brought me here." She glanced around, shook her head. "Everyone's life is so normal and Annabelle is dead. Doesn't seem fair."

"It's not." Jackie held up her notepad. Now that Natalie had agreed to talk, Jackie didn't intend on spooking her with recording her. "Do you mind if I take notes?"

"No, that's fine."

"Thank you. Was Annabelle having any issues with anyone? Clients or boyfriends maybe threatening her?"

"Not that I know of. She wasn't dating a lot. They were more...um," she rolled one hand.

"Hookups?"

"Yes. The divorce was taking it out of her. She liked sex, she just didn't want the drama that came with relationships. She kept things with men casual. Not that she slept around. She had a couple of guys, that's it."

"I see. So nothing, outside of the divorce, in her personal life was cause for concern?"

"She never mentioned anything."

Jackie jotted a note. "All right. How about clients? I know the two of you started your accounting firm together a few years back."

"Yes. We both worked for a bigger firm and decided to go out on our own. With all of Byron's political connections, Annabelle thought we could make a bundle." Natalie let out a small sigh. "She was right."

"How so?"

"With the influx of business from Byron's friends, we had to add two more accountants, which was good. That allowed Annabelle and me to do the big picture stuff. Forensic accounting, audits, the bigger projects while the associates handled tax preparation. We were just starting to see enough income where we could give ourselves raises."

"I see." And since Natalie opened the door... "In terms of the forensic accounting, were there any cases she testified in that could have perpetuated bad feelings?"

"Meaning, did her testimony earn her any enemies?"

"Yes."

"She enjoyed that type of work and that end of the business was picking up. I suppose it's possible someone was upset with her."

"All right. Would you be able to provide me with a list of projects she worked on recently?"

Natalie shrugged. "The court cases are public record so I don't see why I couldn't."

The couple at the next table got up to leave and Natalie glanced over at them then to the door. She'd been skittish from the time she'd sat down and before her anxiety sent her running, Jackie needed to reel her back in.

"Okay," Jackie said. "Can you tell me anything about her dealings with DTC?"

The woman did a double-take, her head literally snapping back. "DTC? What about them?"

"My investigators found an email regarding Annabelle auditing DTC's records. According to the email, she resigned the account days before her murder. I know Dikko Travathian and Byron are friends. I'm wondering why she would do that."

Another long sip of her soda ensued and Jackie's pulse kicked up. Even the mention of DTC had Natalie squirming.

Jackie waited. That soda wouldn't last forever. Finally, the woman gave in and unlatched herself from the straw. "I..." she said. "Huh. I'm not sure I should be discussing that with you. It involves DTC's proprietary information. Definitely not public record."

"I understand."

Really, she didn't. Natalie was holding out on her. Time to up the pressure.

Jackie leaned in again and pasted on her best I'm-the-good-girl face. The one where she opened her eyes wide and offered a reassuring smile. She'd won her father's favor during many arguments with that face. "Natalie, if there's anything at all that you can share with me, I promise I'll keep you out of it as much as I can. This is for Annabelle. If you know something, you might be able to help convict her killer."

The woman sat back, her shoulders drooping enough to make Jackie believe she carried a whole lot of agonizing tension there. Part of her ached for this woman. She'd lost her friend and business partner and now found herself in the middle of a murder investigation that might force her to compromise her professional ethics.

Jackie placed her pen on top of her notepad and pushed it

to the side. "I can see this is tearing you up. I'm so sorry. Please, let me help."

The woman's eyes ping-ponged between the notepad and her soda and then – upsy-daisy – she popped out of her chair.

"I have to go."

Dammit. So close.

She yanked her purse strap over her shoulder, gripping with enough force to make her knuckles protrude. Again, she glanced at the door, ready to bolt.

Let her go. The woman was tuned up right now. Showing sympathy and giving her the opportunity to bail might earn Jackie points.

"It's okay," Jackie said. "I know this is hard. Why don't we take a break and maybe I can call you later?"

Natalie took one step, turned back again. "There were problems with the inventory valuations and Travathian's personal expenses. Anna questioned Travathian about it, but he had a million excuses with nothing to support any of them."

"What about documentation?"

"He had *nothing*. Anna wasn't comfortable with it. Plus, with him being Byron's friend, she didn't want any impropriety rumors floating about us."

"So she resigned the account."

"Yes. She emailed Travathian and his management team telling them she'd finish her report, but that was it. What they chose to do then was on them." Natalie glanced at the door again. "I have to go."

She rushed out just as Beck swished through the circular door. He'd dressed down today in a white T-shirt and jeans that wrapped nicely around his long legs and lean hips. Oh, those hips. Magic. Jackie's suddenly insatiable hormones flew into a frenzy and her nipples got hard.

God, the man.

Two women, maybe mid-thirties, walked by the table, the

taller blonde angling back to her friend. "Meri, look at this one at the door. When I get home tonight, I'm telling Jake I have a new freebie. Forget Chris Hemsworth. If I had a shot at this guy, I'd totally do him."

A freebie. Funny.

Jackie had to smile. "It would totally be worth it," she said. "Believe me."

15

*B*eck pulled up short after walking in the side door of the restaurant and just stared. Across the way, the sun shining through the plate glass window at the front of the place glinted off the auburn highlights in Jackie's hair.

The restaurant smelled like bratwurst and noise from the lunch rush deafened his ears. Jackie met his gaze over the crowd and smiled. Her hand rose, giving him a small wave.

God damn, she took his breath away.

Gone was the gut-wrenching sadness from her face. Today, she was more relaxed, more Jackie.

The man-eater is back.

Which he'd known last night after she'd ravaged him multiple times, barely letting either of them get any sleep. But come six a.m., she was ready and raring to go.

Thank God I didn't go with Fleming.

The thought made Beck snort as he scooted past a couple gals picking up a takeout order and paying their check. The previous harassment by the cop seemed like a lifetime ago.

Midday traffic eased by outside the window as Beck made his way past the packed tables and booths. Out front on the sidewalk, a dark-haired woman hailed a cab. Others hustled by, some on lunch breaks, others on business.

He was halfway to Jackie's table when a noise from outside drew his attention. The woman on the sidewalk suddenly went down. Just boom, one second she was waving a hand in the air, and the next, she dropped like a box of rocks.

Before she hit the ground, Beck saw the reason.

Blood bloomed on the back of her dress. The people around her on the sidewalk screamed, the sound barely noticeable over the noise in the restaurant, but he saw their expressions, saw the way they started running and diving for cover.

Gun.

He had a split-second of *oh shit* and then, instincts pounding, he launched himself at Jackie.

The tackle knocked her clean off her chair and took her to the ground. The only thing that stopped her head from smacking the floor was his hand cupping the back of her skull. At the moment of impact, the window above them exploded.

Pieces of glass rained down and Beck tucked Jackie under his body, every cell inside him screaming as loud as the startled patrons in the restaurant. For half a second, no one moved. Then a stampede started for the door.

Not the door. Shooter's out front.

Jackie sucked in a gulp of air. He must have knocked the oxygen from her lungs and his weight probably wasn't helping, but she managed to get enough air to yell, "What the flying crap was that?"

Shifting back, he looked down into her scared eyes. "Are you okay?"

A jerky nod. He kissed her forehead, then climbed off her, peering carefully over the broken window at the street. No shooter in sight. No more bullets flying either.

Sliding Jackie away from the window and toward the wall, he helped her gain her feet. People were scattering, some pushing toward the side entrance where he'd entered. "Everyone, get to the rear of the restaurant," he yelled. "The kitchen. The restrooms. Doesn't matter. Don't go outside! Stay inside!"

He gave Jackie a gentle shove. "Get to the kitchen and make sure any doors leading outside are locked, got it?"

She didn't argue—which was a first—and took off, hustling the other patrons toward the rear of the building.

Punching 911 on his cell phone, he headed for a young woman hiding under a table with her daughter. "Come on," he said, bending down and holding his hand out to a young girl who couldn't have been more than three or four. "You have to move. Let's get you to safety."

As he carried the girl and hustled her mother to the back, his call connected with the operator. Jackie stood at the door of the kitchen, waving them in. He gave the operator the details, and then handed his cell to Jackie to stay on the line while they waited for the cops to arrive.

"Where are you going?" she asked as he started back to the restaurant floor.

"There's a lady out front that was shot. I need to see if I can help her."

"Oh my god," Jackie said. She started forward with him. "Was it Natalie?"

He grabbed her by the arms and set her back. "Stay here. I'll find out."

He dashed for the front door against Jackie's arguments, surveilling the area as he ventured out.

Right, left, up. No sign of any shooter. Far off in the distance he heard sirens. Someone had probably called in the attack before he did.

Random shootings seemed to be happening daily anymore, but Beck had a feeling this one hadn't been so random.

The woman was still exactly where she'd fallen. One shot

had gone through her ribs and another through her forehead. He probed her neck for a pulse.

It was faint, slowing.

A man dropped to his knees next to Beck. "She alive?"

"Barely. You a doctor?" Beck asked, checking the woman's wallet.

"Yep."

Watching the blood pool on the sidewalk, he doubted it would make a difference, but he stripped off his jacket and gave it to the man to apply pressure to the chest wound. "EMTs are on the way."

A glance at the driver's license inside the wallet confirmed his worst fear. Natalie Wong.

Leaving the doctor to tend to her, Beck scanned the street, evaluating. Where had the shot come from?

Glancing back at the woman and the direction she'd fallen, he tried to figure out where the shooter had been. He turned in a slow arc, looking for the optimal spot, and...

There, the building to the west. Three stories, sun behind it. The perfect place for the shooter. Up off the street, good cover.

First Natalie and then...

Jackie.

Shit.

Beck sprinted for the alley.

Turning the corner, he saw a guy in cargo pants, a tan jacket, and a black ski mask jumping down from the fire escape. Beck didn't bother yelling. At this point, screaming at the guy would eliminate any chance of sneaking up on him.

The guy hit the ground and glanced behind him – shit – spotting Beck hauling ass across the street. Nixing the whole sneaking up thing, the guy took off for all he was worth. What looked like a rifle case caught on the edge of the dumpster and rather than slow down, the runner let it fall to the ground.

Same guy, same guy, same guy. The chant looped in Beck's

brain as he raced after the man. It had to be the same creep who'd broken into Jackie's place. The one Beck had chased for blocks into the park.

B&E, evasion, and now an attempt on Natalie. Another shot at Jackie. The asshole was upping the ante.

The man disappeared into another alley. By the time Beck reached the corner, the shooter was gone.

Frustration burning in his stomach, he slammed both hands into the brick wall of the building.

Get back to Jackie.

Same guy or not, the shooter had been trying to take her and Natalie out. Sharpshooter?

Possibly. It appeared this guy had enough training to be highly dangerous.

Same guy. Beck knew it in his gut.

If Beck hadn't knocked Jackie to the ground, would she be alive?

A cop pulled up at the end of the alley. "Doc said you went after the shooter," the cop said through his open window.

"Guy went west and left evidence behind." He pointed at the rifle bag. "Get someone to watch it until the crime scene techs get here."

He didn't wait for the officer to say anything else and sprinted for the restaurant.

Was the shooter former military? A cop? Some survivalist freak who had weaponry far more advanced than he needed and thought he was above the law? Why would that kind of guy have a hard-on to kill Natalie or Jackie? What did Natalie know that could possibly get her killed in the first place?

Or was this asshole FBI?

The idea made Beck pause.

Not Byron, but maybe a friend? Someone who'd washed out of Quantico?

Maybe the Director had thought the creep was good enough to hire to shut up Annabelle and Natalie.

Get to Jackie.

Beck ran all out. Whoever it was, they weren't playing games anymore. They were serious about stopping this investigation.

Dead serious.

Natalie was dead.

Jackie sat on her office sofa, head cradled in her hands while visions flashed of the restaurant's plate glass window exploding. She shook her head, tried to focus on next steps. That's what DelRay's did. They bullied their way through.

The only way to the other side is through it.

True, but...what in the hell had happened? One minute she and Beck had been talking and the next – chaos.

Beck set a mug on the coffee table in front of her, its contents sending a swirl of steam into the air.

"Drink this," he said.

Another one of his concoctions, no doubt.

"What is it?"

"Chamomile tea. It'll relax you."

She looked up at him, trying her damndest not to pop off because – dammit – taking her frustrations out on him wouldn't help. "You think I want to *relax*? We just witnessed a woman get murdered. Shot down right in the goddamned street." Jackie held her hands out. "It'll take a whole lot more than tea to relax me."

"You don't think I know that? Drink the tea. It'll at least help."

When eyeballing him for a solid ten seconds didn't back him off from his hovering, she grunted. Reached for the effing tea because why not? Couldn't hurt. "Fine." She took a gulp, scalded the roof of her mouth and swore.

"Be careful." He lit off a sarcastic smile. "It's hot."

"Oh, *fuck* you.

"What are you pissed at me for? Because I was late?"

"I'm not pissed at you." She flapped her arms. "You're just...hovering. I can't deal with it. What we do is ugly business, I get that. I just don't usually see it happen live and I need a second. That woman left my table, stepped out onto the street, and now she's dead. Somehow, I don't think that's a coincidence."

"You're right."

"About?"

Beck shrugged. "All of it. I can't change it. What I can do is make sure you're okay. You see it as hovering. I see it as taking care of you. Get used to it."

He dropped next to her, slid his arm over her shoulder and pulled her close, locking her against his chest.

Damned man. A lame attempt at elbowing her way free failed and he tightened his grip.

"Please, Jackie. Be still for two minutes and process it. I get that you're the big, bad DelRay chick, but I got news for you. You're still human and we mere mortals experience trauma. Not to mention the emotional ramifications of it. So sit here, shut up and be still. Let me be here for you this time."

That tore it. Damned man adding that little 'this time' in there. She elbowed him again, but shifted closer. "I hate you."

"Excellent."

She buried her face against him, sucking up every ounce of heat and strength she could find in his solid presence. The clean scent of his cologne settled her frazzled nerves. *Sanctuary.* Somehow it always came back to that with Beck.

Jackie DelRay, a woman who tore the toughest of the tough to shreds in court, had been reduced to a sniveling wuss.

Well, too bad.

She lifted her head and met his gaze, the two of them lost in those few seconds of quiet. "I can't believe this happened," she said.

"Me neither. It's fucked up, for sure."

"I think that woman died because she met with me, and she was trying to help us. We have to stop it."

"I know. How did you communicate with her?"

"I called her office. Talked on the phone."

"Her phone could be tapped. If the shooter knew she was meeting you, he could have followed her."

Sitting so close, she couldn't focus. Couldn't wrap her mind around a strategy. She should be at her desk, advising her client. Not sitting on the couch in his arms.

This was the problem with emotional entanglements. They created mental bedlam. Intersecting lines where there shouldn't be any.

What am I doing?

She levered away from him and slowly got to her feet. He hooked a finger around her wrist. "You leaving me?"

"I can't concentrate when I'm trying to crawl inside you. How am I supposed to defend you with," she flapped her hands between them, "with this. It's too much. I'm your *attorney*, Beck."

"Who's just been through an ordeal."

That's what he was going with? "And that makes it right? What we're doing? I don't think so."

"For a few minutes it does."

Dream on, fella. She rolled her eyes. Idealists. Always so relentlessly positive. She pulled free of his hold and walked to her desk. "Fine. We'll agree to disagree."

She spun her chair, smoothed a hand over her slacks and settled into the soft leather. Much better. *Shark Jackie.*

"But," she said, "I'm going on record that we're being bad here. Really bad. I should turn your case over to someone else."

"No."

Idiot. "Yes. I'm no good to you when all I can think about is putting my hand down your pants."

He laughed. Did someone say something funny? "I'm not kidding. The Bar Association has a problem with this sort of thing. Rule 1.8, letter J to be exact, of the Rules of Professional Responsibility. I looked it up." She grabbed her phone, held up the note where she pasted the rule. "I quote 'A lawyer shall not have sexual relations with a client unless a consensual sexual relationship existed between them when the client-lawyer relationship commenced.'"

Beck didn't miss a beat. "Technically, thanks to spring break, a sexual relationship already existed."

"That was twelve years ago. You're trying to spin this and it won't work. We weren't in a relationship when I took your case. Nice try though." She tossed the phone on her desk. "How can you be so calm?"

"I've been handling shitty situations my entire life. Starting with my family. I've learned to deal with it. And, yeah, if it makes me feel better, sometimes I twist it to work for my benefit. I'll admit that. With the crap I see – saw – at the Bureau? If I didn't develop coping skills, I'd be insane by now. For shits and giggles, let's consider you a coping mechanism. One I care very much about."

Coping skills, she understood. As a criminal attorney, she'd seen her share of rapes, murders, and crimes that had no place in the world. She'd learned to separate herself. To become clinical in her approach. Anyone in this business would have to. Survivalist mentality.

Sitting back, she dug her heel into the floor and swiveled her chair side to side as she tried to ignore the part about him caring.

That was beside the point. She cared too. Probably too much or they wouldn't be in this mess. "I'm crazy about you," she said. Before he could speak, she held up her hands. "Don't say anything. We'll deal with that later. Right now, as your attorney, going with your theory that Natalie was followed to the restaurant, I think it's safe to assume, given her business partner was just murdered, they both knew something the killer didn't want them to."

"Reasonable assumption. Walk it back. Natalie was coming to meet you and you're defending the guy accused of murdering Annabelle. You're investigating. And not quietly. Killer thinks by following Natalie, he can..."

Beck stopped talking, blew out a hard breath.

He didn't want to say it and that was the problem with sleeping with one's client. Suddenly, the filtering, the limiting of information, started. And that had no place in a murder investigation.

Might as well help Beck along here. "He could take us both out," she said.

Jesus.

Beck gave her a hard look. Too bad. She pointed at him. "Hey, don't give me that. Trying to spare my feelings will put you in a cell for the rest of your life. Then what? Conjugal visits? I think not."

"Christ, you're tough."

Damned straight. "You'll thank me when I keep you out of Sing Sing. Natalie told me Annabelle resigned the DTC account because the inventory valuations and personal expenses didn't jive. When Annabelle questioned Dikko, he couldn't provide documentation to support the numbers."

"So he's cooking the books. He's not gonna kill two people over it."

"You don't think? Please. I've seen people murdered over ten dollars. We're talking hundreds of millions here." She sat forward, propped her elbows on the desk and held up a finger. "I want everything we can find on DTC's financials."

Beck lifted one hip and dug his phone from his front pocket. "Hang on. I'll text Taylor and Matt. See if they can get us copies of DTC's 10-Ks from the past few years. That'll give us everything."

The Securities and Exchange Commission required businesses to report a company's financial performance, including audited financial statements, every year. "Yes, good idea."

"We'll start there. See what we can find. I already talked to her about the shooter."

"What about him?"

"If it's the guy I saw running from the building, he took Natalie out with two shots." Beck pointed to his head, then his chest. "Boom, boom. From that distance, he's not a weekend warrior. He knows his way around a weapon. Someone who spends a lot of time at the range. Either as an amateur marksmen or – "

" – law enforcement."

"Possibly. Think about what DTC does."

"Military supplies."

"Bingo."

"You're thinking the shooter might be former military?"

Beck cocked his head. "I'm curious if Travathian has friends or associates who play with long-range automatic rifles."

Jackie's cell phone rang and she sat forward, snatching it from the desk. "Debra Johansen. This should be good." She tapped the screen. "Debra, what can I do for you?"

"Well, you can start by giving me a statement about the sex tape starring Jackie DelRay. Then we'll get to today's shooting."

What now? She bolted upright, her gaze shooting to Beck. The only man she'd had sex with in over a year. Just last night in fact.

He wouldn't.

Would he? After so many years apart, how much did she really know about him? No. Couldn't be. Not with a murder charge hanging over him. Only an idiot would make a sex tape of his lawyer and release it to the press.

"Debra," Jackie said, her narrowed gaze still on Beck. "I have no idea what you're talking about."

The reporter let out a soft snort. "Nice try, Jackie, but believe me, you'll want to give me some kind of comment and rather quickly. Whoever sent me this video gave me a thirty minute head start before unleashing it on the internet. Pretty soon the world at large will see your client sucking on your nipple through a bra."

Jackie leapt out of her chair sending it crashing against the credenza. "What!"

"Jesus. What is it?" Beck was out of his chair and moving around the desk, but Jackie pointed at him to stay put.

"Girl," Debra drawled, "he's a hottie for sure, but I must say, I'm stunned that hard-nosed Jackie DelRay would risk a case like this. Are you in love with him?"

Oh, she might be. She glanced at Beck, who propped a hip on the edge of the desk and, ever the FBI agent, stared at her, measuring her actions.

She should have warned him not to head shrink her. He'd fry his brain trying to figure her out.

"Send me the video," she said to Debra. "Then I'll see about a comment."

She punched off the call and held the phone up. "I'm trying not to freak out right now, but if this is what I think it is, we have a huge problem."

Her phone dinged and she brought up the email containing a link to a shared file service site.

Beck sidled up to her and she pushed her shoulders back, steadying herself before tapping the link. Frozen on the screen was an image of Jackie – in her sports bra – with her head

MISTY EVANS & ADRIENNE GIORDANO

tipped back, mouth partly open in what could only be described as sexual euphoria as Beck suckled her breast through her bra.

Dear God. Bile swirled in Jackie's stomach and she pressed her hand against her forehead. She poked at the arrow on the screen and the video rolled, showing them in her office just the other night when she'd spilled coffee on her blouse and they'd shared that crazy hot kiss.

A low moan came from the phone and onscreen Beck's hand moved down her throat to her cleavage and even in her horror, Jackie felt something stir.

"Shit," Beck said as he watched himself move between Jackie's legs.

"Oh, my God," she said. "This is bad."

She closed her eyes, thought back to that night and what came next. *Son of a bitch.* The thumbnail photo at the beginning of the video. Beck's mouth on her. Sucking her breast.

Another moan came from the phone and then, "God, yes. More. Harder."

With that, the humiliation was complete. Jackie set one hand on the desk, steadied herself against it.

"Holy shit," Beck hissed. "How the hell...?"

A small squeak left Jackie's throat and a burst of panic, mixed with the spinning bile in her stomach rocked her. The room spun and she tipped left. Beck grabbed her, sliding his arm around her and absorbing her weight.

"You're okay," he said. "Sit down."

Sit? He wanted her to *sit*? Like a weak little girl who'd let her rational mind take leave while she dry-humped her client against her desk. The big bad attorney turned sex kitten.

Her mother. *She'll never forgive me.*

"I can't sit!" she screamed. "Someone is about to release this. And, and..." She flung her arms around, gesturing wildly with the phone. "How the hell did they get it? Oh, son of a bitch. I will *murder* the fucker. My *parents* will see this! My mother is the Mayor of Philadelphia! Her PR people will be on this the second it gets released."

"I swear to you, it wasn't me."

"Of course it wasn't. You have nothing to gain from this. If anything, it makes you look like a schmuck. And me a bigger one!"

Beck turned, facing the entrance to her office. He pointed. "Josh walked in on us."

"Josh? No way. He wouldn't."

"Are you sure?"

Right now, not of anything. "Well, as sure as I can be at the moment. He'd have no reason to release it. I gave him a career."

"Maybe he's trying to ruin you. Take over your clients."

Maybe.

But...no. She'd helped him. Saved his damned career when that court reporter accused him of sexual harassment after he'd rejected her. Jackie had gone to bat for him with the Bar, proving the woman had a history of revenge against men. Jackie shook her head. "It's not Josh."

"How do you know?"

She eyeballed him. "Trust me. It's not him."

"Chessie?"

"Oh hell no. We're too much of a good team."

Jackie tapped the phone's screen again. Five minutes since she'd hung up with Debra. The clock was literally ticking before this video was released. She poked at Debra's name. Seconds later the reporter picked up.

"Quite the imagery, aye?"

"First of all," Jackie said, "obviously this video was taken without my or Mr. Pearson's consent. It's private."

"It *was*. In about twenty minutes, it won't be. Do you have an additional comment?"

What could she say? There was absolutely no defense for

this. Besides, in twenty minutes, it would supposedly be released to the general public. Compared to that, Debra was small potatoes.

A fresh bout of horror descended and Jackie dipped her head, squeezing her eyes closed as a wicked pounding settled at the base of her skull. "Other than to reiterate that this is an illegally obtained video, I have no comment."

"You're no fun, Jackie. What about Pearson? Any comment from the bombshell?"

"He has no comment either."

"Alrighty then. I'm rolling with it."

"Gee, Debra, thanks."

"Oh, please. It's going to be out there anyway. I might as well get the scoop."

"Well, I'll remember that. Just so you know."

Before Debra could comment, Jackie disconnected.

Beck held his hand out. "Let me see that video again? Let's figure out how they got it."

He watched it a second time while Jackie tried to hold down her stomach contents. The chamomile was trying to exit stage left.

"Here." Beck pointed at her monitor sitting on the credenza behind her desk. He sat and started typing. "He hacked into your computer's camera and microphone, the bastard."

Less than a minute later, Beck had discovered how the hacker had compromised her computer and used it to spy on her conversations. And record her movements. "Looks like he could see who you've texted and emailed from this computer too. You're going to need a full system scan and security update. I'll call Teeg…"

Jackie didn't hear the rest. She ran to the bathroom and vomited.

16

The landline rang off the hook for the next hour. Jackie's cell phone too. The only call she'd taken so far was from her mother. When she came up for air from that conversation, Beck could see the troubled look in her eyes again.

"Oh. My. God." Jackie banged her skull back against her chair. "I love my mom to death, but threatening to show up here and drag me home to Philly is a little over the top."

"You *were* shot at and had a sex tape leaked to the press," Beck said, "and she's your mother. She's more than a little freaked out, and rightly so. You're being targeted."

I wish mine cared that much.

"I know, I know." Jackie rubbed her eyes and sat up straight again. "But going home to Philly won't solve anything. She knows that. She's just...scared for me."

"Can't say I blame her."

"So back to this shooter. How do we find out if Dikko hired him?"

Work was her coping mechanism. Beck understood. He'd used it on many an occasion to help him deal with shit. Since the hacker who'd done the sex tape might be connected to Annabelle and the rest of the case, they might as well keep looking into Dikko and the shooter. "I'll hack into DTC's employee files and see if there are any with military backgrounds. Cyber experts, too." He stood and stretched, his calves cranky from hauling ass earlier. "Do you need a refill on the tea?"

"I'm going to need something stronger if you're hacking into DTC's records from my office. That's illegal, you know."

"I have a laptop Teeg gave me. It's got some funky software that will ping the IP address off ten different towers around the country. He thought I might need it if I had to go on the lam. If Dikko figures out he's been hacked, no one will be able to trace it to your office, and I actually have decent hacking skills, so don't look so worried."

Jackie laughed. It was subdued but he'd take it. "Go on the lam? Ye of little faith."

"We're talking Teeg here. He probably belongs in Federal lockup for the cybercrimes he's committed, and I have no doubt he's ready to go all *Fugitive* on Grey at the drop of the hat. He's like a prepper in the cyberworld. He could do an e-death on himself without blinking an eye."

"I'm sorry, e-death?"

"The top shelf black hats can redact warrants, BOLOs, person of interest flags, etc., to clean a fugitive's files. It's tricky, but it can be done. Even more extreme are the ones who can make a fugitive dead to the government and give them an entirely new identity. Like cyber WITSEC for those on the run."

"And Teeg is one of the hackers who does this?"

The things Teeg could do were downright scary. "Neither you nor I want to know what all Teeg can—and does—do, trust me. That's for Grey to worry about."

Her lips blew out on a hard sigh. "Do you need a desk?"

"Nah." He grabbed the backpack with the laptop Teeg had

provided and made himself comfy on Jackie's office couch, kicking off his shoes and setting his feet on the coffee table in front of it.

Jackie stared at her desktop, unseeing, and Beck had to bite his tongue not to offer her more tea again. Or a massage. Her landline rang, startling her out of her funk and she reached for it like it was a lifeline.

"Chessie?" She sat back in her seat and rocked. "Yeah, I'm fine... No, no, everything's okay. Seriously. Beck was there to save me. I didn't even get a scratch."

As she continued to fill in her investigator on the details of the shooting, Beck booted up the laptop. Her words—*Beck was there to save me*—swirled in his head. Everything had happened so fast, so unexpectedly, he was still twitchy. What if he hadn't gotten there in time? There would be two bodies in the morgue right now.

Focus on the problem at hand.

Acid ate at his guts, but he took several deep breaths, zeroing in on the screen in front of him and trying not to see the replay of Natalie dropping to the ground over and over again.

"You saw the video, huh?" Jackie's gaze met Beck's. "Yeah, a hacker is targeting me. I know, I know...yeah, got it handled. Thanks, Chessie."

Josh popped in and opened his mouth to say something to Jackie, then stopped, seeing she was on the phone. She held up a finger and the kid turned as if to take a seat and noticed Beck. "Hey, your friend is here."

Friend? "My friends are few and far between these days, but I still need you to be more specific."

At that moment, a blond head peeked around the doorframe. "Thought I might find you here."

"Taylor?" Beck jumped to his feet, setting the laptop aside and slipping his shoes back on. "What are you doing here?"

She hugged him and he saw Jackie narrow her eyes. Josh ducked out the door.

"Special delivery from Matt." Taylor shoved an envelope at him. "I never touched or saw this, just so we're clear."

"Absolutely." He took the manila envelope, eyeing it suspiciously. "Thank you... I think?"

"A little bird might have told me Dikko's 10-K forms filed with the SEC are in there."

"Any discrepancies?"

"I wouldn't know since I have *absolutely* no involvement in this exchange." She batted her eyelashes, giving him a fake innocent look. "But I'm guessing the reason you're holding them is because they contain important information or Matt wouldn't have sent them."

He grinned. "Roger that."

She turned serious. "Ballistics aren't back yet on the rifle, but the preliminary evidence suggests it was the one used on Natalie Wong." Taylor cocked her head at Jackie, who was hanging up the phone. "She okay?"

"*She* is fine," Jackie said, standing and straightening the edge of her bland suit jacket. He really needed to get her a new wardrobe. Some nice tight skirts and blouses rather than the ultra-boring suits. "You must be Beck's boss."

Beck made introductions and Taylor shook Jackie's hand. "Sorry to barge in like this," Taylor said, "but I needed to see that he was all right with my own eyes. I'm glad you're both okay. It was a traumatic event for sure. And the video, we'll see what we can do about that."

Jackie eyed the envelope in Beck's hand. "Please tell me that's evidence that will tell us who killed Annabelle and her business partner."

Taylor chewed her bottom lip. "For the record, I'm just the messenger. Matt was going to bring it to Beck, but I offered since I wanted to check on him. Off the record, I think you're onto something with Dikko Travathian. Keep digging."

"Any thoughts on who took the shot at Jackie?" Beck asked. Taylor had no doubt been brainstorming on the culprit with the rest of the team. "Any of the traffic cams catch him?"

She shook her head. "We're waiting on DOT to provide us with access to the videos in that area. At this point, the police are labeling it a random shooting and saying we're lucky the guy didn't kill more people in the restaurant."

"Seriously?" Jackie leaned on the desk. "They think it's a random occurrence that Annabelle Lockhart's partner was shot?"

"Because the guy shot up the restaurant, they're saying they think he's mentally unstable. That's all. There's been no official link between this and Annabelle's death."

Unbelievable, but so was the rest of this case. "So I'm still their number one suspect then," Beck said.

"Afraid so." Taylor's cell buzzed and she looked down at the screen. "Lockhart's on my case. Gotta run. Remember, if anyone asks where you got that envelope..."

Beck drew his fingers across his lips. "It magically appeared under Jackie's door like the picture of Byron and the President."

Beck handed Jackie the envelope. "I'll see you out."

As he and Taylor walked down the hallway, he lowered his voice. "What's Lockhart on your case about? Me?"

"You were inside the restaurant when the shooting happened, so he's trying to figure out if you hired someone to take out Natalie in order to make it look like you're innocent, or if you really *are*. His stress level is through the roof. I think deep down, he knows you didn't kill his wife, but if you didn't? Then he's got a whole other can of worms to dig into and it's making him nuts."

"*His* stress level is through the roof?" Beck chuckled at the irony. "Poor baby."

Taylor gave him another hug when they reached the entryway and he opened the door for her. Cold air blasted in. "Thanks for checking up on me, Taylor."

"We'll get this figured out. You're not alone, you know." Just as she stepped out into the cold, she drew up sharp. "Director?"

Beck swore under his breath as he saw the man coming up the walk. *Great.*

Lockhart's cheeks were flushed, his trench coat unbuttoned and blowing back due to his aggressive gait. His hair was mussed like he'd dragged his fingers through it, and he looked like he hadn't slept for days.

Welcome to my world.

Crossing his arms over his chest, Beck blocked the door. "I'm guessing this isn't a social call, but I'm pretty sure if you're looking for an attorney, you'll have to go elsewhere. Ms. DelRay is booked."

"I'm not here for you or your lawyer," Lockhart scowled. "I was looking for Sinclair."

Surprise flashed across Taylor's face, followed by indignation. "How did you know I was here? Were you *following* me?"

He ignored her questions. "I put a rush on the ballistics for the Wong shooting. Thought you'd want to know that the bullets that killed her came from the weapon Pearson found." He didn't even glance at Beck. "No fingerprints on the rifle, scope, or bullet casings. Nothing found on the rooftop except the casings. If there weren't dozens of witnesses at the restaurant claiming Pearson was inside when the shooting started, he'd actually look pretty damn good for it."

The Director's stance and tone suggested he still wanted to believe Beck was six shades of guilty. Beck stepped out of the doorway to stand next to Taylor. "Seems like you could have told Taylor all that over the phone."

Byron glared at him, but there was something different in his stare. Less defiance. More weariness. Just a touch of...was that dismay at the fact Beck might be innocent? "Watch your-self, Pearson. There's a killer on the loose and I'm still not convinced of your innocence."

Unbelievable. "Come on, Lockhart. You're a smart guy. With all this evidence you still think I murdered Annabelle?"

Lockhart turned on his heel and started back to his parked car down the block. "Agent Sinclair?" he yelled over his shoulder as he walked away.

"Yeah?" Taylor called.

"Get the hell back to work already!"

She gave Beck a half-smile. "Told you he was reconsidering your guilt."

"He sure has a funny way of showing it," Beck said.

"Beck?"

He turned to find Jackie in the doorway, papers in hand. He knew the look on her face. "What is it?"

"There's something here you need to see."

"I'm off." Taylor waved and hopped down the steps, heading for her vehicle. "I heard nothing, I saw nothing, I know nothing."

Beck followed Jackie inside. "What's up?"

"The 10-K numbers for DTC are totally screwy compared to the tax returns. I'm not an accountant, but Dikko's either falsi-fying the SEC forms or the tax returns. Which totally jives with what Natalie told us about Annabelle being uncomfortable with what she found during DTC's audit."

"Maybe we should pay a visit to the DTC offices. Ask Rachael some questions and see if she'll slip up."

"Exactly what I was thinking. It'll at least take my mind off Natalie."

He had other ways to distract her, but she needed to work. Needed to follow the yellow brick road until she felt stable again on her home turf once more. Interviewing DTC employees, scoping out the place, anything to keep her mind off the shooting, would do the job.

"Hey," he said when they got back in her office. He pulled her into his arms and was relieved when she melted into him instead of pulling away. Lockhart's warning rang in his head. "I need to be the voice of reason here. There's somebody out there taking shots at you. Maybe it would be best for you to stay here. Or go back to my place. I can grab Chessie and go to DTC."

Now she did draw back. "Fat chance, buster."

Stomping over to her desk, she reached into the top drawer and took out her gun. "Let's do this."

Jackie and Chessie once again left Beck in the car. The poor guy wasn't happy with her, but putting him in front of Rachael might spook the already nervous woman. Well, Jackie supposed she'd have to make it up to him later.

Privately.

Heh, heh, heh.

Feeling guilty over leaving the hunkster behind, they'd wired Jackie so he could listen in. This attempt at eavesdropping came with an added bonus. The listening device tucked in her ear allowed Beck to ask questions or make inquiries. Even if he couldn't be in the room, they'd use his experience and instincts to trip Rachael up.

Either the woman knew her husband was defrauding the government or she was blind as a friggin' bat. Right now, Jackie wasn't sure which, but she intended to find out.

Beck's voice erupted in her ear. "Can you hear me?"

Lordy, that was loud. Jackie paused five feet from DTC's entrance and rifled through her purse. "Yes." She kept her head down to avoid any busybodies from inside seeing her lips moving. "Can you hear me?"

"Yeah, all good. Be careful."

"We will."

After all the time apart – and the vitriol between them during her prosecutor days – they'd somehow fallen back into the easy rapport they'd shared on their first night together. Why did it have to take the brutal murder of a woman to bring them both to their senses?

Who knew? Certainly not Jackie. And she couldn't spend too much time dwelling on it. There'd be time for that later. Once she got Beck cleared of murder, maybe they could give a shot at this couple thing. Spending time together. Learning each other's habits. And whether they could tolerate them enough to deal with it for a lifetime.

If that's what he wanted. For all she knew, this could be some sort of twisted attorney-client worship going on. She'd seen it before.

But...nah. Not Beck. A career in law enforcement clued him in to the risks associated with what they were doing. How it might affect his chances of beating a murder charge.

Jackie took the last step toward the DTC offices and peered up at the one-story, squat brick building. Compared to the Travathian's home, this was downright generic.

What am I doing?

Oh, she knew. The levelheaded, career girl in her had taken a nasty tumble into the land of the stupid. Insanely stupid. Actually, no. She couldn't even claim stupidity. She'd known all along getting involved with Beck, her client and the father of her lost baby, was a mistake that might have devastating consequences.

Somehow, she'd done it anyway.

Jackie, Jackie, Jackie.

Chessie stepped ahead and set his hand on the door. "You ready for this?"

Did she have a choice? They needed to find a killer and save

Beck's rear. His extremely fine rear that Jackie wanted her hands on every day. And evening.

"Ready," she said.

Her investigator held the door open for her and she stepped inside only to find an empty desk in the reception area. One red light flashed from the phone, but other than that, zero activity. No stacks of paper on the desk, no blotter, no nameplate.

She scanned the small room where four cheap chairs lined the wall across from the reception desk.

Chessie rolled his bottom lip out. "Guess they don't get a lot of foot traffic."

"Guess not."

He moved to the archway leading to what looked like a hallway. "Hello?"

A few seconds later, a male voice responded with an "Oh, hey. Sorry. We weren't expecting anyone. Can I help you?"

Chessie moved back and the man belonging to the voice appeared in the doorway. He wore a pair of black dress pants with a pressed white shirt over shoulders that might double as the side of a building. A fact he was obviously aware of given his erect posture and a focused gaze Jackie had often seen on S.W.A.T. guys. The I-will-kick-your-ass confidence was hard to miss.

He met Jackie's appraising eye and his full lips quirked.

Relax, stud, I've got my own hunk.

Chessie held his hand out. "I'm Chesley Morton from DelRay and Associates. This is Jackie DelRay."

After shaking Chessie's hand, the hottie's gaze came back to Jackie. "DelRay. You're the one defending the FBI agent."

"I am," she extended her hand. "And you are?"

"Roane Hodges."

Jackie repeated the name to herself, hoping Beck was already doing an Internet search on his phone. Roane shook her hand, releasing it quickly and without any suggestive squeezing that told her just what a manly-man he was.

"Nice to meet you," Jackie said. "Are you an employee?"

"Consultant," he said. "I help with the government contracts."

Interesting. Exactly what he consulted on, she'd have to find out. She studied the slope of his shoulders, his thick forearms. Muscular guy.

Like the one who'd broken into her house.

Could this be him? Her mind ticked back a few nights. To the man throwing her against the wall. The wiry muscle.

Different.

The intruder was leaner, not as jacked. And he was shorter than Roane by a good three inches. Still, Roane deserved a look, and a quick background check.

"Got him," Beck said. Of course, among his other talents, he was psychic. "He's not on the employee list I pulled. Probably because he's a consultant. I'll see if Taylor can run his name."

"Mr. Hodges," Chessie said, "Is Rachael here?"

"Yeah," he jerked his thumb. "She's in her office on a call. Have a seat and I'll see if she's done."

Chessie pointed to the empty desk. "Receptionist off today?"

"No receptionist. Usually there's no need. Rachael has an assistant who answers phones. She's out on an errand."

"Carly Ingrams," Beck said. "*She's* on the list."

Jackie led Chessie to the guest chairs and the two of them sat, patiently waiting while Roane checked on Rachael. A minute later Rachael appeared in the archway with Roane behind her. Her protector. Except something was...off.

The distance.

If roles were reversed and it had been Beck standing behind Jackie, he'd have stayed close. Beck would have made sure everyone understood he'd offer support as necessary. Roane?

He stood a foot back, creating plenty of space for Jackie to form her own assumptions about his dedication to his employer.

Had Chessie noticed that too? Or was she hallucinating? Hoping for something, anything that might offer up a clue to what Rachael knew of her husband's misdeeds.

"Hello," Rachael said in a tone that dropped the temperature a digit or fifty. "I'm in the middle of something. I do wish you'd have called."

Jackie stepped forward. "My apologies." *Not really, but whatever.* "We have a few more questions for you." She shifted her gaze to Roane then back to Rachael. "It's of a personal nature."

After a brief pause, Rachael nodded. "Of course. Come back to my office." She faced Roane. "We're fine. Thank you."

"Sure," he said. "I'll be in my office."

Jackie and Chessie followed Her Highness down the hall. At the third office, Roane hooked a right and Jackie peeped inside. A pole in the corner held an American flag. Not an altogether unusual sight considering DTC's government work, but...

Roane.

His build, his posture. His confidence.

Military? Could be. No doubt Beck would find out.

Rachael led them into her nicely appointed office and Jackie's feet sunk into a Persian rug as she made her way to the leather guest chairs. A giant oil-painting adorned one wall, anchoring a sizeable cherry bookcase that matched the desk. The oversized marble sculpture of a bird in flight was a nice touch, but rather than giving the office a warm, homey feel, it screamed wealth and over-consumption.

Unlike the reception area, the Travathians had spent some money here, but similar to their home, it was more a statement, a collection of material things rather than a love of art.

Rachael took a seat behind her desk and keeping her face strategically stoic, folded her hands. "How can I help you?"

Getting right to business. Excellent.

Jackie pulled copies of the financial reports from her briefcase. "I wanted to show you these. See if you could explain them?"

Her gaze still on Jackie, she took the reports. "What is it?"

"DTC Financials."

Rachael blinked. "My husband handles the money."

"Your signature is on them."

"Well, of course. I'm a partner."

"Then maybe you can explain why, when Annabelle did her audit, she discovered the inventory valuation for last year had been inflated."

This revelation gave the woman pause. *Gotcha.* Explaining that away wouldn't be so easy.

Slowly, she glanced down at the stack of papers in her hand. "Inventory valuation?"

"If you look at the 10-K form, you'll see the totals don't jive with the 10-Q."

Blink, blink, blink.

"Go get her, Jackie," Beck said in her ear.

If his freedom wasn't on the line, Jackie would have laughed at the amount of blood draining from Rachael's face.

She shuffled through the reports, then shook her head. "I don't understand."

"The 10-K is the annual report," Jackie said. "The 10-Q is quarterly. Quarterly reports are less detailed. When Annabelle did the audit, she discovered inconsistencies related to DTC's inventory. It appears your company's gross profit has been, shall we say, overstated. Obviously, if DTC is submitting false reports to the government, well, that's not a good thing."

Rachael shuffled through the papers again, shaking her head. "I...I have to talk to Dikko."

"You do that. While you're at it, ask him how much jail time you could get for financial fraud since all these inflated numbers drove the price of DTC stock up."

"Ha!" Beck said. "You're a beast."

Jackie fought a smile. Really, there was nothing to be smiling about in this whole mess.

"That's ridiculous," Rachael said.

"It's true." Chessie circled a finger. "Your husband put the screws to you here, lady. You gonna let him get away with that?"

Rachael's head snapped up, the panic clearly taking over. "I have to speak with my husband. You need to leave."

Jackie stood, slinging her briefcase over her shoulder. "Sure. Call me when you're ready to get yourself out of this mess." She waved a hand. "You can keep those copies. I have another set."

They headed for the door, but—wait—Jackie angled back. "My client is facing a murder charge. I'm not about to let an innocent man go to prison. At the very least, based on the financial fraud we've barely scratched the surface on, I can destroy DTC. Never mind the connection to Annabelle's discovery of said fraud. Be smart here, Rachael. I'm coming for you. And your husband."

17

*B*eck winked at Jackie as she and Chessie got back in the car. "You're sexy as hell when you're threatening people. I'm totally turned on right now."

"That?" She cocked her chin at the building. "That was nothing. Wait 'til I channel my mother. She taught me all the best tricks to scare people."

Beck was pretty sure she was serious. "What do you think Rachael will do now? Call Dikko or go see him in person?"

Chessie tapped a thumb against the steering wheel. "She'll confront him face-to-face. I say we hang out and see if she goes to him or makes him come here. Either way, we can follow him, put him on the spot next."

"If this doesn't make him squirm, I'm not sure what will," Jackie said. "But if he *is* the killer..."

She shivered.

"Yeah, we need to be careful. No threatening Dick—that will be my job." Beck's phone buzzed. "It's an email from Taylor on Hodges."

He scrolled through the info and recited the pertinent facts. "Roane Hodges, former Green Beret, got out several years ago, did some consulting for the Defense Intelligence Agency, and works for DTC and a few other contractors."

"What did he do for DIA?" Chessie asked.

"Intelligence, both overt and clandestine."

"Interesting," Jackie commented. "With his military background, he could be our shooter."

"Him or Jones Ashley, Jr., who also works for DTC. He's on the team that designs...get this...helmets. He's an employee, not a contractor, and is also a former Green Beret. I had Taylor check into him too. Looks like he was dishonorably discharged."

That got Jackie's attention. "For what?"

"Um..." Beck scanned the file. "Sedition."

Chessie stopped tapping. "Espionage-type sedition, or something less extreme like disobeying orders?"

"Doesn't say, but since he's not in prison, I'm guessing it's not the former." Beck continued reading. "Now, this is interesting."

"What?" Jackie turned in the seat to look at him.

"Jones was a sniper."

She smacked the armrest. "He could be our guy."

"There are plenty of former military snipers in this town," Chessie said. "Current ones too."

"What about Roane?" Jackie asked. "Any mention of sniper training in his file?"

Beck shook his head. "He took a sniper course like most Spec Ops, but he was the Intelligence Sergeant on an A-Team with Jones. Jones was their Weapons Sergeant."

Jackie didn't look surprised. "So they worked together as Green Berets."

A beat-up black truck rolled into the parking lot and slammed to a stop, taking up two spots near the back of the building. Beck recited more of the file Taylor had sent. "Looks like Roane started contracting for DTC about six months before Dikko hired Jones. Maybe Roane got the guy the job?"

"Might be worth talking to him." Chessie motioned at Roane who had emerged from the back door. "Since Rachael hasn't bailed yet, we could follow this character instead."

The driver of the truck got out and slammed the door, tossing a cigarette butt on the ground and grinding it out with his boot heel. Roane, walking toward a silver Sequoia, shifted direction and headed for the guy, saying something they couldn't make out.

"That's Jones," Beck slid forward to see out the windshield, showing Jackie the photo of the man in the file.

Jones didn't seem to like what Roane had said and met him in the center of the parking lot with a sneer on his face and his hands flapping at his sides as he talked back.

"Someone's not happy," Chessie murmured.

Jackie rolled down her window. "I need some air. It's hot in here, isn't it?"

Like she needed an excuse to eavesdrop? Beck smiled to himself.

They all three strained to hear what the men were saying, but they were too far away. It wasn't difficult to understand the body language, though, especially when Roane grabbed Jones by the collar of his jacket and pushed him against the black truck.

"Okay, then," Jackie said, voice lowered. "Could Jones be the guy who broke into my place? The height is right, but he has that jacket on so I can't tell by his build. And I thought these two were friends."

Roane pointed a finger at Jones' face, a definite threat.

"If they were, they aren't now." Beck sat forward, analyzing Jones' movements. "You're right about his height. Could be him."

Jackie cocked her ear closer to the open window. "Do you think this has to do with DTC or is it personal?"

Jones shoved Roane away and beelined for the building's back entrance. Roane watched, eyes narrowed, hands on hips.

"Maybe both." Beck considered his options as Roane turned toward his vehicle. "I don't know, but let's see if I can find out."

He grabbed the door handle.

"Beck!" Jackie whirled. "No."

Bounding out and slamming the door on her warning tone, he jogged toward Roane, catching him before he could get in the Sequoia. "Mr. Hodges?"

Roane turned, eyed Beck, and then his attention slid behind Beck where the slam of a car door sounded. Damn it. Jackie wasn't going to be left out of the fun. "Yeah?"

"Can I talk to you for a minute?"

"Depends." The man's jaw worked. "What do you want?"

Beck pointed at the black truck. "Can you tell me anything about your friend there?"

"He's not my friend."

Jackie came stomping up. "Funny, since you two have known each other since your Army days."

Roane glanced at the building, back at Beck. "I got nothing to say."

But as he turned to get into his vehicle, he murmured under his breath. "Meet me at the Zippy Mart at the end of the block."

He climbed in and the vehicle roared to life. Beck and Jackie exchanged a look and hurried back to Chessie's car.

"Zippy Mart," Beck told the investigator. "Follow that Sequoia."

Roane blew out of the lot and Chessie followed at a slower pace. "What's going on?"

"Not sure," Beck said, "but I have a feeling Mr. Hodges has something to get off his chest."

"And what a chest it is," Jackie said. "Let's hope he has something juicy for us."

Beck scoffed at her. "You were checking out his chest?"

She grinned over the seat. "Down boy. I'm just saying, it was hard to miss."

"Let's remember this guy could be our shooter," Chessie said, "regardless of his penchant for intelligence or his *big chest.*"

The silver SUV pulled in behind the convenience store and Chessie parked beside him.

"You should stay here," he said to Jackie, pulling a handgun from his shoulder holster and checking the magazine.

"Good luck with that," Beck said under his breath, drawing his own personal weapon and doing the same.

Jackie's gun made an appearance and she waggled it in the air so they both could see it. "I'm not missing all the fun."

Before any of them could get out, Roane hauled out of the Sequoia and jogged over to Chessie's car. He pulled open the back passenger door and slid in next to Beck. "Holy shit, it took you guys long enough."

All three of them looked at him.

Chessie stated the obvious. "We got here the same time you did, chief."

"Not that." He shifted uncomfortably as if he were too big for the seat. Beck knew the feeling. "Figuring out about the bogus finance numbers. I thought you were never going to put two and two together and interrogate Rachael about them."

Jackie frowned at him, keeping her gun in view. "You overheard our conversation with Rachael?"

"I overhear a lot." He glanced out the window, his hand rubbing on his thigh. "I knew about the funky numbers."

"Tell us," Beck insisted.

Roane took a deep breath, his eyes continuing to survey their surroundings as if the boogeyman were about to jump them. "I came on board at DTC after the investigation into Travathian and the faulty helmets. Dikko wanted to land better contractors to ensure the equipment was up to spec and a friend referred me. Dikko needed help digging out of the hole he'd made with the DOD and I had connections. I believed he was legit and wanted to make things right, and the money was good. At first, everything seemed normal, and I was only in the office a few days a month, consulting on some of the overseas contracts. Then I realized things were off. I overheard conversations between Dikko and the CFO. She was asking questions about finance numbers. Then Annabelle Lockhart came into the office for a meeting. The conference room is right next to my office and well, the walls are thin."

"What did you hear?"

"Annabelle had concerns about the tax reports. Something about the lack of documentation. Dikko blew a gasket, claimed Annabelle wasn't being a team player."

"So you looked into it?"

"I spoke to Annabelle, you know, off the record, just a friendly little conversation to see if I could find out what was going on. She wouldn't talk about it."

"And?" Beck prompted.

"I did some digging—I have contacts in a lot of places. Things were fishy with all the connections between the Travathians, Lockharts, and POTUS. I didn't like the smell."

"So why didn't you quit?" This from Chessie. "Or go to Justice with your suspicions?"

"I did go to the Justice Department. A friend there thought I should stay on and see what turned up. That guy you saw me with back there?" His gaze finally swung to Beck. "He's former military like me. We have history and it's not all grins and giggles. I thought he might be up to something aside from the funky finance numbers and inventory stuff, and since I took pity on him when he got kicked out of the Berets and got him this job with DTC, I felt responsible if he was doing anything underhanded."

"You were investigating your friend," Beck said.

"Like I said, he's not my friend. Maybe once, back in the day when we were part of a unit, but not for a long time. I thought he'd changed after getting kicked out of Spec Ops, but... I've reconsidered my position on that."

"Someone broke into my home," Jackie said. "This person also stole my notes on Annabelle's case. Could it be him?"

Roane nodded. "I think so."

Jackie dug the picture of Lockhart, Dikko, and the President out of her briefcase. "You know anything about this?"

He glanced down at his lap, then back up at her. "Yes, ma'am. I slipped it under your door after Mrs. Lockhart was killed."

"Because you think Dikko killed her?" Beck asked.

Roane's focus switched to him even as he pointed at the photograph. "I don't know for sure who killed her, but I'm pretty damn sure it's one of them. Thing is..."

His gaze went back out the window and he rubbed his pants-clad thigh again. "I don't think any of them had the balls to pull the trigger. Or swipe the glass in this case."

Beck knew where this was going. "But you know someone who does."

His sigh could have sunk the Titanic. "Jones Ashley has nineteen kills to his name while he was in the Green Berets, and only half are listed on his official record."

"Dikko hired him to take care of Annabelle, didn't he?"

"I believe it's a strong possibility, but I have yet to find the proof. I was hoping you were going to do that."

Jackie snorted. "We are. Thank you, Mr. Hodges. We'll take it from here."

Roane nodded and offered his hand to Beck. "Good luck. If you need anything, you know where to find me."

. . .

Hodges exited the car and Jackie turned to Beck. "Wow."

"Yeah." He stared out the window. "Now we know where the photo came from."

Chessie fired up the engine and drove from the parking lot. "I'll drop you two at the office and chase a couple people I know at the phone company. Maybe we'll get lucky and I can pull Ashley's phone records. See who he's been talking with."

Behind them, Beck made a humming noise. "If he's smart, he has a burner phone."

"If you get his records," Jackie said, "check the night of Annabelle's murder. Maybe he was communicating with Dikko around the time Annabelle died. I would think, if he were the hired gun, he'd want to tell his boss the deed was done."

"Will do."

Ten minutes later, Chessie pulled away from the curb, leaving Jackie and Beck standing outside Jackie's office. Chances were he wouldn't find anything on Jones' phone from the night of the murder, but maybe there'd be a pattern of calls, constant communication, something she could use to bolster a possible Plan B defense.

Briefcase in hand, she ran her teeth over her bottom lip while her mind worked possible scenarios.

"What are you thinking?"

"If we can find something in Jones' phone records, we should be able to create enough reasonable doubt for a jury. I'd like something solid though. Indisputable evidence that will clear you."

"You and me both."

A bird whizzed by. Beck glanced up, squinting against the evening sun as the bird dipped and soared then came to rest on top of the street lamp. He let out a snort. "You got some life, buddy."

And there it was. The worry. Maybe he didn't talk about it, but they both knew – how could they not? – his future was far from safe.

She set her hand on his chest, gave him a pat. "You know I'm doing everything I can think of, right? I won't let you go to prison."

Not now that they'd finally reconnected. She wanted a chance with him. Some time to hopefully recapture the fun and excitement they'd shared in Fort Lauderdale. They were older now, both experiencing successful careers and maturity they didn't have twelve years ago. Back then they were ambitious dreamers. Now they could have it all.

If she kept him out of prison.

Beck covered her hand with his and squeezed. "Nothing's guaranteed. Even for you."

"True, but I don't give up. And we have resources. Dikko Travathian is in the middle of this mess. We just have to prove it."

"I think," Beck said, "we should call Debra Johansen."

"Are you kidding? After what she did putting our sex tape out there for God and country?"

"We'll leak DTC's financials and Annabelle's involvement to her. If nothing else, it'll put pressure on Metro to start looking in that direction."

Not a bad idea. Jackie paused to ponder the benefits as well as the possible downsides. "It's risky, but I like it. First, we'll be messing with evidence. Second, we could piss off a judge by trying our case in the press. I'm not opposed, but you have to be ready for the consequences."

Beck shrugged. "At this point, I've got nothing to lose."

True dat. Jackie nodded. "Let's go inside. We'll call and send her copies of the reports."

"I'm hungry. Can we order dinner while we're dealing with Debra?"

Probably a good idea since it was after seven o'clock and the day gave no indication of winding down.

Hand-in-hand, they walked up the path to Jackie's office. Halfway there, she lifted their joined hands. "A girl could get used to this."

"Holding hands?"

That, plus some. "All of it. The companionship, the affection. It's nice."

For a few seconds, the career girl in her mourned the niceties that came with a relationship. Building her law practice had consumed her, kept her mind always moving ahead. She'd had no time or patience for men. Over the last few years, the men who'd come into her life quickly disappeared. Too needy or requiring her attention.

Was it fair to them? Probably not. She accepted it and steered clear of anyone even hinting at a relationship.

At least until Beck burst back into her life. Now she wanted whatever she could get of him. That meant keeping him out of prison.

Failure, as her mother often said, was not an option.

Beck held the exterior door open and Jackie walked through. She flipped the switch on the wall, illuminating the reception area.

"Hello?" she called, just in case Josh was hibernating in his office.

Blessed silence.

She'd been running on adrenaline since the shooting, but the quiet gave her mind a few seconds to pause, to recognize the ache in her limbs.

Damn. Shouldn't have stopped to think. If she focused too much on the fatigue, she'd collapse.

"Everyone's gone," she said. "Come back to my office."

She smacked another light switch and the wall sconces lit up. Together, they moved down the short hallway and she pointed to the small break room at the opposite end. "Last door on the left is the kitchen. Check the top drawer next to the sink for menus. Why don't you order us something while I track Debra down? The Chinese place is good."

While Beck busied himself with their dinner order, Jackie dropped into her desk chair and closed her eyes. Just a few seconds, that's all she needed to recharge. Beck's voice drifted from across the hall and she took in the simplicity of a man ordering dinner for her. Another thing she could get used to.

If she won his case.

Win it.

She snapped her eyes open. What the hell was she doing daydreaming like this? It was a total waste of precious time.

She dug out her cell phone and searched her contacts for Debra's number. The phone went straight to voicemail so Jackie left a message indicating it was a 9-1-1 situation.

That should get the feisty reporter moving.

She tossed the phone on her desk and stared at the solid crystal paperweight her mother had given her. The thing weighed eight pounds – yes, she'd checked – and at certain times she imagined slamming it against her head.

Times like now when mind-melting self-doubt crept in. Should she have done that? A reporter, for God's sake. Really? That move so early in the game could easily backfire on her.

It was Beck's idea of course, but she needed to be the voice of reason. The one who talked the emotionally charged suspect out of rash maneuvers.

Except, by allowing herself to get involved, she was just as emotionally charged. And way more apt to make mistakes.

She set her palm against her forehead and pushed. *Think, Jackie. Think, think, think.*

Movement in the doorway caught her attention. Beck rejoining her.

"I think," she said, looking up. "Whoa."

A man – Jones – stood in the doorway dressed in black jeans and a black long-sleeved T-shirt.

A backpack was slung over his shoulders, but her eye went to his side.

Gun.

He raised his arm, pointed the weapon straight at her and panic exploded, sending stabs of pain down her neck into her shoulders. "What...What are you doing?"

He brought his free hand up, placing his finger against his lips in the classic *ssshhh* signal. Silently, he stepped into the room, keeping his back to the wall, his gaze ping-ponging between her and the doorway where any second Beck would be walking in.

Using his free hand, Jones slid the backpack off his shoulder and set it on the sofa next to him. "You're a pain in the ass," he said. "Always interrupting my work."

She swiveled in her chair, tracking his movements as Jones adjusted his aim. Center mass, the cops called it.

"I..." she stopped, then took a breath, and curled her trembling fingers into tight fists. "Listen, I can help you. Whatever Dikko has you wrapped up in, you don't have to do this. I can *help* you."

"Hey, Jackie."

Beck's voice. Coming closer. *No.* "Beck! Run!"

Too late. Beck swung into the room, spotted Jones and halted, hands rising in the air. Jones brought the weapon around, aiming it at Beck and...*now.*

Jackie grabbed the crystal paperweight and flung it at Jones' head. Despite its weight, it flew from her hand. Jones side-stepped and avoided the blow. But Jackie was on the move, leaping toward him as he brought the gun up. From his angle, Beck charged and –

"No!" Jackie said

Ooff. Beck slammed into Jones, tackling him.

Still, he raised the gun, aimed at Jackie and...boom. The gun went off, the sound reverberating in her ears. A shot zipped by her, but somehow she kept moving. A moving target was harder to hit.

Beck gripped Jones' wrist with one hand, cocked his free arm back and slammed his fist straight into the man's temple. His head snapped sideways.

Still, Jones held on to the gun. Dammit. Jackie lunged just as his finger found the trigger again and squeezed.

18

———————

*B*eck was already shoving all his weight into Jones to pin the bastard down when the gun went off a second time. Lucky him, he caught the bullet in his shoulder.

A fiery sensation ripped through his upper arm where it grazed his skin, but Jackie was okay, and that was all that mattered. He could still make a fist and, with it, he punched Jones in the face and then ripped the gun from the man's hand.

Jones' eyes rolled up in his head and he went limp.

Ears ringing with the echo of the gun's report, Beck sat back on his heels. He slammed the safety on the gun and tossed it over to the couch. "Are you okay?" he asked as Jackie fell to her knees beside him.

She touched his bleeding shoulder. "Oh my God, you've been shot."

"Not the first time." He looked her over from head to toe, taking her hand and pulling her up off the floor. "That's a killer fastball you've got there, Ms. DelRay."

Her brow knit with worry. "I definitely need to get better security around here."

"Call the police. I'll call Taylor. She can be in on the interrogation of this weasel down at the station. She'll get him to confess and expose Dikko."

"You need an ambulance." Jackie went for her phone.

"Meh. It's nothing but a graze. Some peroxide and a bandage, and I'll be good to go."

She punched numbers, and at first, he thought the muted beeping noise was from her phone. But the sound wasn't matching her finger movements and it was too rhythmic.

Beep...beep...beep.

Tugging on his earlobe to clear the gunshot echoes, his eyes strayed to the sofa where a black bag sat.

Beep...beep...beep.

"What is that?"

The phone to her ear as the call connected, she shook her head, eyes wide. "Jones brought it with him."

Fuck. He prayed it wasn't what he thought.

Carefully unzipping the top, Beck peered in. Red numbers winked back at him.

Numbers counting down from thirty.

His stomach dropped. The bastard had brought a bomb.

God, I hate bombs.

29

28

27

Of all the things he'd studied, he knew little about explosive devices. What he remembered from his training was sufficient to know this device was stable enough for Jones to transport in a bag.

But there was no way Beck had the expertise to disarm it.

25

24

23

He glanced back at Jones, still out for the count. *No help there.*

The man's coat had been ripped open, a small cream-colored box that looked like a pager was hooked on his belt. Beck bet anything that pager had gotten jammed during their fight and had triggered the bomb.

Someone on the other end of Jackie's call had answered, and he heard a sharp, tinny voice. *"Is anyone there? Hello? What is the nature of your call?"*

19

18

17

Beck zipped up the backpack, considering his options.

Not a fucking one of them did he like. "Put an order in for the bomb squad, Jackie."

Snatching up the bag, he ran.

Get outside.

Get away from Jackie.

As he hit the front stoop, he ran on full instinct, adrenaline pumping hard. The construction across the street had halted for the weekend. Street lights glinted off the machines. Scaffolding rose high in the air against the building being revamped.

Dumpster.

The dark green dumpster was filled with broken concrete slabs from the parking lot that was also getting a makeover. The dumpster sat next to a big, hulking bulldozer.

Beep...beep...beep.

Heavy, dense. Concrete and metal. It was the best—and only—solution he could see. Otherwise the bomb could take out Jackie's office building or the one next to it. Quite possibly, the entire block.

Vaulting over the concrete barricade, Beck skirted a backhoe and hurdled a set of pylons. The entire site was a giant obstacle course, reminding him of the Academy. Skidding to the dumpster, he tossed the bag inside, burying it deep between the broken slabs of concrete.

"Beck!" Jackie screamed from the steps of her office building.

Sprinting all out, he waved his good arm at her. "Get the fuck back inside!"

Instead, she ran toward him, right down to the sidewalk.

Clearing the concrete barricade once more, he ran across the road, the timer in his brain still *beep-beep-beeping* at him.

He hit the sidewalk and tackled Jackie, taking them both to the ground.

A heartbeat before they hit, the explosion rocked the night.

Lights flashed off and on over the front of Jackie's office building as police cars, ambulances, and the bomb squad blocked the street and parking lot.

Over the noise, Beck heard bits and pieces of Jackie arguing with a cop while an EMT bandaged his arm and checked his pupils.

"You should let us take you to the ER," the guy said. "You might have a concussion on top of the GSW."

Although Beck was pissed at Jones for trying to kill Jackie a second time, he couldn't take his anger out on the paramedic. "Nah." Beck patted the man's arm and stood from his seat on the edge of the ambulance. "I'm good, and I appreciate you bandaging me up."

The EMT ran through the concussion protocol and Beck just nodded. No frickin' way he was going to the hospital, and the bump on his head would be gone before morning. "We done here?"

He'd already given his statement to the police and Jackie had done the same. Taylor was on her way to the station to meet Jones—he had a broken nose and a few bruises, but had been conscious when the cops put him in their cruiser.

"I need to check your blood pressure again."

Don't have time for this, but since Jackie was still speaking to the police officer on the steps of her building, he offered up his good arm for the cuff. It could be another hour or more before the cops would have what they wanted and clear out. After what had happened only the previous day, the police were antsy about him being on the scene of both crimes. Thank God, Jones was in custody—at least the cops weren't looking at Beck like he was a prime suspect anymore.

The bomb squad was taking care of the aftermath and trying to decipher the explosive's components. The head of the construction company had also arrived, bitching his ass off about the damage done to his bulldozer and dumpster.

Better that than Jackie.

Her hair was matted on one side and sticking out on the other. Mud stained her pants from hip to knee, thanks to Beck taking her on a home run slide through the little piece of yard in front of her office building. She'd thrown a jacket over her destroyed blouse and had her shaky hands buried in the pockets.

He saw her look down and draw her cell phone out of the right pocket, eyeing the screen. She said one more final thing to the cop, then waved him off as she answered a call.

Her body stiffened and her gaze swung to Beck's.

Just like when he'd seen the bomb, his stomach sank. He ran.

Jackie didn't put much stock in coincidences. She liked to think of them as the result of various events set into motion.

Like Rachael Travathian calling her right after DTC's employee tried to blow. Her. *Up.*

Jackie bolted inside the office building as Beck bounded up the steps, waving him in before she took the call. Because, holy hell, this should be good.

She tapped the screen just as Beck ripped the blood pressure cuff from his arm.

"Rachael," she said, loud enough for Beck to hear. "Hello."

Beck drew up close. "No way," he mouthed.

Jackie nodded, turning the phone so they could both hear.

"Oh, my God," Rachael said, her voice lit with panic. "What's going on. The police just called me and said Jones *attacked* you."

"He did more than that. He brought a bomb in here and shot Beck Pearson."

"No! The police didn't tell me *that*. Did he..."

This woman. Such a damned flake. Jackie rolled her eyes. "Kill him? No. Beck is alive and well. Jones has a shattered nose and, as we speak, is on his way to an interrogation room. Rachael, I'm not your attorney, but I'm telling you, you are knee deep in whatever is going on here. I know how these detectives work. They'll leverage everything they have, they'll promise reduced sentences, better cells, whatever it takes to get Jones to talk. Because right now, with all the evidence we've collected about DTC's shady accounting and Annabelle's refusal to take part in financial fraud, he looks damned good for her murder. Natalie's too."

The phone line went silent and Jackie checked the screen. Still connected. Beck held up a finger, the universal wait sign. No problem there. The one who spoke first usually lost and Jackie was in no mood for losing.

Not with Beck's freedom on the line.

"I can't *believe* it," Rachael said.

"Well, honey, you'd better start. And worse, I'm pissed. Before I'm done with Jones, he'll be squealing like the pig he is. If you were smart, you'd take my advice and hire a lawyer. By making you an officer of the company, your husband, at the very least, has you on the hook for not only financial fraud, but possibly insider trading as well."

"What are you talking about?"

The woman could not be this naive. Then again, people in love did stupid things. Jackie pinched the bridge of her nose, praying for patience. She needed to flip Rachael. Spousal privilege only went so far in criminal cases. Given the situation Dikko had put his wife in, Rachael could easily testify against him to save herself.

"Rachael, your husband made you the Chief Executive Officer of DTC. He then, without your knowledge, manipulated *your* company's accounting reports to make it look like you were profitable. Then he sold his stock when it reached its high-point. He did all this knowing the reporting was bogus. Right off the top of my head, he's violated the Securities Act, the Securities Exchange Act, and a slew of rules related to those acts. And you, as the CEO, by signing the tax forms, are a co-conspirator."

Beside her, Beck flashed a smile and gave her a double thumbs-up. If nothing else, she was damned good at her job.

"Look," Rachael said, "if what you say is true and Dikko screwed up on the financials, that's one thing. Jones killing Annabelle has nothing to do with us."

"Oh, please, Rachael!"

"Don't yell at me! I hate yelling!"

The cop Jackie had been speaking to was in the doorway finishing his notes. He glanced over at her. Okay, so maybe she got a little loud. She moved down the hall to Josh's office, signaling Beck to follow. He shut the door behind them and reclaimed his spot next to her so he could eavesdrop.

"Rachael," Jackie said. "I'm sorry I raised my voice, but honestly. You need to take a second here and follow the logic. Jones is an employee of DTC. According to what we've uncovered, he helped design the helmet that put your company on the map. Based on that, I'm assuming he has a financial stake in the success of your company. Now, if I'm the prosecutor, which I *was* in this town, here's what I'd do. I'd look at all the players involved. I'd see that Annabelle resigned the DTC account because of shady financial reporting. I'd also search her files and talk to everyone she worked with. In this case, I'd find out Annabelle threatened to turn Dikko in for fraud." It was a stretch, but worth the lie. "She ends up dead and then her business partner, the one who knew Annabelle made threats against Dikko, winds up murdered. By a high-powered rifle shot from a distance. Which means the shooter was damned good with a weapon. And, oh, gee, Jones Ashley, who works for DTC and has just as much to lose as Dikko, happens to be former military." Jackie held out a hand. "Rachael, are you picking up what I'm putting down, here?"

Again Beck smiled. *Step aside, big boy, and let me work.*

"He couldn't have," Rachael said, her voice hitching with desperation.

"Rachael, I don't know your husband, but you do. Ask yourself if he's capable of sending Jones after Annabelle and her partner. If your answer is yes, then you'd better get a lawyer because your world is about to collapse."

19

$\mathcal{J}$ackie pushed through Beck's front door and poked a finger at the steps leading to the second floor. "Be quick about this. Please. We have a lot to do."

He dropped a kiss on the top of her head, and passed her, heading upstairs. "Give me two minutes to shower and change clothes."

"Whatever." She dug her phone from her briefcase and damn near threw herself onto the couch. "Unbelievable," she muttered. "Leave it to me to fall in love with a neat freak."

"Did you say something?"

She looked up, finding him peering down at her from the top of the stairs. Whether he heard her or not, debatable. Did it matter? She knew what she wanted and Jackie DelRay had never been one to let an opportunity cruise by.

"I did say something. I *said*, leave it to me to fall in love with a neat freak. I mean, seriously, we need to track down Dikko and you're worried about a little blood? Can we get a move on before this guy hops on a plane to Costa Rica and we lose him for good? Because listen up, I want you out of prison and in my bed. For a long time."

He stood on the steps staring at her as if she'd lost her ever-loving mind. Which, in fact, she probably had, but after twelve years of life without Beck, she didn't intend on another twelve.

"Beck!"

"What?"

"Get going!"

"I am, but – "

She snapped her fingers at him. "Move it."

"You just said you loved me."

"And what? Now you want a medal? I love you. At least, I'm pretty sure I do, but hey, with all this dawdling you're doing while I'm trying to keep that fine ass of yours out of jail, I might be changing my mind." She gave him the DelRay evil eyes. "Quite rapidly. Get. *Going.*"

Shaking his head, he laughed. "You're twisted, but I love you too."

She stared up at him, forcing the trapped air from her lungs. *He loves me.* She couldn't remember the last time a man had said that to her. Not a sober man anyway. And here was Beck, probably the most hard-working, protective man she knew, proclaiming his love.

How the hell did she get this lucky?

"Finally," he said, "I've muted her."

She smiled up at him. "Ha! Nice try." She waved him off. "Glad we're in agreement on this whole being in love thing. Can we discuss it later? Maybe find a killer first?"

He let out an exaggerated sigh. "Don't forget Monroe is on the way."

Taylor had texted Beck a few minutes earlier alerting them that Mitch was on the way to offer any backup they might need.

What they needed right now was to find Dikko.

"I'm on it," Jackie said. "You get in that shower."

A minute later she heard the shower go on. Good. She

checked the time on her phone. Three minutes. That's how long she'd give him to hose off. After that, she'd start yelling.

While waiting, she punched up Grey. He answered on the first ring.

"Jackie DelRay, what can I do for you?"

"Hi. This thing is coming to a head."

"I heard. Taylor called me. The PD updated Byron, who updated Taylor. Let me guess, you're looking for Dikko Travathian."

Lord, she loved a man who got right to the point. "I am. My guess is Jones Ashley, Jr. has already lawyered up and is trying to work a plea deal. Which means, if he killed Annabelle on Dikko's orders, we'll hear about that real quick."

"Did you talk to the wife?"

"Yes. She's a bust, for now. I think when she wraps her head around how her beloved husband screwed her over, she'll tell us what she knows. But, honestly, I don't think she knows anything about Annabelle's murder. Dikko kept it from her. Along with a lot of other things."

"You seem pretty sure he's behind it."

"Based on the evidence we've found, you bet your life. It's no coincidence Annabelle was murdered right after she resigned his account. I think Dikko saw his life coming apart and decided to prevent it."

"What do you need from me?"

"Any chance you can figure out where he is? Maybe track his cell phone or something?"

"Give me five minutes."

The line went dead. "Alrighty then," Jackie said. "Good talk."

She checked the time on her phone. *Time's up.* She set the phone down and headed for the stairs, reaching the landing just as the doorbell sounded.

At the door, Jackie checked the peephole and spotted the top of a blond head. Whoa.

This is it. Jackie's heart slammed and the whooshing in her ears set her back a step. *Get it together here, DelRay.*

Upstairs, the shower went off. Finally. In another two minutes, Beck would be downstairs. The doorbell rang again and Jackie deactivated the alarm before opening the door. On the other side stood Rachael. Rather than her usual elegant clothing, she wore jeans and a short trench coat over an untucked blouse. Her normally silky blond hair fell in stringy clumps around her shoulders and black liner bled from the corners of her eyes.

Crying.

Oh, Beck, hurry up. This might be it. That moment when Rachael flips on her husband.

"Rachael," she said. "What are you doing here?"

Not bothering to wait for an invitation, she pushed by, moving quickly into the house. "I tried your place first. Figured you might be here. Shut the door. I'm not sure where Dikko is and I don't want him to find me."

Oh, yes. Here we go.

"All right." Jackie closed the door and turned the dead bolt. The lock snapped into place, echoing in the quiet room. *This is it.* Got him.

When she turned back, Rachael stood midway between the back of the sofa and the staircase. She faced Jackie, slowly lifting her blouse, revealing a handgun at her waist.

Another spurt of adrenaline flooded her and Jackie threw her arms up. "Hang on."

But Rachael slipped the gun from the holster and aimed it straight at Jackie's chest. In her lifetime, Jackie had never had a handgun pointed at her. Today? Twice.

"I'm done," Rachael said. "This ends now."

· · ·

The doorbell had gone off twice. *Impatient.*

Beck looked down at the towel hugging his waist and cursed under his breath. Fucking Mitch Monroe. Had to be him, sent express mail by Taylor and Grey for another round of bodyguard duty.

Jackie had been so fired up, Beck figured they'd be gone before Mitch arrived and that was fine with him, but if the jerk did make it, it wouldn't be bad to have him for backup when they went to talk to Dikko.

Kill me now.

As Tink circled his ankles, Beck dragged on clean dress pants, his time up a good five minutes ago but then his cell buzzed. Taylor.

Hopefully she had forced a confession from that sack of shit Jones.

"Not yet," she said when Beck answered. "He's demanding medical treatment and his lawyer, which both take time. As soon as I have anything, I'll send Metro to grab Dikko. Promise."

Beck, like Jackie, suspected it might be too late by then. *We have to stop him.* Couldn't tell Taylor that though. "Thanks. Hey, Monroe is here. You didn't need to send him."

"The hell I didn't."

Snagging his shirt off the hanger, he put it on, then grabbed his gun and started downstairs. Gun in one hand and his cell in the other—Taylor still talking— he halted on the second step.

Jackie was speaking loudly, her voice strained, anxious. "Just tell me the truth. Who killed Annabelle?"

The low chuckle that came in reply wasn't from Mitch. "Annabelle was a nice person. Stupid, and a whore, but a whore with a heart of gold, as they say."

He knew that voice. *Rachael?*

She chuckled again, this time full of cynicism. "Dikko had

the hots for her, you know, but because we were friends, she wouldn't screw him. That's what friendship meant to her."

Taylor's voice was a distant buzzing in his ear, asking him what was wrong. "Ssh," he whispered and held up the cell for her to hear.

"I warned him," Rachael continued. "I told him not to screw up and put DTC in the spotlight, but he wouldn't listen. He was so incredibly pissed at Annabelle. First, she wouldn't fuck him, and then she wouldn't finish her audit because of 'irregularities.'"

Warning bells went off in Beck's head. Rachael didn't exactly sound like the upset, crying woman he'd heard on the phone earlier. She sounded pissed, but...

Calm.

Jackie's anxious, Rachael's calm. What was wrong with this picture?

Clang, clang, clang, the warning bells grew louder.

After everything that had happened in the past few days, he wasn't about to ignore the clanging. Easing back up to the landing, he whispered to Taylor, "Hang on. Got a situation."

He slid the phone in his front pocket and checked the gun's magazine—six bullets. The chamber held an additional one. Tink sat and eyed him.

He closed her inside the bathroom with a mental apology. Back on the stairs, he avoided the one that always popped from his weight and hugged the wall as he descended cautiously.

Jackie's voice drifted up. "Jones is in custody. He's going to turn on you. Killing me won't stop the police from finding out about your role in all of this."

Killing...?

The bells went sonic. He eased another inch down the wall to where he could peek into the living room.

His blood ran cold as he saw Jackie sitting on the couch with a gun to the back of her head. Rachael stood behind her holding a small Beretta—the perfect handgun to conceal in her designer purse, but its 9mm bullet could stop nearly any threat.

And point blank to the back of the head?

Dead. Lights out.

He gripped his weapon tighter.

"Call your friend," Rachael demanded. "Get him in here."

"I told you he's not here." Jackie had removed her jacket earlier when they'd entered and laid it on a chair. Her face had lost its color, now nearly as white as her blouse. "He dropped me off and went to the police station to give his official statement about Jones. He was injured and needed medical treatment. He won't be back for hours."

The gun shoved Jackie's head forward. "You think I'm that gullible?"

Her gaze swept around and Beck ducked back out of sight.

"He's upstairs," Rachael said. "I heard a voice when I came in."

Jackie's shaky voice firmed, edged with that signature brand of DelRay irritation. "Rachael, I told you, I'm the only one here. That was the TV. Do you really think if Beck was upstairs, I wouldn't be screaming my lungs out right now to get him down here?"

Sell it, Jackie.

Beck snuck another peek. Jackie had Rachael's attention again and was pointing at the alarm system panel next to the door. "He thought it would be safer for me here than at my place since I don't have a security system and he does."

The light on the panel blinked rapidly, in time with Beck's crazy pulse. Jackie hadn't reset the alarm after opening the door.

Rachael noticed the blinking light too. "Set it." She waved the pistol, motioning Jackie to get moving. "I don't want any surprises."

It looked like Jackie had tried to wash the grass and mud

from her pants. Large, wet stains decorated the drab gray material as she walked across the floor. The hem of her shirt hung untucked from her waistband showing she'd tried to get the stains off that too.

As Rachael skirted the end of the couch to follow Jackie to the entryway, Beck crept down the final step, stopping at the bottom. *One surprise coming up.*

Jackie's fingers punched buttons, but she got the code wrong and the system beeped loudly, asking her to re-enter the numbers.

"What's the matter?" Rachael asked. "Hurry up."

"Sorry, but when someone's holding a gun to my head, I get a little nervous. Why don't you put that thing down and let's talk. Whatever Dikko's got you into, I can help."

"Dikko? Ha!" The scorn in Rachael's voice was thick. "Do you really think he's this smart? This calculating? Please. The man thinks with his dick and only cares about his bank account. He wants to be rich and screw every whore who comes along. He thought I'd let his endless affairs slide because the money was good. Let me tell you something, I'm no fool. I've got plenty of financial resources now, and Jones will be free soon. Dikko's going down for everything, just like we planned."

Jackie curled her fingers into a fist. "Why kill Annabelle?"

"She was going to blab about the embezzlement. Can you imagine? Because of Dikko's connections, he got away with insider trading, faulty helmets, you name it, and she was going to blow everything over false inventory records."

"He didn't falsify them, did he?" Jackie asked. "You did. You set him up. He was ripe for it, because of his previous run-ins with the Justice Department."

"Annabelle said she was my friend," Rachael fumed. "And then she betrayed me. Her and her audit—she was going to ruin everything."

Jackie faced her. "She told you she thought Dikko was

embezzling and she was going to turn him in, so you figured, why not? Let Dikko take the fall, but you were afraid his connections would get him off the hook like they had before, so you needed to up the ante."

Rachael pressed the gun against Jackie's forehead and Beck's breath caught. "And then your friend got in the way, but in the end? It's all going to work out just fine."

Jackie's voice was barely above a whisper. "Did Jones kill Annabelle or did you?"

Rachael drew the gun back, though it was pointed at Jackie's chest now. "I tried talking to her the night of the auction, but she wouldn't listen. I offered her money, a job working for me. She said she wouldn't be bribed. What a joke. Byron had been bribing her for years, trying to get her to stop whoring around. He and I—two of the same, putting up with our lousy, cheating spouses. He tried to get her to stop the affairs, but no, she milked him for money and anything else she wanted, and she kept right on throwing herself at men, just like she did with Beck Pearson. So, to answer your question, I killed her. She deserved it. She *wasn't* my friend. Never had been."

Rachael grabbed Jackie's arm and whipped her back around to face the alarm panel. "Now arm the security system. Since Pearson isn't here, he's going to be my fall guy again - for your murder this time. How convenient that your body will be found in his house."

Jackie's fingers didn't shake as she punched at the buttons. "No one will believe you're innocent, Rachael. You're smart, but you haven't thought this through."

"Shut up."

Staying out of Rachael's peripheral vision, Beck raised his gun and tread one slow, careful step at a time toward them. He hated violence, but some people didn't deserve mercy.

Problem was, from his current vantage point, if he shot at Rachael, he risked Jackie getting hurt.

Get Rachael's attention. Distract her.

Then shoot for the kneecap.

Not FBI SOP—that was all about center mass—but he wasn't your average agent. All he needed was to distract his target...

"Sounds like you have it all planned out," he said conversationally, and both Rachael and Jackie jumped. "Tell me more, Rachael."

Rachael's head spun around, eyes wide.

But the gun stayed leveled on Jackie.

The alarm system started up again since Jackie hadn't finished putting in the correct code, and Jackie—God bless her—used it to her advantage. She twisted, and with Rachael so close, punched the woman's hand, sending the pointed gun to the right.

Boom.

Deja vu. The shot rang in Beck's ears, Jackie falling back and covering hers, as the bullet penetrated the wall. Before Rachael had time to recoil, he stepped in and grabbed her wrist, shoving it—and the gun—straight up. Anger fueled him enough that he lifted her right off her feet, dangling her by her arm.

The Beretta went off again and Rachael struggled against him, pieces of ceiling falling on them. Blinking through the dust and debris hitting him in the face, he pressed a thumb into the tender center of Rachael's wrist and her grip released. The weapon fell, her screaming the whole time.

Whether it was from pain or anger he wasn't sure, and he really didn't care.

He lowered her to the ground and was about to knock her feet out from under her when she buckled. As she went down, Beck saw Jackie standing directly behind her with a nasty grin on her face. She'd kicked Rachael in the back of the knees.

What a scrapper.

Beck used a foot to kick Rachael's gun away and handed

Jackie his. He shoved the woman face-down on the floor, Rachael *oomph*-ing from the impact, her screaming cut short.

But only for a moment.

"It was all Dikko!" The old Rachael was back, sounding scared and freaked out. "I had nothing to do with any of this. Jones will back me up. Dikko killed Annabelle. I'm innocent, I tell you. Innocent! He used me. I came here to warn you, but you're trying to set me up too!" Her voice morphed back to Evil Rachael and she snarled at Jackie. "That's what I'll tell the cops. It'll be my word against yours."

Beck looked around for something to secure her hands with, keeping a knee between her shoulder blades. "Keep the gun on her," he told Jackie, pulling out his cell and hitting the speaker button. "Did you get any of that, Taylor?"

"It was muffled, but I think I got the important parts. Now hang up and arrest that bitch."

"Technically, I'm on suspension."

"Not if I have anything to say about it."

Overwhelming relief washed over him. Jackie was safe. He was free.

The front door flew open and Mitch pulled up short on the threshold. His gaze went from Beck's plaster-sprinkled face and open shirt, down to Rachael being held against her will, and over to Jackie's wet pants and blouse.

"I heard gunshots, thought you were in trouble," he said. "But excuse me, I didn't mean to interrupt your kink party, Pearson."

God Almighty. How in the hell did Caroline put up with this douchebag? "Tell me you have a set of zip ties, Monroe."

Mitch dug around in the back pocket of his worn jeans. His jacket hung open, revealing his latest smartass T-shirt: *I'm going to hell in every religion!* He held up a pair of metal cuffs. "These do?"

Beck snagged them and handcuffed Rachael. "Thanks."

Sirens blared in the distance. Beck hauled Rachael to her feet. Mitch glanced at all of them again and shook his head. "You're either into some weird shit, man, or you're a hell of an agent."

A sideways compliment from Monroe? Hell had frozen over. Beck shoved Rachael down onto the couch and turned to Jackie. "You okay?"

Her jaw was clenched. She limply held out his gun. "I told you two minutes."

She was totally burnt out but the attitude told him she would be okay. "It's not my fault, I swear. Taylor called. Blame her for my tardiness."

Without another word, Jackie fell into his open arms.

20

*J*aniece stood inside FBI headquarters waiting for him.

"Thank God you're back," she said, handing Beck a blue file folder once he passed the security desk. She scrolled through a list on her phone. "No one in this place can make a decent pot of coffee, and we have a slew of meetings all day. I need my damn caffeine—tell me you brought a fresh bag of that Guatemalan organic stuff. And I need you to dig into that file"—she taped it with her phone—"and Taylor wants you to find a suspect or two to browbeat about our missing girl, Coriann Meullers."

It was almost like he'd never left.

She started marching away, leaving him standing there. "Good to see you too," he called after her, "but officially, I'm not back, yet. You know this, right?"

Her well-manicured hand made a hurry-up motion to follow her. "Your first meeting is with Director Lockhart and Taylor. After that, you're mine, so get a move on."

The Missing Persons Unit secretary held the elevator doors

for him and he hustled to catch up. Fellow Bureau members nodded as he passed by.

Hunh. Guess they heard the news.

As Beck swung into the elevator, he felt a smile curve over his face. *I'm back.*

Jamming the file folder under his arm, he straightened his tie. A strange sense of rightness, of belonging, warmed his chest. "There should be half a bag of ground Pico Gesha beans in the cabinet unless you guys drank it all."

"Are you kidding?" Janeice punched the button for their floor. "We've been drinking that crap Leo brings in all the time. There's nothing else in the coffee cabinet."

Well, there was the problem. Leo wouldn't know a decent coffee bean if it choked him. "He probably stole what was left of your coffee, Jan, and substituted it with his crap. I'll bring a fresh bag tomorrow."

"I love you and want to have your babies," she joked, typing away on her phone.

It was her standard response any time he made her life easier. A joke they shared, but one that now felt weirdly...weird. "I love you too, but I have a small request."

Type, type, type. "Oh, yeah?"

"Yeah, can you not declare your love for me in front of my girlfriend?"

That got her attention and her head snapped up. "Girlfriend? You mean you and Jackie DelRay are really a thing? No. Way. I thought Taylor was kidding about that."

"You didn't see the sex tape?"

Janeice's jaw dropped open. The elevator dinged as they hit their floor and the doors opened. "You made a *sex tape*? Why have I not seen this? Oh my god, like all of my dreams just came true."

Beck laughed and it felt good, but the looks on the faces of the two people standing across from him and Janiece, waiting for the elevator, cut the laugh short.

"Joking," he said, guiding Janiece out of the elevator and past their coworkers. Someone who liked him—Taylor, Grey, or most likely Teeg—had made the sex tape disappear. Just poof. Gone. They'd traced it to Debra Johansen, who still claimed she'd come by the video anonymously. Teeg said otherwise. He'd figured out that Debra had been behind it, and Beck reasoned it made sense with the reporter's need to keep her ratings up. "There's no sex tape," he assured his fellow agents.

I hope.

Plenty of people had seen it, or at least heard about it, but all that was left of the thing was a memory.

As he and Janiece entered Missing Persons, the smells of carpet, burnt coffee, and microwave popcorn permeated his nose.

No doubt, Leo had popped it in their kitchen so it didn't stink up the one in the Behavioral Science wing.

Bastard.

Beck's teammates filed out of their offices to say 'hi'. As he accepted back slaps and welcomes, he saw Taylor come out of her office at the end of the hall. She smiled and he returned it, his shoulders relaxing.

Yep. He was back all right.

Home.

At least now, it wasn't the only one he had.

Jackie was also home for him. Wherever he ended up, whatever happened, he knew without a doubt, she had his back. They were partners.

Still hanging onto the case file Janiece had handed him, he met Taylor halfway down the hall.

"Good to see you in one piece," she said, hugging him. "How's the shoulder?"

"Probably won't even leave a decent scar."

"I think you have enough of those already, tough guy."

He held up the file. "Apparently, I'm on the clock. Do I need to sign any paperwork or check in with…"

The smile fell off his face as Byron Lockhart emerged from Taylor's office. His gaze went from Beck's head to his toes. "You coming or what?" he barked, disappearing back inside. "I don't have all day, Pearson!"

Beck canted his head at Taylor. "You could have warned me."

She pushed him toward the office. "What fun is there in that?"

Inside, he sat in one of the chairs across from her desk as she took her seat. He wanted an apology from Lockhart, but knew he'd never get it.

But maybe, in some small way, he owed Byron one too, for believing he'd killed Annabelle.

Nah. Not gonna happen. At least not until Beck could look at him without feeling betrayed.

Lockhart, as per normal, took up a spot at the window, gazing out on the traffic below. "I've already sent out an interoffice memo that all charges have been cleared and you've been reinstated."

Beck swallowed his pride. He didn't feel any gratitude to the man, but he had to play his part. Make this as quick as possible. "Thank you, sir. I'm ready to get back to work."

"And I'm ready to have you," Taylor said, pointing at the stack of files on her desk. "We fell behind even more than usual while you were gone."

"I'll triage what you've got." Beck reached for the pile, his fingers itching to get busy. "I can work overtime for a while to make some headway."

"Yes, well." Byron turned from the window and walked past the desk. "Good to have you back, Pearson."

A bit of sympathy for the man tweaked Beck's breastbone. He rose from the chair. "I'm sorry for your loss, Director."

Byron stopped at the threshold of the door and turned back, his brows slightly raised. "Thank you. I..." His Adam's apple worked. "I appreciate you bringing Annabelle's murderer to justice, and just so you know, Debra Johansen dug up the info on your family. I would never release anything personal like that to the press."

The man's gratitude was better than an apology. Beck watched him walk out, his shoulders slumped.

"He won't say it to your face," Taylor said, drawing Beck's attention back to her, "but he was pretty impressed with what you did."

"What *we* did. You, Matt, Grey, Teeg, even Mitch. Jackie and I couldn't have done it without all of you."

"She's quite the fireball."

Beck chuckled. "You have no idea. I'm totally nuts about her, Tay."

"She seems pretty enamored with you too."

He couldn't keep the grin off his face. "I'm not one to do the whole Sunday dinner kind of thing, but Jackie is. I'd like all of you—Matt, the sisters, Grey and Sydney, everybody—to come have dinner with Jackie and I on Sunday if you're up for it. I'll make something special."

Taylor's eyes widened. "You've never invited me to your place before."

He grabbed Janiece's folder and took the stack of files from Taylor's desk. "Yeah, well, you know. We're family. That's what families do, according to Jackie."

Taylor smiled. "Look at you, turning over a new leaf."

He glanced down at the files. *Too many.* There always were. Too many families missing a member. He wondered if his family ever missed him, but the ache he usually felt over them had mellowed. His situation with them hadn't changed, but that was okay. *He* had. "I better get to work on the Coriann Muellers' case, and Janiece is waiting for her coffee."

"You didn't bring me tea?"

"Tomorrow, boss. I will tomorrow."

She got up and came around the desk to follow him out. "Then I'll take a cup of that coffee when it's ready."

As he stepped into the hall, he saw his coworkers had gathered at the other end.

"Well?" Janiece called.

"It's official," Taylor said.

A cheer went up and clapping echoed down the hall.

She patted Beck on his good shoulder. "Welcome back, Agent Pearson. Welcome back."

Clothes.

Clothes.

Clothes.

Skirts and pants, blazers and cardigans. Edgy blouses with pops of color. *Prints* for heaven's sake.

Jackie stood over her bed shaking her head at the array of combinations Beck had artfully arranged for her. Lost under it all was her smothered comforter, probably begging for oxygen. It wasn't enough that Mr. Vogue dragged her—literally—to his favorite clothing store in Georgetown, but he'd forced her to spend five hours there. Five long hours of stripping down and redressing over and over and over in every item he'd brought her. The man was relentless. With the way he liked to shop, and let's face it, his excellent taste, he should be the woman in their relationship.

All that aside, her fantasy of burying him alive in a landfill was overtaken by the amazing wardrobe he'd just outfitted her with. Even if that wardrobe set her debit card ablaze.

She needed this. This moving on from her plain suits and

grinding routine that she blamed on a lack of time for anything but her career. In short, Jackie needed a life. With Beck, the man who knew how to spice things up in oh-so-many ways.

A vision of him from inside her shower that morning, all rugged muscle and five percent body fat, brought a burst of heat to her cheeks. Maybe, after the damned fashion show Beck insisted on, she'd strip out of these clothes and do him right on her sofa. Talk about spicing up her life.

"Yes, ma'am," she said. "Spicy, spicy."

She picked up the emerald blue blouse and white pencil skirt he'd paired together. The skirt was too tight. At least she thought so. Beck, of course, squashed that, insisting it fit perfectly. So she liked things a little roomy? Apparently her days of comfort were gone. She shimmied into the skirt, sucking in her stomach as she zipped and then adjusted it the way he'd instructed. She'd need an extra twenty minutes in the morning for all this primping.

She turned to the full-length mirror, took in the image of herself in the tight skirt and push-up bra she'd tucked into her purchases when Beck was storming the clothing racks. *Holy smokes.* She set her shoulders, tilted her chin up.

That's me.

And I'm sexy.

Go figure. Damned Beck.

Seeing herself like this, her mind skipped back to the night she'd met him. In Ft. Lauderdale where she'd been wearing that stretchy dress that hugged her curves. Oddly enough, she'd never again worn anything as provocative. How could she after the mess it had left her in? Or maybe she simply didn't want reminders of that weekend with Beck. That amazing, exquisite time she'd never been able to replicate.

Until now.

Until Beck came back.

"Jackie!" he hollered from the living room. "Stop thinking so much and get out here. You'll look great. I promise."

He promised. Coming from him, she believed it.

She eased her arms into the blouse sleeves enjoying the brush of delicate fabric against her skin. She'd have to be careful with this one. No more jamming her arms in while running for the front door with a bagel hanging from her mouth.

One way or another, Beck, his herbal tea and good taste, would slow her down, forcing her to live in the moment.

She finished buttoning the blouse, leaving the extra one open as he'd told her. She glanced in the mirror at the hint of cleavage that said confidence rather than slut.

I can do this.

Because, yes, she looked damned good. She swept her hair over her shoulder, making a mental note about her overdue salon appointment. By the time she got done with this little makeover, Beck would beg her for sex every night.

Maybe even lunchtime quickies.

She'd make him insane. Wouldn't that be delish?

Bad, Jackie. Bad.

"Jackie!"

She flinched and spun back. As crazy about him as she was, he'd just about snapped her last nerve. "Hey! Don't rush me. Rome wasn't built in a day."

The bedroom door swung open and Beck stood there, his gaze roaming over her in a slow, dissecting perusal that kicked her pulse up. How pissed could she be when he looked at her with such want?

"Shoes." He pointed. "Try the beige strappy ones."

"Well, if you'd been patient, I was getting to it."

She bent low and rummaged through the shoe boxes scattered on her floor, shoving the lids and boxes aside as she searched for the beige sandals that were high enough to knock her on her ass.

"You're killing me," he said. "When you're done modeling all this stuff, we'll tackle organizing your closet. It'll take a trip to the hardware store for shelving, but we'll get it done."

"Yes, commandant."

Beck laughed and spun away. "I'll wait in the living room."

Oh, come on! He'd already seen the damned outfit, now he wanted her to do that whole catwalk thing?

"Seriously?" she asked.

"Seriously. I need to see you move in those clothes."

"Oh, I'll move in them," she muttered.

She sat on the bed and wrestled with the sandals' ankle straps for a solid five minutes. Forget dragging herself out of bed twenty minutes earlier. If she had to deal with these shoes, it'd be at least thirty.

"Any time now!" her beloved pain in the ass called.

"I'm coming."

Three steps in, her ankles wobbled on the high heels and she set one hand on the doorframe. *I can do this.*

Ruling a courtroom was nothing compared to balancing on these stilts. *Focus.* She sucked in her belly, tightening her core for stability—*got it*—and marched down the hallway channeling Shark Jackie, about to deliver her summation. She swung into the living room, head high, shoulders back. The new clothes, somehow, matched her courtroom style. Direct and no-nonsense.

"Holy crap," Beck said from his spot on the sofa. "Those shoes are hot."

"Good, because putting them on sucks."

He lifted one finger, whirled it in the air. Now he wanted a 360 view?

Come on, really?

"You promised," he said.

Yes, she had. As his payment for styling her, she'd promised him a fashion show. God help her. But the way he was looking at her, Beck didn't seem all that interested in the clothes.

Maybe she'd exact her revenge by driving him half mad with lust. Make him wait until she'd modeled every damned outfit before she got within five feet of him. That'd teach him.

Slowly, she eased around, giving him her back and pausing to cock one hip so he'd get a nice long look at her ass. The one he'd told her that morning he loved having his hands on.

"Oh, man," he said. "You are evil."

Calling on her inner sex kitten—who the hell even knew she had one?—she peered over her shoulder, waited for his hungry eyes to meet hers. "You think this is bad," she said, "it's only going to get worse."

Then she pushed it a tad further, breaking eye contact and staring at his crotch where the unmistakable bulge of an erection gave her another rush of heat. And satisfaction.

Only, the latter didn't feel so sweet. It felt...lonely. As if her plan shouldn't be the plan at all.

Ignoring Shark Jackie and her passion for the win, she turned again, went for the top button of her blouse. *Totally off-script here.*

The second button popped and Beck took a sharp inhale. "Oh, God. Are you gonna...?"

"You bet I am." Another button. "I'm going to strip for you. Inch, by tiny little inch. By the time I'm done with you, Beck Pearson, you'll be begging."

A lecherous smile flashed. So much for bringing him down.

"Bring it on, babe," he said.

He wanted to play. Good for him. So did she. In no particular rush, she worked her fingers down the remaining buttons, popping each one while keeping her gaze on Beck's. He blew her a kiss along the way, letting her know he was enjoying the show. That made two of them. Who knew Shark Jackie had it in her?

Maybe she just needed the right man. This man.

She peeled the blouse off, letting it slide down her arms. Beck watched as it dangled from her fingertips, but then shifted his focus to the lace push-up bra.

He rested his head against the sofa and let out a long breath. "Look at you, going rogue and buying something extra."

"I thought you'd like it," she said.

"You thought right."

She let the blouse drop to the floor and took two steps toward him, working the zipper on the skirt as she walked. By the time she reached him, she'd hooked her thumbs into the waistband of the skirt, ready to do away with it. Ready to have Beck's hands on her. And hers on him.

"Wait." He sat forward, reaching for her hips and their eyes locked for a few long seconds that sent Jackie's body temp soaring. "I'll do it," he said.

Jackie let go of the skirt, but the crazy urge to touch him was too much. Bending over, she cradled his face in her hands. Her breasts spilled over the tops of the bra cups and left absolutely nothing to the imagination. He touched her, pressed the backs of his fingers against her nipples before unclasping the bra. In seconds, it was gone, tossed away. She kissed him, gently at first, then used her tongue to tangle with his until her nipples went so rigid it became painful.

How did this man do this to her?

Her skirt hit the floor and she stepped out of it, carefully kicking it to the side as Beck's fingers slipped into the waistband of her underwear. Her plain cotton ones because she absolutely refused to put the matching pair to the bra on before washing them. At the sight of them, Beck smiled. He knew.

He gripped the panties with both hands. "Jackie?"

"Yes?"

Rrrrippppp. He tore the underwear off her. Just like that, shredded them into two pieces and discarded them over his shoulder.

"I guess I know how you feel about cotton."

He pulled her closer, kissed her belly while cupping his hands over her rear. After a minute, he looked up again, held her stare. Something in his eyes changed, a shift from the amped up heat of just seconds before. Something softer. She ran her hands over his cheeks. "What is it?"

"I love you," he said.

He loved her. All these years, she'd waited to hear those words. Fantasized about it. Could it be? Finally?

Yes.

She straddled him, kissed him again. Hard. Nearly sucked his face off because holy, holy cow, after that amazing spring break together they'd found their way back.

She broke the kiss. "I love you. I always have. Even when you hated me, I loved you. Now get those damned pants off."

With her still on top of him, he lifted his hips. She helped him with the zipper and then worked him free of his boxer briefs, more than ready for him. She wrapped her fingers around the hard length of him and he groaned.

"I want you," he said.

She let go, propped herself over him, more than ready for the orgasm she knew would happen. "Ditto that."

Beck dug his fingers into her hips and pushed her down. He arched up, filling her and she gasped at the lovely intrusion.

He moved in a slow agonizing pace that left her somewhere between frustration and ecstasy. The only one to ever do that to her.

I love him.

Yes, she did.

Finally, he pumped his hips faster and faster and she met the challenge, moving with him, damn near grinding against him and the heat, *ohmygod*, the scorching heat was insane. She gripped his shoulders, hanging on so she wouldn't tumble sideways and...*yes, here we go.* "I'm so..."

She looked down at him, but his eyes were closed, his brows drawn with concentration. He lunged forward, locked his lips around her right breast, tugging on her sensitive nipple and she cried out, arching and grinding against him. Harder and harder and harder and...*oh, yes.* The explosion pulverized her, sent her mind reeling and she screamed his name, over and over as her body broke apart. He met the furious pace, hammering into her. She opened her eyes, let the last of the orgasm take her to that perfect place while she watched Beck's face go taut.

He squeezed his eyes closed, pumped one last time before his body stiffened under her and he reared up, gripping her ass so tight she might have finger marks for a week. Who cared. He cried out from the force of his own release and Jackie slumped forward, gasping as she cuddled into his chest.

He wrapped his arms around her, pulling her even closer. "I want you," he said again. "Like this. Forever."

"It's not a bad gig," she said.

"I'm serious."

She sat up, cocked her head. "What?"

"Marry me."

Huh?

Before she could speak, he plowed forward. "I've waited years for you. Even convinced myself I hated you. You know that saying about the fine line between love and hate? That's me. With you."

Whoa. Jackie snapped her hands up. "Okay. Just hang on. Normal people smoke a cigarette or have a drink or whatever," she rolled her hand, "you know, to enjoy the euphoria. Generally, they don't ask a girl to marry them."

"I know what I want. Marry me."

He couldn't be serious. Couldn't be. But, oh, if he was. She cupped his cheeks, ran her thumbs over them while she searched for any sign of doubt.

"Beck," she said, "please. What if I say yes?"

"I'd be the luckiest man alive."

"Ssshh. If I say yes and you realize you're caught up in the moment, I'll be devastated. If you change your mind, I'm telling you, I may bury you alive in that landfill after all."

"I'm not caught up. Not in the way you think. I love you. From that first night, you were everything I wanted. Funny, educated, smart-mouthed, and passionate. All of it in one nice, tidy Jackie ball. Marry me."

She studied him again, stared right into his eyes, Shark Jackie searching for the deception. She was good at that. Pegging the liars.

Not this one. This one was rock solid and showing zero doubt. "If I say yes, promise me you won't change your mind."

"I swear to you. I know what I want. It starts with you and ends with a bunch of babies. Jackie miniatures that'll make me laugh and frustrate the goddamned daylights out of me when they don't believe what I say."

Baby Jackies. She pictured it. The two of them running herd on a gaggle of stubborn kids.

"I believe you. There's a problem though."

He huffed. "Of course there is. Because nothing is easy with you. Look, if you don't want to, just say it."

"The problem is, I want Baby Becks too. It's a negotiating point. You agree or I leave the table. Or," she waved a hand, "I suppose the sofa is our negotiating table. It's a combo deal or we're at a stalemate."

"You know," he said, "you're a pain in the ass."

"I know. Do we have a deal?"

He held out his hand. "Deal. Marry me."

"Deal." Ignoring his hand, she threw her arms around him, slammed him with a soul-sucking kiss. "I love you," she said.

"Good. Because we forgot the condom." He smiled wide. "We might be working on that stable of kids already."

The condom! She sat back, met his smile with her own. "I think, Special Agent Pearson, you're who I've been waiting for all these years. Even if my mother does kill us when we tell her we may be doing a shotgun wedding."

Ready for a new adventure?

Thank you for reading *Defending Justice*! If you'd like to follow the Schock sisters on their adventures, check out *1st Shock*, A Schock Sisters Mystery, Book 1.

Elite forensic sculptorMeg Schock is obsessed with solving cold cases and bringing justice to victims. When the local US attorney brings her the skull of a young murdered woman with similarities to one she's already reconstructed—but not identified—she and her sister, Charlie, dive head-first into a chilling investigation.

The twisted killer is clever, drawing closer and closer when he discovers the sisters on his trail. Another body turns up... and another... but his *modis operandi* points to a convicted murderer already behind bars. Together, Meg and Charlie must face the fact this copycat is taunting them, leading them on a gruesome quest. He's picked up where his mentor left off—and he's coming for one of them next.

READY FOR YOUR NEXT ADVENTURE?

*M*eg and Charlie are back in *1st Shock* Two very different sisters. One killer team.

Chapter 1

My name is Megan Eleanor Schock and I rebuild the dead.

I'm not being dramatic either. As we speak, I'm contemplating Emily, a woman who sits in the corner of my office where I greet her every morning and promise justice. She's young. Probably a teenager, tossed away like trash and left to the utter warfare imposed on a human body when animals and Mother Nature feast on it.

I'm not even sure Emily is her name. All I know is when they come to me, usually via a law enforcement official trying to solve a cold case, I need to give them life. An identity someone stole from them.

My sister, Charlie, thinks I'm obsessed.

I damn well might be.

Ask if I care.

We formed a private investigation firm and share equal partnership in it. Charlie, a forensic psychologist and one hell of a profiler, does most of the investigating while I do the sculpting. Forensic sculpting is one of my specialties and I, unfortunately, have a steady stream of subjects to further hone my skills on.

One of those is Joseph—at least, that's the name I've given him. He was brought to me by a sheriff from Louisiana. It's yet another cold case that needs to be solved so I've volunteered my services to see if we can get this man identified. Maybe find his killer.

I peel my gaze from Emily and focus on Joseph. The chime of the back door sounds. Only staff and a certain other few come through it so this must be Matt, an investigator we hired to help with our caseload. Our only other employee is Haley, the receptionist, and I can hear her fielding calls at her desk near the front.

A second later, JJ Carrington, steps into my doorway. As usual, he's dressed to kill in an expensive gray suit, a crisp white shirt, and blue print tie. His dark hair is neatly combed and the artist in me itches to sketch him, to capture the perfect lines of his cheekbones and jaw.

At least until my eye snaps to the plastic shopping bag he's holding. "Swear to God, JJ, if that's what I think it is, I'll stab you."

Unruffled by my threat—he's dealt with far worse than me —the U.S. Attorney for the District of Columbia, aka the Emperor of Cold Cases, steps to the worktable beside Joseph and clears a small space amongst my sculpting tools. He gingerly sets it down and I know, without a doubt, he's brought me yet another victim.

In a goddamned shopping bag.

For that alone I should maim him. Who am I kidding? JJ

only brings me the ones investigators are absolutely stumped on.

Or that are possibly related to another case.

A case like the one from when I was in sixth grade and nine —I remember the number quite clearly—other sixth graders in the area went missing. My mother cried every time a child vanished and I spent the whole of my sixth grade paranoid I'd disappear too. That turmoil still sticks. No matter how old I get, it sticks.

To this day, none of those children have been discovered.

Not one.

I guess I keep hoping someday one of their skulls will come my way, and I'll be able to help give them justice.

That case has made me a freak about my loved ones and the idea of a family having to live with the heartbreak of a missing person. Add to that my artistic talent and watching my older sister immerse herself into the justice system and here I am. Ready, willing and completely able to help. I can't say it's fun, but it satisfies something in me. Makes me feel as if I'm doing my part in some small way.

JJ points to the bag. "Found eighteen months ago in Rock Creek park. Zero leads. If we don't come up with something, the case will go unsolved. There's some public safety group making noise about the area being unsafe."

"Crimes happen in plenty of parks."

"Tell me about it. We're getting pressure from the National Park Service who doesn't want this case used for propaganda."

I peek inside and see a cast of a human skull. When it comes to my work, I'm only ever brought duplicates made from molds taken of the actual victims.

"And you put him in a shopping bag?"

"I didn't say it's a him."

I like JJ, but his years as a prosecutor have gobbled up the last of his sensitivity. "Well, I'm not calling him—or her—*it* so until I determine a gender, he's a him."

I peel back the sides and, using both hands lift him, studying the eye sockets and teeth. It's small and I immediately question myself. A woman then, perhaps. Just like Emily, who has sat in my office, each day reminding me her killer is still out there. Her case has suffered dead end after dead end, each lead fizzling and leaving investigators at a loss. For that reason, I can't let her go. Or give up on her. Maybe because she's young and pretty and deserved an ending far better than the one she got. All I know is I'm determined to help her.

"Small head," I comment.

"A child?"

"I didn't say that. Maybe a woman. We'll see."

I set Avery—a nice, gender neutral name—back on the table and walk to the narrow storage closet where I keep extra sculpting stands.

"Tell me about her," I say as I place the skull on one. "Do we have the rest of her?"

"Not all, but some. ME has them."

"Animals got to her?"

JJ shrugs. "I'm guessing. They searched the area around the body, but we're still missing twenty-five percent of the bones."

Like I said, the wrath of the elements. "Cause of death?"

"Based on fractures in the neck area, ME says asphyxiation."

Interesting. "Can I see what you have?"

I have a process and part of it is seeing all the bones, getting the measurements and figuring out the person's height and age.

JJ nods. Of course. He knows I'm good. The myriad of awards hanging in our reception area attest to it. Plus, this isn't his first rodeo.

I circle the stand, examining the back, running one hand over the smoothness. I reach the front, my fingers lightly touching Avery's cheek and lower jaw and something inside me fires.

"JJ."

At the sound of my sister's voice, I glance at the doorway where Charlie's gaze is glued to the Emperor. He smiles at her and the energy in the room changes. Charlie and JJ have a...thing. Insane chemistry that crackles between them every time they get within ten feet of each other. I'd like to tell them to get a room, but their relationship is complicated. He's in the process of a divorce and my sister doesn't screw married men. He's been separated over a year, but until he works out his marital issues, Charlie has deemed him untouchable.

Even so, I'm a little jealous. I haven't felt that kind of passion in a long time and I miss the buzz that comes with it. Unfortunately, I have too many victims parading in and out of my life to focus on any living, breathing man that might spark something.

Like I said, Charlie thinks I'm obsessed.

As the stare down between them continues, she leans against the doorjamb and crosses her legs. She's wearing one of those fitted pencil skirts she likes and a blouse straight out of Vogue. Me? I play with paints all day. I'm a ripped jeans and T-shirt girl.

Charlie appears relaxed, but inside she's seething. I sense it in her slightly puckered and expertly lipsticked mouth.

"If you've brought her that skull," Charlie says, "I'll kill you."

Poor JJ. First I threaten to stab him and now Charlie will kill him. Our threats come for two very different reasons. I'm pissed about the shopping bag.

Charlie the skull.

JJ holds up both hands. "We need help with this one."

"I'm sure." Charlie nudges her chin at me. "But look at her, she's already bonding."

"I'm fine," I say.

My sister rolls her eyes. She knows me. Understands the second I put my hands on someone, they become part of me.

I look back at Avery. "This is Avery. She'll be staying for a bit. JJ tell the ME I'd like to come by in the morning. After that, I need to finish Joseph." I point to the other skull. "Once I'm done with him, I'll work on Avery."

Charlie straightens and points at JJ. "You. In my office."

Grab your copy of *1st Shock*.

WANT MORE OF SEXY THRILLERS?

The Justice Team Series

Stealing Justice

Cheating Justice

Holiday Justice

Exposing Justice

Undercover Justice

Protecting Justice

Missing Justice

Defending Justice

SCHOCK SISTERS MYSTERY SERIES

1st Shock

2nd Strike

3rd Tango

MORE BY ADRIENNE GIORDANO

SCHOCK SISTERS MYSTERY SERIES w/MISTY EVANS

1st Shock

2nd Strike

3rd Tango

STEELE RIDGE SERIES w/KELSEY BROWNING
& TRACEY DEVLYN

Steele Ridge: The Beginning

Going Hard (Kelsey Browning)

Living Fast (Adrienne Giordano)

Loving Deep (Tracey Devlyn)

Breaking Free (Adrienne Giordano)

Roaming Wild (Tracey Devlyn)

Stripping Bare (Kelsey Browning)

Enduring Love (Browning, Devlyn, Giordano)

Vowing Love (Adrienne Giordano)

STEELE RIDGE SERIES: The Kingstons w/KELSEY BROWNING
& TRACEY DEVLYN

Craving HEAT (Adrienne Giordano)

Tasting FIRE (Kelsey Browning)

Searing NEED (Tracey Devlyn)

Striking EDGE (Kelsey Browning)

Burning ACHE (Adrienne Giordano)

MORE BY MISTY EVANS

SEALs of Shadow Force Series

Fatal Truth

Fatal Honor

Fatal Courage

Fatal Love

Fatal Vision

Fatal Thrill

Risk

SEALS of Shadow Force Series: Spy Division

Man Hunt

Man Killer

Man Down

The SCVC Taskforce Series

Deadly Pursuit

Deadly Deception

Deadly Force

Deadly Intent

Deadly Affair, A SCVC Taskforce novella

Deadly Attraction

Defending Justice

SCHOCK SISTERS MYSTERY SERIES w/Adrienne Giordano

1st Shock

2nd Strike

3rd Tango

The Secret Ingredient Culinary Mystery Series

The Secret Ingredient, A Culinary Romantic Mystery with Bonus Recipes

The Secret Life of Cranberry Sauce, A Secret Ingredient Holiday Novella

ACKNOWLEDGMENTS

Thank you to Jeanie and Amy, beta readers extraordinaire!

"We are not here simply to bandage the wounds of victims
beneath the wheels of injustice, we are here to drive a spoke
into the wheel itself."
~ Dietrich Bonhoefer

Defending Justice

Copyright © 2018 Misty Evans and Adrienne Giordano

Excerpt *1st Shock* © 2019 Misty Evans and Adrienne Giordano

ISBN: 978-1-942504-24-5

Cover Art by Fanderclai Designs

Formatting by Katherine Hahn

Editing by Gina Bernal, Elizabeth Neal, Cheryl Giebel

ABOUT ADRIENNE

Adrienne Giordano is a *USA Today* **best-selling author** of over forty romantic suspense and mystery novels. She is a Jersey girl at heart, but now lives in the Midwest with her ultimate supporter of a husband, sports-obsessed son and Elliot, a snuggle-happy rescue. Having grown up near the ocean, Adrienne enjoys paddleboarding, a nice float in a kayak and lounging on the beach with a good book.

For more information on Adrienne's books, please visit www.AdrienneGiordano.com. Adrienne can also be found on Facebook at http://www.facebook.com/AdrienneGiordanoAuthor, Twitter at http://twitter.com/AdriennGiordano and Goodreads at http://www.goodreads.com/AdrienneGiordano.

Don't miss a new release! Sign up for Adrienne's new release newsletter!

ABOUT MISTY

USA TODAY Bestselling Author Misty Evans has published over seventy-five novels and writes romantic suspense, urban fantasy, and paranormal romance. Under her pen name, Nyx Halliwell, she also writes cozy mysteries.

When not reading or writing, she embraces her inner gypsy and loves music, movies, and hanging out with her husband, twin sons, and three spoiled puppies. She's a crafter at heart and has far too many projects to finish.

Don't want to miss a single adventure? Visit www. mistyevansbooks.com to find out ALL the news!

Check out her humorous pen name Nyx Halliwell for magical mysteries https://www.nyxhalliwell.com .

www.ingramcontent.com/pod-product-compliance
Lightning Source LLC
Chambersburg PA
CBHW071004280626
47160CB00016B/2479